Valerie and the CURSE of the Diamond Necklace

Valerie and the CURSE of the Diamond Necklace

by

Bruce Dulany

Printed in the United States of America
ISBN 978-1-958434-80-2 (sc)
ISBN 978-1-958434-83-3 (hc)
ISBN 978-1-958434-84-0 (e)

Library of Congress Control Number: 2023904706

2023.03.28

MainSpring Books
5901 W. Century Blvd
Suite 750
Los Angeles, CA, US, 90045

www.mainspringbooks.com

TABLE OF CONTENTS

CHAPTER 1

EELLAGOFUSCIOUHIPOPPOKUNURIOUS

(Extra good or fine)

Sixth grade was over, Valerie was growing up. Her popularity lasted a few short months after her success at Parkview hospital. She was yesterday's news after Amari recovered from his injuries and returned to his obnoxious conceited ways. He was eellagofusciouhipoppokunurious, star of the football, basketball and track team and he acted like it. Valerie couldn't argue about his talents, he did score three touchdowns every football game, he averaged 44 points every basketball game and had school records for the 100-yard dash and 200-yard hurdles. He was a good athlete, no, a great athlete, but a terrible human.

Coach Stephen pampered him like he was God's gift from above because he was eellagofusciouhipoppokunurious. Valerie never saw him study for a test, let alone take a test but he had a solid B grade point average. Suspicious? On the bus every morning he had two seats reserved for Amari and was given breakfast every morning. No, not cold cereal and juice, but steak and eggs. Suspicious? For lunch, he had the center table reserved every day for him and his inner circle where they were given a menu to pick and choose their meal. The Principal, Doctor Higginbottom came into the lunchroom every day and talked to Amari and Amari only, Suspicious?

Camilla had moved, yes, the prettiest girl in school had moved over the summer. Where? Nobody knew, but it was rumored she did land a modeling contract with California's biggest and best modeling company, Eve St. Lawrence, she too was eellagofusciouhipoppokunurious. Either way she left all of her "friends" behind. However, her position was quickly filled by the new girl from Orlando, Florida, Emma Lindusky. This blonde haired, blue eyed young lady came in like a tiger replacing Camilla very quickly. Obviously, she too was eellagofusciouhipoppokunurious.

Emma quickly impressed the cheerleading coach, Ms. Wanderby, and was made captain of the team immediately. Ms. Wanderby was highly impressed by her tough leadership skills, her awesome athletic abilities, and her creative cheerleading calls. Like Amari, she knew she was good at her cheerleading skills and was very quickly accepted into Amari's inner circle. Like Amari, she treated people poorly, a true teratism, but the admirers still loved and adored both of them. It was rumored Amari and Emma were dating and were calling themselves Amma.

Valerie thought they were too young to be dating. Valerie kept busy with her classes; she was very serious about becoming a nurse and nothing was going to stop her. She spent very little time with anybody except her books. Biology, Chemistry and Physics became her best friends. Although she only spent one day a week being a candy stripper at Parkview Hospital, she loved every minute of being in the hospital. Valerie watched every move the nurse's made. It didn't matter what they were doing, changing a bandage, giving medicine, taking their blood pressure, Valerie was taking notes and learning.

Everything else faded to the rear side, nothing else mattered, Valerie was going to be the best nurse possible, in terms of nursing she was going to be eellagofusciouhipoppokunurious . No disease was going to stop Valerie, no hospital cutbacks were going to stop Valerie and no negative comments from friends and family were going to stop Valerie. Eventually, there was no more friends and family to even mention. Most of her life, Valerie was a loner. She didn't connect with many people mostly because she was incredibly shy. Valerie also found out early in life people used the "friend" label very loosely. Valerie thought friendship meant being honest, trustworthy, and respectful. She discovered people were not honest with her, she discovered people were not trustworthy and she discovered how many people did not show her the same respect she showed them. Her friends should have had her back in the past, she learned the hard way, that when a problem appeared, her friends disappeared. In Valerie's life there were always a problem, nothing in life came easy for Valerie. She finally decided that people did not know how to be a true friend, so she didn't care if she had any friends.

Valerie was so busy with her studies and her volunteer job that the family also took a back seat. Biology, the study of living organisms, was intriguing but took long hours away from her schedule. Chemistry, the branch of science that deals with the identification of substances of which matter is composed, was perplexing and took many hours away from her schedule. Physics, the branch of science concerned with the nature and properties of matter and energy, was mind blowing and took many hours away from her schedule. The merciless tests, the unique projects and the never-ending assignments were sometimes overbearing.

Giving up family for a few years was a small price of becoming a nurse. Mom would understand giving up going to Target, mom would understand giving up the special talks, mom would understand not getting a birthday present from her daughter, right? Dad would understand when she took his car and did not put gas in it, dad would understand not helping him clean the garage, dad would understand not getting a Christmas present from his daughter, right? Vivian would understand giving up spending quality time with her sister, Vivian would understand not talking with her sister, Vivian would understand not seeing her sister until she received her nursing license, right?

Vivian eventually got tired of waiting for her sister to spend time with her. Vivian found new friends. They drifted apart. Vivian spent time after school with the art teacher, Ms. Penelope, learning to become a better artist. They drifted farther apart. Vivian spent more time practicing her violin hoping to become first chair in high school. They drifted even further apart. Vivian made new friends and spent time shopping at the mall and seeing movies together with them. The two sisters drifted miles apart.

Valerie thought Mr. Dulany was yesterday's news, something from her childhood that could be left behind as a memory like kindergarten, sippy cups, and crayons. Although he was getting older, struggling with Parkinson's, and lived next door, Valerie made no effort to keep in contact with him. Although she had wonderful memories of gardening, becoming a nurse was her dream, and not a florist or farmer. Unfortunately, Mr. Dulany was an innocent casualty in this quest of becoming a nurse.

This quest, like everything else in Valerie's life would be difficult, especially if she wanted to be eellagofusciouhipoppokunurious. Nothing came easy for Valerie. In gym class she was always picked last. She never won any prizes at school; she could have 99 entries in the box and Vivian could have 1 and the picker would pick Vivian. When she was in the car with her parents she would always be caught by red lights. She never won in rock, paper, scissors. Whenever she went to the beach it would rain. Thinking about this made Valerie angry. Mom didn't have bad luck; dad didn't have bad luck and Vivian didn't have bad luck. Valerie asked herself, "Why, why do I have such bad luck?"

CHAPTER 2

GADZOOKS

(An exclamation of surprise or annoyance)

Valerie woke up hoping for a better day. Getting dressed in a very casual white blouse and her new "designer" blue jeans, she felt confident in her modest look. Valerie applied her blush, her light red lipstick and brushed her long black hair. Unlike most girls her age, she never wore much makeup. First, she didn't like how it made her look and her mother always told her girls under 18 should never wear makeup, all she needed was a great smile and a pleasant personality.

Valerie was a little late in coming down the stairs for breakfast, she didn't see Vivian nor her mom. With the Covid 19 pandemic over, dad was back to work and mom was trying to find a job. The girls were growing up and didn't need constant attention. "Mom, Vivian? Anybody home?" she called out. Nobody answered. Valerie didn't see any breakfast, so even though it wasn't Saturday, she decided to treat herself to Eggo Waffles. "Mom? Vivian?" she called again.

Grateful there was peace and quiet, Valerie put the two golden treats into the toaster. While she waited for the best breakfast ever, she took out her science book and started studying Chapter 5, The Human Body. Today, Ms. Cassaundra was giving the big test. Soon Valerie became immersed in reviewing what she had learned, she was fascinated reviewing the nervous system, the digestive system, the skeletal system, the muscular system, and the respiratory system. She absorbed the fascinating information like a sponge.

Relentlessly she turned the pages. She laughed at the fact that, like fingerprints, everybody has a different tongue print. She was fascinated that humans shed about 600,000 particles of skin an hour. She wondered how babies start with 350 bones and as adults we have only 206 bones in our bodies. Valerie didn't understand how the human body replaces its stomach lining every 3-4 days. And she couldn't believe a sneeze comes out of your nose at 100 miles per hour. Becoming a nurse was going to be great.

Suddenly, running down the stairs ran Valerie's mom screaming "Valerie! Valerie! What's burning?" Smoke filled the small kitchen, yet Valerie was unphased. Valerie's mom tapped Valerie on the shoulder, "What is wrong with you? You have to pay attention!" Her mom quickly unplugged the toaster, opened the windows, and turned on the quaint celling fan. Then she pulled the two burnt waffles from the toaster and threw them in the sink.

Valerie was embarrassed and still hungry, but this was her life. The kitchen smelled like a campfire and since it would take hours for the air to clear, mom told her they could stop for breakfast when she drove Valerie to the middle school. Vivian was already at school, practicing her violin for the big concert Thursday night.

While they drove Valerie's mom reminded Valerie that her, dad and Vivian were going to visit Aunt Eva next week and Uncle Bruce would be coming to stay with Valerie. Aunt Eva was 93 years old and in failing health. Valerie kept her eyes glued to her anatomy book and nonchalantly said, "Okay, Mom."

Although Valerie was running late, her mom still stopped at the Mr. Bagel to get herself a cup of coffee with a hint of hazelnut cream and get Valerie her breakfast a caramel Frappuccino with a hint of ginger and a mist of whipped cream plus two blueberry bagels sliced with cream cheese. The drive thru line went quickly and soon as they received their order, they wasted no time in getting to the middle school.

Unfortunately, they didn't double check the order before they got onto busy Army Trail Road. As mom maneuvered her 2018 Chevy SUV through the busy rush hour traffic Valerie handed her coffee with a hint of hazelnut cream. Her mom smelled the nectar of Gods and exclaimed, "Mr. Bagel makes the best coffee" and continued driving eastward down Army Trail Road.

Valerie smiled in agreement as she grabbed a "blueberry bagel" out of the bag. Much to her surprise, it was a whole wheat bagel, "GADZOOKS!" she exclaimed. Hoping for a miracle, she reached for the other "blueberry bagel" and was very upset to discover a cinnamon raisin bagel, "GADZOOKS!" she exclaimed as her mother hit another red light.

Hoping to save the day she still could enjoy the cream cheese, she quickly discovered they gave her apricot jelly instead of cream cheese. "GADZOOKS!" she hollered. Traffic was backed up and Valerie's mom kept hitting the red lights. Could things get any worse? Valerie hoped not. She grabbed her caramel Frappuccino with a hint of ginger and a mist of whipped cream and went in for a taste of heaven, she closed her eyes and took a giant sip. "GADZOOKS!" she exclaimed as Mt. St. Valerie erupted spitting it out all over the dashboard, "This is a caramel cappuccino with a hint of mint and a mist of whipped cream, not a caramel Frappuccino with a hint of ginger and a mist of whipped cream. Nothing could bother mom as she drank her coffee. This was the life of Valerie.

Still fuming as Valerie's mom pulled up to the school, hungry and frustrated, Valerie got out of the SUV madder than a hornet. "Have a good day honey!" mom said as Valerie slammed the car door shut. Valerie was late and the principal, Dr. `Higginbottom was at the front entrance to greet her and hand Valerie a tardy slip, "Morning Crystal, please don't make this a habit!" Some things never changed. She rudely grabbed the white slip out of the principal's hand and headed to her English class. This was the life of Valerie.

Walking late into English class, Valerie slithered into the room while Ms. Maria took morning attendance. The new girl Emma was surrounded by a slew of young men trying to impress her. Valerie slipped Ms. Maria the tardy slip and quickly sat down. Unfortunately, Valerie caught Emma's attention. "Nice designer jeans!" she said boldly across the room.

Valerie waited for more, the jab, the insult, the joke but nothing came. Valerie misjudged Emma, maybe Emma was nice, maybe the earth is flat. Eager for a friend, Valerie turned around and said, "Thank you!" Then it came, the shot heard round the world, "You left the tag on from Uncle Bob's knock off designer store. You only paid $19.99 for those pair of imitation BD jeans compared to $299.00 for a real pair of BD jeans. I only buy original BD jeans! I wouldn't be caught dead in a fake pair. How embarrassing!" This was the life of Valerie.

Uncle Bob's knock off designer store was a very busy store located just south of I-355. Most of the kids in Glendale Heights couldn't afford $299.00 for a pair of jeans. Most of the kids shopped at Uncle Bob's for all their clothing. Who could afford $199 for an original Tommy Linuci Designer blouse? A copy went for $9.99. Who could afford $500 for a pair of Lady Alicia designer high tops, when a Lady Angelica which looked exactly like the Lady Alicia's went for $29.99? Most parents want to dress their children in fancy designer clothes but can't afford the ridiculous prices.

Despite the popularity of Uncle Bob's clothing, everybody laughed at Emma's joke. Trying to fit into the popular girls, Mariah, Aaliyah, and Chloe all laughed hysterically at the expense of Valerie. Trying to impress the new pretty girl the boys, Daniel, Ethan, and Roger all laughed childishly at the expense of Valerie. Trying to avoid Mt. St. Valerie from erupting, Valerie ran out of the room crying uncontrollably.

She ran past the Principal, Dr. Higginbottom where he told Valerie, "Slow down Betsy!" Valerie ran into the bathroom locking herself into a stall. She pulled out her cell phone and called her mother to bring her a pair of joggers. It didn't take long for her mother to bring the red joggers, so she switched pants quickly and went to her next class, honors algebra.

Unfortunately, the rest of the day went eerily similar. After Valerie ate her lunch, she wanted to treat herself to an M&M ice cream sandwich, so she waited in line. There were 12 people in line and 11 ice cream sandwiches, Valerie never got one. In Chemistry class they were going to have partners to do experiments and projects with, there were 23 students, 22 students received partners, Valerie never got one. When the end of the day bell rang, Valerie tripped on her untied gym shoe, By the time Valerie picked herself up, picked her books and laptop off the ground and tied her gym shoes, every student got a ride home. Valerie never got one.

Principal Higginbottom walked by and asked, "Why are you still here Samantha? There are no after school activities today." Somethings never changed. As Valerie walked home, she wondered what she did wrong in her past life to cause such terrible bad luck. Was she a bank robber, was she a mean girl, was she a tax collector? She wondered why her sister had an easy life, her mother never had bad luck and her father won small amounts in the lottery constantly, Valerie wondered if she was adopted. Was she an ugly baby? Was she a crying baby? Was she a fussy baby?

Nothing made sense. They could send an astronaut to the moon, but Valerie couldn't figure out why she had such bad luck. They knew how to send a submarine to the bottom of the deep blue ocean, but they couldn't figure out why Valerie had such bad luck. They knew how to send a radio signal 200 million miles in space but couldn't figure out why Valerie had such bad luck. It was a complete mystery.

Either way Valerie was determined to find the truth, good or bad, when she got home. Her mom and dad would have to tell the truth of Valerie's misfortunate life. Valerie asked herself, "Why, why do I have such bad luck?"

CHAPTER 3

KAPOW!

(The next action you take automatically succeeds)

Determined to find the truth about her ancestry, Valerie came into her small house, demanding to find mom, "Mom, mom where are you?" Dad quickly replied, "She went to the grocery store for dinner. She should be back soon." Furious at her parents for keeping her past a secret, Valerie continued to rant and rave, sometimes making no sense at all.

Poor Dad didn't know what hit him. Finally, able to sit down and watch one of his favorite shows on Netflix, he heated up eight mozzarella sticks, four chicken and cheese taquitos and six mini tacos, poured himself a nice tall glass of ice-cold Pepsi, "Finally, peace and quiet," he said to himself and turned the television on. That's when the walls of Jericho came tumbling down.

Storming in determined to find an answer, Valerie demanded to know, "Where did I come from? Am I from the planet Zuru 225? Am I adopted? Was I an unwanted baby? Why am I the only one who has bad luck? Why? Why? Why? Finally taking a breather, Valerie was silent. Her dad stood frozen, unable to move, unable to speak. He was unable to comprehend what was happening.

Valerie was relentless, "Am I an experimental test tube baby? Did someone drop me at the fire station? Why am I so different than the rest of you? Why do I lose every time in heads and tails? I have never won in rock, paper, scissors. I never find money on the sidewalk like Vivian, last week she found a $100 bill when she took

Kiara for a walk. Whenever mom goes to the store, she is always given the freshest fruits and vegetables, remember those delicious, sweet strawberries? I always get the old stale vegetables, remember that bag of rotten potatoes I picked up last week? You always brag about being the green light king, but when I get in the car, we always get stuck by every red light. You know you call me the red-light queen. I beg you, please tell me where I came from. Where do I come from? Where is my good luck? Where was mom?" Somebody needed to sound the emergency alert system, Mt. St. Valerie was beginning to erupt.

Dad was completely caught off guard, where was mom? He needed back up; the devasting effect of Mt. St. Valerie was no match for one innocent man. He wasn't sure what to do, Valerie was too young to know the truth, Valerie was too small to know the truth, Valerie was too nice to know the truth. The deal between mom and dad was to tell Valerie on her 18th birthday, then as an adult she could decide her own fate. Where was mom? Like a deer frozen in time staring at headlights, dad stood there unable to move while Mt. St. Valerie erupted.

Mt. St. Valerie continued spewing ashes of demands towards her dad, "When is mom coming home? I need to know why I have such bad luck. Am I adopted? Do I come from a distant galaxy far, far away? Am I from the planet Zuru 225? Or when mom was pregnant with me, did she walk under a ladder while walking a black cat on Friday the 13th?" With his hands in his pants pockets, dad stood there frozen, still unable to move or talk.

Like the calm before the storm, silence dominated the room. Was dad safe from the hot lava of Mt. St. Valerie? Only time would tell. Then without warning, Mt. St. Valerie exploded yet again, "Are you going to tell me? Are you going to be honest? Why do I have such bad luck?" There was a slight pause, then it continued. "I demand you tell me and tell me now!" Over and over the record played. Then like a bolt of lightning, it hit dad.

Dad had his keys in his pockets. On his key chain somebody had given him a furry white and grey rabbit's foot for good luck. "Honey, don't you carry a good luck charm?" He showed her the fake rabbit's foot. "Most people have and carry a good luck charm with them all the time, something they believe brings them good luck. Abraham Lincoln carried a shiny penny whenever he went to the theater, Emelia Earhart wore a blue hat every time she flew an airplane and John Lennon carried a lucky medallion whenever he went out to walk his dog!"

Mt. St. Valerie cooled down for a minute. Dad's examples were terrible, not one of his examples were good, but Valerie did not have history class until the second semester, so for now, he looked like a genius. Valerie thought about what a great President Abraham Lincoln was, she knew about Emelia Earhart flying across the Atlantic Ocean and John Lennon's great talent of singing and smiled. "That's it!" she exclaimed. "All I need is a good luck charm!" She quickly exited, thanking her dad in the process.

Dad was relieved, back to his cold appetizers and warm glass of soda. He missed his television show Jeopardy, but was ecstatic he temporarily solved his daughter's bad luck, or did he? He knew sooner or later they would need to tell Valerie the truth.

Valerie's mind immediately thought of the four-leaf clover. Everybody knew the four-leaf clover was lucky. She searched on the internet and verified the rumors. For years people had used the four-leaf clover to ward off bad luck. Perfect! In the Middle Ages children used the four-leaf clover to see fairies and mythical creatures that would bring good luck. Perfect! In 1620, Sir John Melton found gold while he possessed a four-leaf clover. Perfect!

Valerie discovered that four-leaf clovers are offspring of the very common three-leaf clover, which are found in most forests and bushes. Where there were three -leaf clovers, there were four-leaf clovers. Excited and determined Valerie yelled, "Kiara! Time for a walk", Kiara came running and she put a leash on her. "Dad, I'm taking Kiara for a walk, be back soon!" she ran out the door with Kiara and headed straight to the forest preserve next to the park.

Determined to end this bad luck, she was relentless in dragging Kiara to the forest preserve. Kiara wanted to chase squirrels, Kiara wanted to sniff everything, Kiara wanted to lick and be petted by everyone she saw, especially the children. Valerie wanted no part in allowing Kiara to enjoy the great outdoors, in fact every time she went pee, Valerie pulled her leash. Valerie searched and searched for clovers, but there was nothing.

Despondent, Valerie started to cry. She let down the leash for a millisecond to wipe her tears, out of nowhere a grey bushy squirrel raced swiftly through the forest. Kiara noticed and took off like a race car at the Daytona 500. The squirrel went right past some old oak trees, Kiara followed, Valerie tried following. The squirrel zigzagged and made a sharp left after a tall patch of grass, Kiara pursued the squirrel with Valerie not too far behind. Tired, the squirrel found the tree where his dad built their family nest.

Up the tree the squirrel went, very close behind stood Kiara at the base of the tree. She barked and barked, hoping to catch the furry beast. Tired and aggravated with Kiara and unable to find any clovers, Valerie began to scold Kiara, "ba......", then she saw it, a large patch of clovers, "Good doggie! Good doggie!" She got on her hands and knees determined to find an elusive four -leaf clover.

She scoured the forest floor for what seemed hours, plenty of weeds, plenty of ragweed, but no four-leaf clovers. With darkness quickly approaching, her hands dirty from the dead leaves and Kiara wanting to play, this mission seemed futile. "Stop Kiara! This is important, no time to play!" Dejected, Kiara walked away.

In tears, almost ready to go home, almost ready to admit failure, the very aggravated Valerie stood up. Kiara began to bark; Valerie commanded her to stop. Refusing to listen, Kiara continued to bark, and bark and bark. Annoyed at this point, Valerie yelled, "STOP!" and whispered to herself, "stupid dog." Now ready to go home,

Valerie told Kiara to "come", Kiara ignored her and stood barking in the same spot.

Mt. St. Valerie was getting ready to explode yet again, with no four-leaf clover and a disobedient dog, Valerie had had it. Walking intently in the mud towards Kiara, Valerie called, "Come here Kiara!" Kiara stood barking. Frustrated beyond belief, Valerie told Kiara, "When we get home you will be grounded forever!" Valerie stomped through the mud flabbergasted at Kiara's rare bad behavior.

Finally arriving where Kiara was standing, Valerie grabbed Kiara's collar and put the leash on her. "Why don't you listen to me? You st . . ." that's when she saw it. Kiara had found a four-leaf clover, "You wonderful, beautiful dog!" she exclaimed. She kissed Kiara, smiled, and gently pulled the good luck charm out of the ground. Ready to go home, Valerie held her new life in her hands. "Thanks Kiara, let's go home!" Kiara proudly listened and followed Valerie out of the woods.

Walking briskly in the diminishing sunlight, Valerie's right arm began to itch. She scratched it, soon the left arm began to itch, she scratched it. Still tightly holding the four-leaf clover, she noticed her legs beginning to itch, she scratched the red patch on them. She couldn't decide what to itch first, her arms, her legs, her hands, her feet, or her neck. With only one arm, she struggled frantically trying to catch up with the scratching, it was no use. Still holding the four-leaf clover as she walked home, she started scratching with both hands. It was dark and she was home, nothing was going to stop her.

Finally arriving home, Valerie's mom opened the back door, "where have you been?" Valerie proudly held her hand up to show her mom. "My luck needed to change so I went to get this", there was nothing, Valerie continued to itch as she looked frantically for the elusive four-leaf clover.

"Carumba!", mom exclaimed, "you have poison ivy!" Valerie's luck had not changed. "Go upstairs, change clothes and I will get the calamine lotion. No more scratching!" Valerie spent the next few days with socks on her hands and pink spots all over her body. She missed two days at school, two fun days, movie day and treat day, her luck had not changed.

Not ready to give up on changing her life of bad luck, Valerie was determined to find something that would bring her good luck. Obviously the four -leaf clover didn't work, and no way was she going to carry a cut off rabbit's foot in her purse, she was perplexed at what she would try next. She checked the internet and found a section on witchcraft, too spooky, a section on voodoo, too scary and a list of things to keep bad spirits away. Besides a rabbit's foot, there was cat's tongue, bats eyes and an elephant's tusk. EW! EW! And EW!

She asked around at school and people said they kept their cut toenails, they had lucky pencils, they had lucky seats, lucky footballs, lucky shoes and lucky hats, the list was endless. She asked at the hospital, people said they had lucky days, lucky numbers, and lucky food. Valerie had none of these. Several people even said they had lucky coins. BOOYAH! She remembered her neighbor once told her he picked up loose coins on the ground and told her shiny pennies with the heads up were the luckiest, but you didn't touch the head down ones, those were considered very unlucky.

Feeling confident, Valerie headed down the sidewalk with a sense of premeditated relief. Pennies were a thing of the past; many people didn't want or need pennies. Nothing cost a penny, why did they even make them? With her head down, she scanned the sidewalk back and forth, nothing but old disgusting cigarette butts, used candy wrappers and unwanted soda cans.

Relentless in her pursuit of a shiny penny heads up, she ironically kept her head down. Block after block she walked in pursuit of a shiny penny. Totally focused, Valerie crossed busy Glen Ellyn Road, cars beeped, cars braked. Drivers yelled from their open windows; drivers swerved to avoid the mysterious young lady with her head down. Valerie was determined.

The journey continued to North Avenue where she avoided all traffic with the complicated light system. Drivers stared, bikers were confused, other walkers avoided the strange girl. She dangerously walked through Wendy's drive thru hoping to find the shiny penny, cars slammed on their brakes, all she found was a dirty 2015 quarter and two faded nickels from 2008 and 2018. The drivers yelled, but Valerie heard nothing. She was determined.

As she continued westward, a bicyclist swerved and fell on his side, breaking his wrist. Valerie kept walking oblivious to his fall. An ambulance and the police were called. Valerie kept walking despite the dangers. With her eyes peeled to the ground, Valerie noticed how much litter was on the ground, one day if she was lucky enough, she would join the Earth Club at school which helped clean up the streets of Glendale Heights.

Walking west, she crossed a small street, the green SUV turning right did not see Valerie and slammed on their brakes, the small white box truck couldn't stop in time and ran into the back of the green SUV. Nobody was hurt, but the police were called. Valerie was oblivious to the situation and kept walking, hoping to get lucky enough to find a shiny penny with its head up. Next was Portillo's, despite the huge number of cars Valerie followed the drive thru lane, employees asked her to leave, cars honked, and drivers yelled. Nothing was going to stop Valerie, nothing. Eventually, a distracted driver hit a light pole near the drive through lanes. Nobody was hurt, but the police were called. Valerie kept walking.

Crossing Bloomingdale Road, Valerie caused an eight-car pile-up. With cars going 50 mph the first car broke hard, skidded, and ran into a Volkswagen beetle. Another car hit the Ford Taurus broadside and then the pile-up began. Not sure if anyone was hurt, but the police were called. The search quickly began for the unusual young lady wandering around town with her head down.

Still walking, Valerie saw Burger King and headed for the drive thru. Suddenly, six police squad cars came squealing towards her, lights flashing and sirens blaring, loud enough to wake up the dead.

Valerie was oblivious, she was focused on finding a shiny penny. The officers screamed at her, nothing, they commanded her to stop, nothing. Eventually they convinced her to stop, by standing in front of her.

Although she committed no crimes and was not arrested, Valerie was considered a safety hazard and was immediately brought home. The concerned officer handed Valerie over to her mom and suggested she get some rest and see a "doctor", soon. Valerie was embarrassed and went to her room where she quickly gave up the idea of finding a shiny penny with its head up for good luck.

Valerie was grounded for two weeks for her unwise decision. Her dad offered his lucky horseshoe which had been hanging in the garage for twenty years safe and untouched, bringing mostly good fortune to his precious family. Valerie initially declined, but was having second thoughts, at this point anything would help with her bad luck.

Not sure of what a horseshoe was good for, Valerie got on the internet and did some research. Searching why horseshoes are considered lucky? Valerie read the information. Good luck is attributed to horseshoes because blacksmithing is considered a lucky trade. Perfect! It takes seven nails to attach a horseshoe to a horse's foot. Perfect! Horseshoes are considered magical because they're made from iron and iron resists fire. Perfect! Finally, hanging a horseshoe in the U shape helps keep out bad luck. Perfect! Time to get the horseshoe.

Out of the garage Valerie traveled. Concerned, her mother asked where she was going. Sadly, and with little hope of getting rid of her bad luck anytime soon Valerie replied, "Just out to the garage, can't do much damage there." While she was out getting the horseshoe, her mom told dad, "We have to tell her the truth, it's not her fault, it's tearing her apart." Dad agreed but they couldn't decide when.

Desperate, Valerie headed out to the small garage in a last-ditch effort to have good luck, or at least not to have any bad luck. She quickly found the horseshoe, hung in front, high above her dad's pride and joy, his brand new 2022 blue Nissan Sentra. There was nothing else in the garage, the car barely fit. Having nothing to lose, she shimmied her way to the front of the garage, poor Valerie couldn't fit between the car and the wall.

Politely, Valerie took off her red gym shoes and gently walked across the hood of her dad's new car. Careful not to dent her dad's "baby" she tread lightly. She reached up, slipped a little but regained her composure and grabbed the heavy horseshoe proclaiming, "Goodbye bad luck, Hello good luck!" Excited, Valerie started walking back across the hood of the Nissan carrying the heavy horseshoe.

Wearing only her white cotton socks, Valerie walked gingerly across the huge hood. Suddenly she began to slip and slide, trying to balance` herself she waved her arms, eventually dropping the horseshoe on her dad's pristine car hood. KAPOW! The horseshoe bounced off the damaged hood and onto the cold cement floor. THUD! The horseshoe was okay, the hood was not. This horseshoe has not started off so luckily.

Valerie ran into the house carrying the heavy charm. As she ran past mom and dad, she said, "Mom you are home! Dad I…". very calmly dad replied, "I know, I called the insurance company!" Valerie went directly to her bedroom. While she was upstairs deciding where to put the horseshoe, mom said to dad, "You know we have to tell her, we can't wait until she turns 18." Dad smiled at mom, sarcastically asking, "Why? What else can go wrong?"

Then like a hurricane, Valerie came racing down the stairs. "I need the hammer and a nail." Mom quickly answered, "in the kitchen drawer closest to the wall." Valerie found the hammer and a small nail and went back upstairs. Mom watched as she ran back up the stairs. Mom waited a few moments before telling dad that for everyone's safety they should tell her right before they leave next weekend to visit Aunt Eva. Uncle Bruce could deal with Mt. St. Valerie. Dad agreed.

Upstairs Valerie centered the old beat-up horseshoe above her headboard for maximum exposure to all the good and lucky vibes possible. She grabbed the small nail and tapped it into the wall. Then she hung the horseshoe, but it quickly fell to the ground taking the nail with it. Mom and Dad heard the loud thud and asked Valerie if she needed help, Valerie quickly declined.

Thinking for a second Valerie knew she had to put the nail farther into the wall, but how far? She quickly decided if she held the horseshoe and nail together, she could nail it perfectly. Holding it perfectly centered, she held the hammer with one hand and the nail and horseshoe against the wall with the other hand. Tap! Tap! Tap! The nail was barely going in the wall. She knew she needed more power.

TAP! TAP! TAP! Went the hammer. The nail went a little deeper into the wall. "More power!" she said to herself. "More Power!" with everything she had she wound up the hammer and swung it. KAPOW! Went the hammer against the wall, completely missing the nail and making a huge hole in the wall. Simultaneously, the horseshoe crashed to the ground, putting a giant hole in the hardwood floor below.

"DAD!" she cried. "Don't worry honey, I have called the insurance company," her dad sadly replied. Valerie sat on the edge of the bed in a sea of despair and asked herself "Why, why do I have such bad luck?"

CHAPTER 4

SUERTE!

(Good Luck in Spanish)

Valerie gave up trying to find a good luck charm, she was content in accepting her fate as one of the unluckiest people on the planet. No rabbits foot, no shiny penny, no four-leaf clover and definitely no horseshoe were going to change her destiny. She promised herself she would renew her membership in the poor, poor me pitiful me club, effective immediately.

After she paid back her father for the "damage" she caused to his new car, the bedroom wall and the bedroom floor she would put this chapter of her life behind her. Hakuna Matata! Unfortunately, the extra chores she would be doing the next few months would not let her embrace this new Valerie anytime soon.

Valerie's future was still bright with the hopes and dreams of becoming a nurse. Today in chemistry class they will be assigned their end of the quarter project. This was no easy class, the homework was hard, and the tests were challenging, but Valerie aced them all. Valerie knew the periodic table backwards and forward and was the only person in class who knew all the symbols. Valerie knew that the periodic table was a graphic formulation of the periodic law which states that the properties of the chemical elements exhibit a periodic dependence on their atomic numbers.

She proudly knew about copper (cu) and the properties of gold, (au). Valerie was intrigued with boron (b), carbon (c), and oxygen (o). She was fascinated with sulfur (s), phosphorus (p) and aluminum (al). Valerie never heard of tungsten (w), samarium (sm) and dysprosium (dy). She wondered where gadolinium came from, as well as ruthenium (ru) and rhodium (rh). Forget bad luck, the periodic table was Valerie's guilty pleasure.

Valerie was proud she could hold a conversation anywhere anytime about anyone of the elements. She knew her classmates would be impressed with her knowledge of plutonium, a dense silvery radioactive metal, used as a fuel in nuclear reactors and as an explosive in nuclear fission weapons. Impressive! At birthday parties, her family would be flabbergasted that she also knew of californium, another radioactive metal first produced in 1950 by bombarding curium and helium 4 ions at the Lawrence Berkeley National Laboratory. Impressive! At church Valerie could start any conversation by telling other members of the congregation about livermorium being a very unstable synthetic element made by high energy atomic collisions. Impressive!

Chemistry class was fascinating, chemistry class was thrilling, chemistry class was awesome. Sitting partnerless in the back corner of the room was stupendous. Nobody bothered her, everyone else had their partners Amari and Emma, David and Joey, Justin and Emily, Ilda and Udo, Ray and Anna, Jon, Louisa, Angelica, and Sam. Each pair worked together, talked together, and had fun together. Only Valerie sat alone. In her quest to become a nurse this was the perfect scenario.

Ms. Crystal was the perfect chemistry teacher for Valerie. She was smart, young, and very pretty. She treated Valerie with respect and dignity. She was an avid reader and often biked the fifteen miles to the school. She was funny and often told chemistry jokes before class to relax her students, today was no different.

After the bell rang Ms. Crystal asked David, "I heard you lost an electron." She paused briefly as the class waited for the punch line, "next time you have to keep an ion it!" Eyes rolled but the class remained silent. Ms. Crystal expected more, so she threw out another science joke, "Do you know why you can't trust an atom?"

The class was quiet, Valerie knew the answer but didn't want the attention, so she buried her head in her chemistry book. Then the classroom door opened, and a handsome young man walked in and proudly said, "Because they make up everything." Only Ms. Crystal laughed.

Girls swooned, girls blushed, and the girls all smiled trying to get noticed by this handsome new kid on the block. Ms. Crystal was impressed and quickly replied, "Very good". The handsome young man handed her a slip of paper. Ms. Crystal read it and quickly introduced him, "Let's welcome our new student Grant to our school". Rudely somebody yelled out "nerd" and Ms. Crystal quickly replied, "That's enough Amari".

The class quickly gave Grant a welcome clap, but the damage was done. Amari did not like the new kid, Amari was jealous of the new kid, so his legions of followers did not like the new kid either. That's middle school. Valerie continued to bury herself in her book. Ms. Crystal proudly told Grant to sit in the open seat next to Valerie. Under their breaths, the class chuckled and made rude comments. As Grant walked toward his seat, he asked Ms. Crystal, "Did you hear? Oxygen (O) went on a date with Potassium (K)."

Valerie didn't look up or even hear the joke, but Ms. Crystal quickly answered with a huge smile answering, "everything turned out OK!" Amari yelled out "teacher's pet!" Ms. Crystal quickly ordered him to the principal's office. It didn't bother Amari; he knew Dr. Higginbottom would do nothing to him, not the star athlete of the school.

Grant sat down in his seat. Valerie kept reading about the different names on the periodic table, radium, scandium, cobalt, nickel, holmium, and americium, such cool names, she wondered what each one was and did. Then Grant slammed his books down on the table, Valerie looked up, Grant looked up. They looked each other in the eyes, Valerie stared, Grant stared. The world stood still for a second.

Ms. Crystal asked everyone to take out their projects. Valerie looked away. Grant looked away. "Please check off what you have finished for week three on the syllabus, I will be around to see how far you and your partner are. Remember there are only two weeks left before you and your partner need to turn in your report. Grant get a blank sheet of paper and a pen out; I will be over shortly."

There was a blue Bic pen on the table, Valerie went to grab it, Grant went to grab it, their hands touched. Valerie got goosebumps and shivered, Grant got goosebumps and shivered. They both smiled. Grant quickly said, "Rock, paper, scissors?" Valerie quickly pulled her hand back and defiantly replied, "NO! I always lose." "That's funny, I always win." Disgusted, Valerie pushed the pen toward Grant and reached in her small red purse for another pen.

Finally, Ms. Crystal came around and checked Valerie's syllabus, nothing surprising, Valerie was a few steps ahead. Ms. Crystal was ecstatic, "more of you should be like Valerie!" The class moaned in disapproval. "Grant, you need to get a copy of Valerie's notes, so you are prepared for the oral presentation next Tuesday. Valerie quickly responded, "Be at my house Saturday morning, 8:00 am sharp. I want a good grade on this projects so be prepared to study. Got it?"

Grant immediately replied, "My family and I won a weekend getaway at the Kalahari Resort in the Wisconsin Dells, we leave on Friday." Inside Valerie was jealous but was not phased outside because she never won anything in her life. Angelica overheard the two talking and asked, "Can I come over Saturday? I am having some problems with my report on the actinide series, I don't know the difference between cerium, samarium, promethium europium and neodymium.

That's easy interjected Grant, "cerium is an iron gray lustrous metal" Very good said Ms. Crystal, "Looks like we have another science geek." Valerie was not happy and yelled "samarium is a rare earth element used to make carbon arc lights used in the motion picture industry." Grant was not going to be embarrassed by some ordinary girl and proudly stated promethium is a radioactive element that was produced in a nuclear reactor!" Everyone gasped, all Grant responded was "checkmate!"

"That's all you got?" laughed Valerie. "Europium is the rarest of the earth elements" Valerie announced, "Checkmate!" not to be outdone, Grant stared at Valerie and Valerie stared at Grant. Simultaneously, Grant and Valerie yelled, "Neodymium is a silvery metal that quickly tarnishes." Ms. Crystal was overjoyed she now had two enthusiastic students in the class. Valerie responded, "checkmate!"

"Okay class, everybody has a partner and in two weeks, you will give an oral presentation on your group from the periodic table. Because I am such a cool teacher, I will give you plenty of class time this week to work on your team project, use your time wisely" Ms. Crystal announced. David raised his hand and asked, "will we get the same grade? You know I will end up doing all the work, Joey will be busy with his Pokémon cards." Ms. Crystal quietly said "Yes, now get to work."

Valerie sat quietly with her head buried in her workbook, she never had a partner before, she did not know what to do or say. There was a moment of awkward silence. However, she was impressed how smart Grant was. She glanced up for a second and noticed how beautiful his hair was. She inhaled and thought how wonderful his after shave smelled. Valerie smiled.

Grant sat quietly organizing his pens and pencils, he never had a girl for a partner before, he did not know what to do or say. There was a moment of awkward silence. However, he was impressed how smart Valerie was. He looked over and noticed how beautiful her long dark hair was. He looked over and thought what a nice outfit she was wearing. Grant smiled.

Ms. Crystal was walking the floor answering questions and maintaining civil order. Emma was struggling working alone. Joey was playing with his Pokémon cards and David was working hard on his set of elements. Jon and Louisa were done and preparing their power point presentation. Ray and Anna were researching their unique set of elements, but Ms. Crystal noticed Valerie and Grant hadn't even started.

Trying to break the ice, Ms. Crystal asked, "Do you know protons have mass?" Valerie sat quietly, thinking about the question. Grant looked puzzled about the question. Ms. Crystal told the two to think about the punch line. That's when it hit the two, simultaneously they stated, "We didn't even know protons were Catholic." They both laughed and Ms. Crystal told the two to split the ten elements into two piles, five for each, and start researching them.

Grant jumped at the chance and stated he would take zinc, copper, nickel, gold and silver, Valerie could have rutherfordium, darmstadtium and the other three that were too hard, to spell, write and speak. Valerie stood her ground and told him that wasn't fair, they needed to put the names in a cup and pull them one at a time. Grant told her it wouldn't matter because Grant always got what he wanted; he had the luck of the Irish. Valerie snickered and told Grant, "If it wasn't for bad luck, I wouldn't have any luck at all." Grant laughed wondering how such a pretty girl could have bad luck.

Together they put the name on paper for each element they were researching. Grant was the perfect gentleman and let Valerie pick first, Valerie was quite impressed. It was not surprising, but Valerie first picked molybdenum, Grant picked gold. Second round, Valerie chose rutherfordium, Grant picked copper. Third round she picked roentgenium, he picked nickel. Valerie rolled her eyes, Grant smiled. Fourth round Valerie chose meitnerium, he chose zinc. Mt. St. Valerie began to rumble. Fifth and final round, Valerie let Grant go first he chose silver leaving darmstadtium for Valerie. SUERTE!!

Grant was smug quickly proclaiming, "See, I told you!" Valerie was speechless, sometimes if you have nothing nice to say, then don't say anything at all. And believe me, Valerie had nothing nice to say. Grant felt the heat coming from Mt. St Valerie and decided to get the laptop computers so they could begin their research. There were only two left, an old ratty one and a brand new looking one. Grant handed Valerie the newer one and he kept the old ratty one. SUERTE!!

Although most of the class was chit-chatting while working together on their research projects, there was complete silence at the back table. Justin and Emily noticed, Ray and Anna noticed, and David and Joey noticed the eerie quiet in the corner of the room. Valerie turned on her computer, punched in her password and waited patiently for the computer to start. Grant turned on his computer, punched in his password and the computer started immediately. Valerie still waited for her computer to begin working. SUERTE!!

Grant had no problem typing his research words into Google search. Zinc, copper, gold, silver, and nickel all were easy to spell and type into the google search box. With all the keys working perfectly in the ratty old computer, Grant would easily be done by Thursday so he could travel to the Wisconsin Dells over the weekend. Valerie struggled typing her research words into the computer darmstadtium? No, darmstadum? No! darstatium? No! darmstadtium? Yes! Molybdium? No! Molydium? No! Molybdum? No! Molybdenum? Yes! This is the way all her research went. With many of the keys sticking, it would be lucky if Valerie was done by next week. SUERTE!!

All week the class worked on their projects. Justin and Emily finished their research projects on manmade metals, printed it and turned in their paper. Ray and Anna printed their paper but kept it so Anna could double-check for mistakes. Grant finished on Thursday and printed his twenty-page report containing illustrations, graphs, and charts, it was beautiful. By the time Valerie finished her section of the project the toner needed to be replaced and her paper kept getting stuck in the printer. SUERTE!!

Friday came, just in time. Most teams were finished with their projects, so Ms. Crystal gave her hard-working class free time. Ray and Anna watched a movie. Sam and Angelica worked on their home economics project. David, Joey, and Justin played video games on their phones. Emily planned a birthday party for her father. Grant was away at the Kalahari resort in the Wisconsin Dells, going down the biggest, coolest water fastest water slide there was, the famous Master Blaster, where roller coaster meets water slide. Only Valerie was still working on her half of the research project. SUERTE!!

Grant enjoyed himself at the Kalahari Water Park, but often thought how lucky he was to have Valerie as a partner in Chemistry. She was hard-working, smart, and awfully cute. Valerie left school on Friday completely exhausted but was determined to memorize the skeletal system of the human body. Friday was her evening to volunteer at Parkview Hospital as a candy stripper. The rest of the weekend her plan was to rest and relax.

Valerie thought about her week in Chemistry class. She thought about how lucky Grant was in everything he did. She thought Grant was smart, charming, a bit overconfident, but extremely handsome. She thought about how hard every step of her research paper was and asked herself, "Why, why do I have such bad luck!"

CHAPTER 5

THE PAPADOPOLUS'S

(A Family Name)

Valerie slept in Saturday morning, well at least till 8:00 am. Vanessa, the new candy stripper at Parkview hospital called in saying she was sick, but Valerie knew she was on a date with Amari. It was rumored Vanessa and Amari locked eyes in English class and the rest is history. Emma found out and immediately broke up with him. Valerie worked the Friday evening shift alone but managed to handle it quite successfully.

This week there was a young boy from Ms. Melody's third grade class at Hallsberry School, Luis, who when playing soccer accidentally ran into a solid 150-pound defender, Carlos. Carlos was not hurt but Luis ran into a brick wall, breaking his right arm, tearing a ligament in his right knee, and bruising his fragile ego. Luis stayed the night, but Valerie played several games of Uno with him. It was amazing how many times Luis plus foured Valerie. She also played Connect Four, Valerie was no match for quick draw Luis.

Then there was 84-year-old Mr. Jonassen, widowed now for 10 years. He loved his wife so much and every year, on the anniversary of her passing, he came to the hospital complaining of pains in his chest. Every year Dr. Durose would run countless tests all which would come back negative, despite the results Mr. Jonassen still complained about his chest pains. Everybody, including Valerie, knew he was suffering from a broken heart. Valerie listened to him talk about all the adventures him and his beautiful wife Barbara had, everywhere from Alaska to the Caribbean and even to Hawaii.

Unfortunately, Ms. Kadion also came in; she had a bad asthma attack after playing an impromptu game of half-court basketball with her ten-year-old son, Patrick. Ms. Kadion was extremely competitive, and no way was her ten-year-old son going to beat her. Well, he did, the score Patrick 10, Ms. Kaidion 3. Completely exhausted, completely embarrassed, and completely out of breath, she reached for her inhaler with no success. Patrick called 911. Valerie suggested she take up knitting instead.

Valerie's mom and dad waited up Friday night till 10:00 pm, but Valerie volunteered till 11:00 pm. Unless it was raining or snowing, Valerie usually walked home. It was a short walk and Valerie liked to think while she walked home. Nine times out of ten they waited up for Valerie to come home, but this was their weekend to help watch Aunt Eva. Aunt Eva was a nice aunt, but age had caught up with her. At 93 she could no longer take care of herself, she needed help with cooking, cleaning, bathing, dressing, and lawn maintenance. Valerie had a close-knit family where everyone helped when needed, at 93, Aunt Eva was the matriarch of the family, and was ALWAYS there for her large family, now it was the family's turn to be there for Aunt Eva.

Valerie loved Aunt Eva, she was always positive and uplifting. She was always encouraging. However, Valerie wanted to focus on learning the human skeletal system this weekend. Aunt Eva would understand Valerie's desire to become a nurse, right?

Mom and dad wanted to tell Valerie the truth 'about her misfortunate life but didn't want to be around for her reaction to the news. Most of the time Valerie was a very sweet young lady, but the other times she had a very small tolerance for bad news. That's where Mt. St. Valerie comes from. Mt. St. Valerie had been around since she was two. For Christmas, she wanted Chef Barbie, the one who cooked, Santa forgot, and the preverbal volcano erupted, the heat, the ashes, the shaking, the hot lava never stopped.

Day after day Mt. St. Valerie exploded, causing widespread damage. It was only after Santa made an emergency after Christmas delivery and the Executive Chef Barbie was securely in Valerie's hand did, she stopped crying, demanding, and throwing a tantrum. Giving into this demand created the monster we now know as Mt. St. Valerie.

Mom decided she would write a letter to Valerie, explaining everything and Uncle Bruce could handle the damage caused by Mt. St. Valerie. Uncle Bruce loved Valerie, ever since she was born the two had been close. Nobody knows why but out of all the nieces and nephews Valerie was his favorite. Their relationship was undeniable.

Uncle Bruce was the fun uncle, the uncle who broke or bent the rules, the uncle who spoiled his nieces and nephews. Uncle Bruce gave the children ice cream before dinner, Uncle Bruce never enforced bedtimes when he watched his nieces and nephews, Uncle Bruce never made the children eat their brussel sprouts. Uncle Bruce colored outside the lines, he threw snowballs, and he let the kids spend all their allowance on candy. Uncle Bruce let them watch tv, he let them play video games, he let them put cups on the counter without coasters, yes big bad Uncle Bruce did not care about coasters. He was a rule breaker, a bad boy, a rebel.

Valerie's mom and dad wanted to leave early Saturday morning, around 3:00 am. It was a four-hour drive from Glendale Heights to Shelbyville, Indiana, a small town just southeast of Indianapolis. Vivian would sleep, Kiara would sleep, Mom would nap, and dad would do the four-hour drive. Being the Columbus Day long weekend, they 'would be back late Monday night if all went well.

Valerie woke up refreshed and ready to study. Having no plans but studying the human skeletal system, she brushed her beautiful long dark hair, brushed her teeth, and put on some jogging pants and a nice comfortable middle school sweatshirt. Valerie wondered where Kiara was, she always followed Valerie in the morning. Shrugging the thought out of her mind she grabbed her anatomy book and headed downstairs to the big soft brown couch in the living room. Valerie wondered where her dad was, he was always in the living room reading the paper every Saturday morning.

She threw the heavy book on the couch, turned on the light, opened the curtains and headed into the kitchen. Totally focused on her studies she headed into the kitchen for Eggo Waffles and a nice cold glass of pulp-free orange juice. Behold on the counter was exactly that. Steaming hot with a pat of butter on top and fresh syrup oozing down the sides of Mt. St. Eggo, Valerie grabbed the plate and the glass of orange juice, said "Thank you, Uncle Bruce" and headed back to the living room to study. She wondered where her mom was for a brief second but was too distracted by the picturesque stack of steaming Eggo Waffles. They looked delicious, smelled delicious and hopefully tasted delicious. This was what Saturday's are all about.

Valerie opened the anatomy book and turned to Chapter 3, page 101, The Human Skeletal System. Simultaneously, she enjoyed bites of information about the human skeleton and bites of her Eggo Waffles. This was the perfect pairing. She shut the world out as she read.

There are 300 bones in a baby, 206 in an adult, they fuse together as the baby grows. She took a bite of the waffles. The smallest bone is in the ear, its's called the stapes bone. She took another bite of the syrup covered deliciousness. The largest strongest bone in your body is the femur, it's in the leg. She took a large sip of the orange juice. Bones are filled with a soft spongy tissue called bone marrow. She cut another small piece of awesomeness and gently placed it in her mouth. She took a moment to breathe.

She continued reading, over half of an adults bones are in the hands and feet, 106 out of 206. She took another bite of the best breakfast ever. She kept reading, the hyoid bone is the only bone not connected to a joint, it holds the tongue in place. Another bite of deliciousness. Although bones are strong, your teeth are stronger and when they do break, bones are natural healers. She took the last bite of those scrumptious Eggo waffles. Then lightning struck.

"Oh my gosh!" she proclaimed; "Uncle Bruce is in the kitchen". Carrying her sticky plate and her orange juice glass she ran rapidly through the house. "Uncle Bruce, Uncle Bruce!" Valerie screamed. Thinking something was wrong Uncle Bruce put his peppermint teacup down and ran toward the scream. Simultaneously, Valerie rushed to the kitchen entrance, and Uncle Bruce rushed to the kitchen entrance. Neither one was able to stop. CRASH! BANG! BOOM!

Valerie bounced off Uncle Bruce and fell to the ground. The dishes first hit Uncle Bruce, then bounced off him and then smashed to the ground, shattering into a million pieces. Uncle Bruce tried to stop, but like a freight train he couldn't stop in time. He slammed hard into Valerie, falling hard on his bottom. "Your mom told me you were accident prone!" He gingerly replied.

Neither one was hurt as they stood up, however Uncle Bruce's t-shirt was now covered in maple syrup. 'They both laughed at what happened and Valerie ran and gave her favorite uncle the biggest hug ever. Still hugging his favorite niece, Uncle Bruce whispered, "You have to pay attention to the road even if you don't know where you are going."

Poor Valerie, it brought back memories, "You sound like my neighbor Mr. Dulany, always giving advice." Uncle Bruce liked Mr. Dulany, "How is doing?" Valerie pulled back and hung her head, "I don't know, I really haven't talked to him for a while." Curious, Uncle Bruce asked, "Why? Did he hurt you? Was he mean to you?" Valerie just said, "NO." "so let me get this right, without any reason, you just pushed a friend of many years out of your life?" he said. Valerie sadly replied, "Yes"

Uncle Bruce was flabbergasted, he thought Valerie was better than that. Stoically, he said karma would come after everyone eventually. I don't think you have bad luck; you have bad karma. What comes around goes around, if you are a mean person now, in the next life you might come back as a common fly and dine on poop. You need to make things right with Mr. Dulany, he is heartbroken."

Feeling guilty, Valerie quickly changed the subject, "So, what brings you here? Where is mom and dad? Where is Vivian and Kiara?" Uncle Bruce was confused, "Didn't they tell you they were going to Aunt Eva's for the long weekend? Didn't they tell you I was coming?" Valerie couldn't remember anybody telling her they were going to Aunt Eva's house for the long weekend, so she shook her head no.

Uncle Bruce was confused telling her that her mom and dad asked him weeks ago to come over and watch her because she wanted to study?" Valerie was appalled, Valerie was insulted, Valerie was mad. Was she becoming the invisible girl in her own house? Mt. St. Valerie was getting ready to explode. Uncle Bruce remembered this and wanted to avoid an explosion at all costs, so he quickly grabbed the envelope that her mom had left. He handed the envelope to Valerie.

What's this?" asked Valerie. "I don't know" replied Uncle Bruce. "All your mom said was to give it to you on Saturday morning when you woke up. Something about finally telling you the truth." This was the straw that broke the camel's back. "I knew it I am from the planet Zuru 225! I am an alien! I am not part of this family!" Crying, Valerie grabbed the envelope and frantically ran up to her room where she slammed the door.

Almost afraid, she tore open the letter and began reading:

GOOD MORNING SWEETHEART,

I WAS REALLY HOPING TO TALK TO YOU BEFORE WE LEFT FOR AUNT EVA'S HOUSE, YOU DO REMEMBER WE WENT TO AUNT EVA'S FOR THE LONG WEEKEND? RIGHT? YOU DIDN'T. ANYWAYS, UNCLE BRUCE IS THERE, I KNOW YOU ARE A BIG GIRL, BUT I THOUGHT

YOU MIGHT LIKE TO SPEND SOME TIME WITH YOUR FAVORITE UNCLE. HE ACTUALLY NEEDS SOMEONE TO WATCH HIM. WE PLAN ON COMING BACK MONDAY EVENING.

PLEASE KEEP THE HOUSE CLEAN AND DO YOUR CHORES, EMPTY THE DISHWASHER, VACUUM AND CLEAN YOUR ROOM. I REALLY HOPE YOU DON'T KEEP YOUR HEAD STUCK IN A BOOK ALL WEEKEND; YOUR UNCLE BRUCE WAS VERY EXCITED TO HAVE THE CHANCE TO SPEND THIS TIME WITH YOU. DO YOU REMEMBER THE TIME HE CAME AND TOOK YOU TO GREAT AMERICA, HOW MANY TIMES DID YOU RIDE THE ROLLER COASTER? DO YOU REMEMBER THE WEEK HE VOLUNTEERED IN YOUR CLASS? HOW MANY PARENTS COMPLAINED ABOUT HIM PLAYING SOCCER? DO YOU REMEMBER HOW MANY TIMES YOU TWO WENT CAMPING IN THE BACKYARD?

DO NOT TAKE ADVANTAGE OF HIM, HE LOVES YOU SO MUCH AND WOULD DO ANYTHING FOR YOU. HOW ABOUT THAT TIME YOU TWO WENT TO BUILD-A-BEAR? YOU COULDN'T DECIDE WHICH BEAR TO ADOPT SO HE GOT YOU ALL 27. OR THE TIME HE WENT BACK TO SCHOOL SHOPPING WITH YOU, I BELIEVE IT WAS 2ND GRADE? HE BOUGHT YOU A NEW OUTFIT EVERYDAY FOR THE FIRST MONTH. HOW ABOUT YOUR LAST BIRTHDAY PARTY? WE LET HIM PLAN IT, YOU HAD FACE PAINTING, A PETTING ZOO, A BOUNCY HOUSE, A TACO TRUCK AND UNLIMITED ICE CREAM FOR EVERYONE ALL DAY, DO NOT TAKE ADVANTAGE OF HIM.

THE MOST IMPORTANT REASON FOR THIS LETTER IS TO TELL YOU THE TRUTH ABOUT

YOUR "BAD LUCK." IT IS NOT BAD LUCK, BUT AN OLD CURSE PUT ON OUR FAMILY MANY YEARS AGO BY YOUR GREAT, GREAT, GREAT, GREAT, GREAT, GREAT, GREAT, GREAT GRANDFATHER'S CLOSE FRIEND, ROGER PAPADOPOLUS WIFE, WENDY. SHE WAS RUMORED TO BE A WITCH. ARE YOU STILL READING? THIS STORY IS ONLY BEGINNING.

WELL WAY BACK IN 1849, THERE WAS A GOLD RUSH HAPPENING IN CALIFORNIA. IN 1849 SAMMY DULANY FOUND A GOLD NUGGET AT THE SUTTER'S RANCH. THE WORLD WENT CRAZY, EVERYONE HEADED TO CALIFORNIA, THE IRISH, THE SPANISH, THE CANADIANS. PEOPLE FROM NEW YORK, DELAWARE AND TEXAS ALL HEADED TO CALIFORNIA TO FIND GOLD. INCLUDING, YOUR GREAT, GREAT, GREAT, GREAT, GREAT, GREAT, GREAT, GREAT, GREAT GRANDFATHER ULYSSES. HOWEVER, HIS BEST FRIEND ROGER WANTED TO WAIT UNTIL THE TIME WAS RIGHT.

ULYSSE'S WIFE MARIA WANTED THEM TO GO BEFORE ALL THE GOLD WAS GONE. MARIA WANTED A BETTER LIFE FOR HER FAMILY. SHE WANTED TO JOIN THE RANKS OF THE RICH AND FAMOUS. THEIR OLDEST DAUGHTER, PENELOPE, DESERVED THE BEST.

IN 1849, ROGER FELT THERE WERE TOO MANY PEOPLE GOING, HE DIDN'T LIKE CROWDS, HIS WIFE, WENDY, ASKED HIM TO WAIT. IN 1850, ROGER'S TEAM OF OXEN WERE SICK. HIS WIFE, WENDY, ASKED HIM TO WAIT UNTIL THE TIME WAS RIGHT. IN THE SUMMER OF 1851, WHILE THE CALIFORNIA GOLD RUSH WAS IN FULL SWING, ROGER HAD HS TENTH CHILD, ABRAHAM, HIS WIFE WENDY ASKED HIM TO

WAIT UNTIL THE TIME WAS RIGHT. IN 1852 THERE WAS THE GREAT DROUGHT OF 1852, OBVIOUSLY HIS WIFE WENDY DIDN'T HAVE TO ASK, THE TIME WAS NOT RIGHT SO HE STAYED HOME.

ULYSSES WAS A PATIENT MAN. IN 1853 WITH PROSPECTORS STILL FINDING GOLD, ULYSSES PACKED HIS BAGS IN PREPARATION FOR HEADING TO CALIFORNIA HOPING TO CHANGE HIS LIFE. WENDY, NOW WITH 13 CHILDREN AND THE FARM HAVING A RECORD CROP DIDN'T WANT HER HUSBAND GOING FAR, THE TIME WAS NOT RIGHT. ALTHOUGH ULYSSES WAS EXTREMELY DISAPPOINTED, HE RESPECTED HIS FRIEND'S WIFE'S DECISION.

IN 1854 WENDY WANTED A VACATION. WENDY SUGGESTED AFTER HARVEST THE FAMILY GO CAMPING. SHE KNEW A PERFECT PLACE THEY COULD TAKE THEIR 13 WONDERFUL CHILDREN. AS A CHILD, HER MOTHER AND FATHER TOOK HER TO DIAMOND STATE PARK, IT HAD A SLOW RUNNING RIVER, SAND DUNES AND A BEAUTIFUL BEACH WHERE THEIR 13 CHILDREN COULD PLAY, SWIM AND HAVE A GREAT TIME. ULYSSES, MARIA AND THEIR FIVE CHIDREN, PENELOPE, PENNY, PAUL, PETER, AND PAULINA WERE MORE THAN WELCOME TO JOIN THEM.

GIVING UP ON EVER FINDING GOLD WITH HIS GOOD FRIEND ROGER IN CALIFORNIA, ULYSSES DECIDED TO JOIN THE PAPADOPOLUS FAMILY ON THEIR VACATION. AFTER ALL, HE LOVED ALL OF THEM, ASHLEY, ARIANA, ADAM, ALICE, AARON, ANGEL, ALLEN, ALLISON, ALYSSA, ABRAHAM, ANABELL, AMANDA, AND ANDREA,

HE LOVED HUNTING WITH ASHLEY AND ARIANA. HE HIKED WITH AMANDA AND ALICE. HE SWAM IN THE LAKE WITH AARON AND ANGEL, ULYSSES BUILT CAMPFIRES WITH ALLEN AND ALLISON. HE LOVED TO BUILD SANDCASTLES WITH THE THREE YOUNGEST PAPADOPOLUS CHILDREN, ANABEL, AMANDA, AND ABRAHAM. ANDREA WAS STILL A BABY AND SPENT ALL OF HER TIME EATING, POOPING AND SLEEPING.

THE TWO FAMILIES HAD A WONDERFUL TIME TOGETHER. EVERYBODY GOT ALONG GREAT, ROGER AND ULYSSES SPENT TIME TOGETHER, MARIA AND WENDY HAD FUN. EVEN ALL THE CHILDREN HAD FUN, IT WAS WENDY WHO CAME UP WITH THE IDEA OF A GOODBYE CELEBRATION AT THE BEACH FOR THEIR LAST DAY OF VACATION.

ON THIS BEAUTIFUL SUNNY DAY, MARIA AND WENDY MADE CHEESEBURGERS AND HOT DOGS OVER A BEAUTIFUL FIRE. LIFE DIDN'T GET ANY BETTER THAN THIS, WHAT COULD GO WRONG? AS MARIA AND WENDY COOKED THE FOOD, ROGER TOOK HIS BEAUTIFFUL CHILDREN AND PLAYED IN THE WATER. THEY SWAM, THEY JUMPED, THEY HAD A WONDERFUL TIME. ULYSSES TOOK HIS FIVE CHILDREN TO PLAY IN THE SAND.

This is where the story gets interesting. DING DONG, DING DONG, went the doorbell. Uncle Bruce reluctantly answered the door. "Hi, I'm Angelica, is Valerie home?" asked the sweet young girl. "Valerie! Valerie! You have a visitor," called Uncle Bruce. He guided Angelica to a seat in the living room. He called Valerie again, "Valerie!". Valerie was unphased and continued to read mom's letter.

ULYSSES TOOK HIS BUCKETS AND DUG IN THE SAND. PENELOPE HELPED HER FATHER WATCH THE CHILDREN, ESPECIALLY THE TWO YOUNGER ONES PETER AND PAULINA, PENNY AND PAUL HELPED THEIR FATHER BUILD A HUGE SANDCASTLE. IT HAD EVERYTHING THE FAMILY WANTED, A HUGE BASEMENT, LARGE KITCHEN, LARGE FAMILY ROOM, SIX BEDROOMS AND TWO BATHROOMS, SOMETHING THE FAMILY DESPERATELY NEEDED. THE ONLY THING THE CASTLE NEEDED WAS A MOAT.

A MOAT IS A BODY OF WATER THAT SURROUNDS THE CASTLE TO KEEP PEOPLE OUT. THE MOAT WAS USUALLY SIX FEET DEEP AND CONTAINED AT LEAST ONE ALLIGATOR. PENELOPE TRIED DIGGING DEEP BUT HER HANDS GOT TIRED VERY QUICKLY. PETER AND PAULINA TRIED DIGGING BUT WERE TOO YOUNG, THEY WERE JUST PLAYING. PENNY AND PAUL GOT SOME STICKS AND TRIED DIGGING WITH THEM, IT DIDN'T WORK.

THE HERNANDEZ FAMILY CALLED THE PAPADOPOLUS FAMILY FOR HELP BUT THEY WERE TOO BUSY HAVING FUN IN THE WATER, THEY DIDN'T WANT TO HELP. HAVING BIG HANDS ULYSSES HAD NO CHOICE, HE BEGAN TO DIG, THE SAND WAS HARD, BUT ULYSSES KEPT DIGGING, IF HIS KIDS WANTED A MOAT, HE WOULD GIVE THEM A MOAT. ABOUT HALFWAY THROUGH HE CAME ACROSS SOMETHING HARD.

HE DUG AND DUG, PENELOPE HELPED, PETER HELPED, PAUL HELPED, PAULINA HELPED AND PENNY HELPED. THE PAPADOPOLUS FAMILY STAYED IN THE WATER AND PLAYED.

WENDY CALLED EVERYONE FOR LUNCH, THE PAPADOPOLUS FAMILY ATE WHILE THE HERNANDEZ FAMILY DUG IN THE SAND.

MARIA CAME OVER BRINGING LUNCH TO HER FAMILY, FINALLY, ULYSSES PULLED THE SMALL WOODEN BOX FROM THE CLUTCHES OF DIRT AND SAND. THE HERNANDEZ FAMILY WATCHED IN ANTICIPATION AS DAD HELD THE BOX, CURIOUS WAS NOT THE WORD, EXCITED WAS NOT THE WORD, BUT ECSTATIC WAS AND INQUISITIVE WAS.

DAD OPENED THE SMALL WOODEN BOX WITH GREAT ANTICIPATION, THE LATCH STUCK A LITTLE BUT ULYSSES NIMBLE HANDS QUICKLY FREED THE STICKY MECHANISM. ALL EYES WERE WATCHING, INCLUDING ADAM FROM THE PAPADOPOLUS FAMILY. ULYSSES OPENED UP THE BOX AND FOUND AN OLD PAIR OF BEAT-UP DAMAGED GLASSES. ADAM WALKED AWAY DISAPPOINTED, PETER, PAUL, PAULINA, AND PENNY ALSO WALKED AWAY DISAPPOINTED, ONLY HIS ELDEST DAUGHTER, PENELOPE STAYED AT HIS SIDE.

AS EVERYONE ATE LUNCH, PENELOPE HELPED HER FATHER UP FROM THE DIRTY WET SAND, AT 6'3" AND OVER 200 POUNDS, SHE GRABBED HIS HAND AND PULLED, SHE SLID, SHE SLIPPED, IT WAS A MESS, WITH ONE LAST PULL HE GRABBED HIS HANDS WITH EVERYTHING SHE HAD, WHICH WASN'T ENOUGH. SHE SLIPPED AND FELL INTO THE MAKESHIFT MOAT. SHE CLOSED HER EYES IN DISBELIEF.

ULYSSES LAUGHED, PENELOPE OPENED HER EYES AND LAUGHED. PENELOPE STRUGGLED, BUT EVENTUALLY GOT HERSELF UP AND

STARTED TO HELP HER FATHER FROM THE MOAT. SHE GRABBED ULYSSE'S HAND AND PULLED, NOTHING, SHE PULLED AGAIN AND THAT'S WHEN SHE SAW IT, ANOTHER BOX, SHE DROPPED ULYSSES AGAIN. PENELOPE APOLOGIZED AND PICKED UP HER FATHER. TOGETHER WITH NO ONE WATCHING, FATHER AND DAUGHTER DUG OUT THE SECOND BOX.

WITH LITTLE CURIOSITY, WITH LITTLE HOPE, THE TWO THOUGHT THEY FOUND ANOTHER PAIR OF OLD GLASSES. WITH EVERYBODY PLAYING IN THE WATER, WITHOUT ANY FANFARE, ULYSSES AND HIS FIRST-BORN DAUGHTER OPENED THE SMALL DIRTY BOX. NONCHALANTLY THEY UNCLASPED THE BRASS LATCH. SURPRISINGLY, THEY FOUND A BEAUTIFUL DIAMOND NECKLACE, PENELOPE CRIED TEARS OF JOY AS SHE HELD HER TREASURE.

IMMEDIATELY, THE AIR BEGAN TO CHANGE. WENDY IMMEDIATELY CAME RUNNING OVER TO WHAT ALL THE FUSS WAS ABOUT. PENELOPE SHOWED HER THE NECKLACE. THE DIAMOND NECKLACE WAS CLEAR AND SHINY. WENDY KNEW IT WAS VALUABLE. WITHOUT HESISTATION, WITHOUT REMORSE, WITHOUT GUILT, WENDY TOOK CREDIT FOR FINDING THE NECKLACE. PENELOPE AND ULYSSES WERE SHOCKED AS WENDY TOLD THEM IT WAS BECAUSE OF HER, THIS IS WHERE FATE BROUGHT THEM AND NOT CALIFORNIA, SHE FELT IT BELONGED TO HER.

THE HERNANDEZ FAMILIES LUCK IMMEDIATELY BEGAN TO CHANGE. THE LAUNDRY MOM HAD DONE IN THE RIVER WAS SUDDENLY DRY. ULYSSES SUDDENLY FOUND

THE WALLET HE MISPLACED WHEN THEY GOT TO THE LAKE. PENELOPE GOT PERMISSION TO GO TO A SCHOOL DANCE WITH A BOY, FROM HER PARENTS. PETER STARTED BEING NICE TO HIS SISTERS. PAUL AND PAULINA FOUND AN ABANDONED GERMAN SHEPARD PUPPY. AND SUDDENLY PENNY STOPPED THROWING TANTRUMS TO GET HER WAY. WENDY PAPADOPOLUS NOTICED THEIR STREAK OF LUCK AND DEMANDED THAT THEY GIVE HER THE LUCKY DIAMOND NECKLACE.

ULYSSES HERNANDEZ REFUSED, SAYING IT WAS PENELOPE WHO FOUND THE DIAMOND AND SHE WAS THE OWNER. THE PAPADOPOLUS FAMILY DISAGREED AND LEFT THE CAMPSITE SAYING THAT THEIR FRIENDSHIP WAS OVER BETWEEN THE TWO FAMILIES. WENDY PROMISED ULYSSES THIS WAS NOT OVER. THEY PACKED QUICKLY AND LEFT THE CAMPGROUND. WENDY PROMISED HERSELF ONE DAY SHE WOULD GET THE DIAMOND NECKLACE BACK AND PUNISH PENELOPE FOR HER GREED.

ON THE WAY BACK HOME, THINGS DID NOT GO WELL FOR THE PAPADOPOLUS FAMILY. THEY TOOK THE WRONG TRAIL BACK HOME, THEY ENDED UP GETTING LOST, ROGER REFUSED TO STOP AND ASK DIRECTIONS. FOR MUCH OF THE RIDE HOME IN THEIR COVERED WAGON, THE CLOUDS POURED GALLONS OF RAIN UPON THEM. THE COVERED WAGON LEAKED MAKING EVERYTHING IN THE WAGON WET, INCLUDING ALL THIRTEEN CHILDREN. BY THE TIME THEY GOT HOME ALL THIRTEEN CHILDREN HAD THE FLU. WENDY WAS NOT HAPPY. SHE HAD TO GET THE NECKLACE.

THE HERNANDEZ FAMILY HAD A FABULOUS TRIP HOME. THEY FOUND THEIR WAY HOME WITHOUT GETTING LOST, THEY ACTUALLY STOPPED FOR LUNCH AND ENDED UP BEING THE MILLIONTH CUSTOMER, GETTING FREE LUNCH AND TONS OF PRIZES. THEY RAN INTO NO RAINSTORMS WHILE TRAFFIC WAS VERY LIGHT. UYLSSES WAS VERY HAPPY WITH THEIR NEWFOUND LUCK WITH HIS DAUGHTER'S DIAMOND NECKLACE.

EVERTBODY GOT HOME OKAY AND THE FAMILIES CONTINUED NOT TO TALK TO EACH OTHER, THE HERNANDEZ FAMILY CONTINUED TO THRIVE. IT WAS ALMOST LIKE THEY HAD THE MIDAS TOUCH, THEY HAD A RECORD HARVESTS ON THEIR FARM, THE CHILDREN ALL DID WELL IN SCHOOL AND WERE OFFERED SCHOLARSHIPS TO PRESTIGIOUS COLLEGES, ULYSSES INVESTED IN SOMETHING CALLED THE TELEPHONE AND BECAME AN OVERNIGHT BILLIONAIRE.

ON THE OTHER HAND, THE PAPADOPOLUS FAMILY STRUGGLED. EVEN THOUGH THEIR FARM WAS RIGHT UP THE ROAD THEIR FARM WENT THROUGH DROUGHT, CRICKET INFESTATIONS, AND LEAF ROT. BECAUSE OF THIS, THEY WENT INTO BANKRUPTCY, EVENTUALLY LIVING A LIFE OF POVERTY. THE CHILDREN ALL DID TERRIBLE IN SCHOOL, TOO TIRED, TOO HUNGRY, TOO POOR, TO EVEN BOTHER WITH HOMEWORK. THERE WAS NO MONEY TO INVEST, NO MONEY TO PAY THE BILLS, NO MONEY TO FEED THE CHILDREN.

WENDY PAPADOPOLUS KEPT TRACK OF THE HERNANDEZ'S STREAK OF GOOD LUCK. SHE WAS CONSUMED WITH JEALOUSLY. THEN ONE

DAY THE TAX COLLECTOR CAME AND GAVE HER FARM THIRTY DAYS TO PAY THE BACK TAXES OR THE FARM WOULD BE SOLD, WENDY WAS FURIOUS AND WAS DETERMINED TO SAVE HER FARM. WENDY PAPADOPOLUS CONOCTED AN EVIL, DEVIOUS PLAN TO GET THE LUCKY DIAMOND NECKLACE INTO HER HANDS.

IT DIDN'T TAKE LONG FOR WENDY TO GET THE DIAMOND NECKLACE, THE HERNANDEZ FAMILY WAS VERY TRUSTING, THEY HAD A HABIT OF LEAVING THEIR DOOR UNLOCKED. ONE DAY WHILE THE HERNANDEZ FAMILY WAS HELPING WITH THE ORPHANS, WENDY STROLLED RIGHT IN AND STOLE THE NECKLACE.

THE PAPADOPOLUS LUCK CHANGED IMMEDIATELY. WENDY FOUND A HUNDRED DOLLAR BILL ON THE WAY HOME. IT RAINED JUST OVER THEIR FIELDS, MAKING THEIR HARVEST BOUNTIFUL. WENDY GOT THE LAST CAN OF PEPSI ON THE SHELF. THINGS WERE FINALLY LOOKING UP FOR THE PAPADOPOLUS FAMILY.

"Valerie! VALERIE! "Uncle Bruce called as he got Valerie's friend a nice cold cup of water. Uncle Bruce apologized to Angelica for Valerie's rudeness, but he continued calling her. Valerie did not care who it was, she was determined to finish reading this letter, so that's exactly what she did.

THE FIRST THING AFTER ACQUIRING THE LUCKY NECKLACE WAS TO FIND A WITCH, DESPITE WHAT PEOPLE THOUGHT, SHE WAS NOT A WITCH. WENDY HATED PENELOPE FOR FINDING THE LUCKY NECKLACE, SHE FELT THAT ONE OF HER CHILDREN SHOULD HAVE

FOUND IT AND THE PAPADOPOLUS FAMIY SHOULD HAVE ALL THE GOOD LUCK. BEING CONSUMED WITH ANGER AND BITTERNESS, SHE WANTED THE FIRST-BORN DAUGHTER IN EACH GENERATION TO HAVE BAD LUCK. THE WITCH LAUGHED AND TOLD WENDY THAT WAS ONLY POSSIBLE IF THERE WAS A WAY TO BREAK THE CURSE.

WENDY CAME UP WITH AN EXTREMELY IMPOSSIBLE THREE-PART RIDDLE TO SOLVE. IF THE FIRST-BORN DAUGHTER SOLVED IT THE CURSE WOULD BE BROKEN, HOWEVER SHE ALSO PUT IN THE CURSE, IF THERE WAS A MISTAKE ANYTIME IN SOLVING THE RIDDLE, DIRE CONSQUENCES WOULD BE SERVED.

WHEN YOU ARE 18, YOU MAY OR MAY NOT DECIDE TO GO ON THIS JOURNEY, FOR NOW YOU SHOULD WAIT. BUT BE WARNED YOUR GREAT COUSIN GERTRUDE WENT TO SOLVE THE RIDDLE AND SHE NEVER CAME BACK. YOUR GREAT GREAT COUSIN AGATHA WENT TO SOLVE THE RIDDLE AND SHE WAS NEVER HEARD FROM AGAIN. AND LET NOT FORGET ABOUT YOUR GREAT COUSIN LILLIANA, YES, SHE TOO HAD BAD LUCK AND WENT ON THE JOURNEY AND YES, SHE WAS NEVER SEEN OR HEARD FROM AGAIN. YOU MUST DECIDE YOUR OWN FATE.

WELL, AS I STATED BEFORE, WENDY PAPADOPOLUS ENDED UP STEALING THE DIAMOND NECKLACE FROM THE HERNANDEZ FAMILY. SUDDENLY THE PAPADOPOLUS FAMILY LUCKED TURNED AROUND, THEY HAD A RECORD CROP, THEY PAID OFF THEIR TAXES AND SAVED THE FARM THAT HAD BEEN IN THEIR FAMILY FOR 100 YEARS. THE KIDS DID

WELL IN SCHOOL AND THEY HAD PLENTY TO EAT.

AT THE SAME TIME THE HERNANDEZ FAMILIES LUCK TURNED AROUND TOO. THE NECKLACE WAS STOLEN AND NOBODY KNEW WHO TOOK IT. SUDDENLY SQUIRRELS INVADED THEIR CROPS, SUDDENLY MARIA LOST HER JOB AT THE NEWSPAPER, SUDDENLY THE BANK LOST THEIR MONEY. THINGS WERE LOOKING BLEAK FOR THE HERNANDEZ FAMILY, BUT THEY HELD THEIR HEADS HIGH.

PENELOPE, BEING THE FIRST-BORN GIRL OF HER GENERATION, WAS HIT THE HARDEST. HER FEET GREW TO A SIZE FOURTEEN, SHE HAD A RECURRING PIMPLE ON HER NOSE. PENELOPE WAS FORCED INTO GETTING A PART-TIME JOB CLEANING UP HORSE POOP AT THE MISTICI HORSE STABLES TWO FARMS DOWN. THERE WAS NOT A DAY THAT WENT BY THAT SHE DID NOT SLIP AND FALL INTO A PILE OF POOH. SHE NEVER MARRIED AND DIED A LONELY OLD CAT LADY, SHE HAD OVER 40 CATS IN HER HOUSE.

I KNOW THIS WILL NOT HELP, BUT I WANTED YOU TO KNOW. YOU ARE OUR DAUGHTER WHO WE LOVE AND ADORE, YOU WERE NOT LEFT AT A FIRE STATION, NOR ARE YOU FROM PLANET ZURU 225, UNFORTUNATELY YOU WERE CURSED BY WENDY PAPADOPOLUS WITH THE CURSE OF DIAMOND NECKLACE. YOU SHOULD WAIT UNTIL YOU ARE 18 BUT HERE IS THE FIRST CLUE.

GENERAL STORE-TICK TOCK-TICK TOCK

Valerie now knew why she had bad luck, unfortunately she was years away from being 18. Now she wondered if she would ever ask herself again, "Why, why do I have such bad luck?"

CHAPTER 6

BUMFUZZLED

(To confuse)

Uncle Bruce was relentless in his attempt to bring Valerie downstairs. "Valerie!" he called over and over again with no response. Angelica was a nice young lady who waited patiently for Valerie to come downstairs. He apologized over and over again for Valerie's rudeness. "Valerie! Valerie! Don't make me come upstairs and get you!" he called out. There was no response.

For some odd reason, her mind wandered to Grant. He was lucky. Not that she cared, but he was smart and did well in school. Grant was the type that didn't have to study for tests, but still managed to do well. Not that she cared, but he had a great personality. He definitely had manners and a great attitude towards life. Not that she cared, but he was a handsome young man, nice well-groomed hair, beautiful smile and well dressed.

In the Wisconsin Dells, Grant's mind wandered to the pretty girl he met at school last week. There was something different about her, there was something unique about her, there was something very special about Valerie. Yes, she was pretty, but there was something more. Grant knew that being the new kid in the school he didn't have a chance with her. She was out of his league; all he could do was admire her from the sidelines and wish she was his. Having her as a friend was better than nothing.

Frustrated, Uncle Bruce called up, "I am going to send Alice back home." Angelica quickly responded, "It's Angelica and I can't go home, since I was planning on spending the long weekend here, my mother and father decided to spend a long weekend in a fancy hotel in Chicago."

Uncle Bruce was bumfuzzled, Valerie's mom and dad said nothing about a sleepover. Very casually, very calmly he asked, "Sleepover?" Finally, Valerie came down the stairs and repeated what her Uncle Bruce had asked, "sleepover?"

"I hope that is okay," asked Angelica. "I know I am not one of the cool kids, but it would be awesome to spend some time together with you." Valerie looked around to see who Angelica was talking too. "You must have me bumfuzzled with somebody else" she gingerly replied. "I have no friends, and I am definitely not one of the cool kids!"

Angelica strongly disagreed, "Don't be so modest, all the kids admire you. Most of us are a jumbled pot of wild hormones, one minute we are sweet children then we wake up in the morning and five minutes later we act like know-it-all angry adults. This month alone, I have dressed in goth, done the urban casual look and now I am dressing in the Seattle punk rock look. Based on our moods we are either super rebellious with our parents or sweet as pie. We don't know why. It could be a gust of wind or the gravitational pull of the moon's orbit, but it flips at a moment's notice. Trust me, the kids all think you are the coolest!"

Valerie was speechless, all that came out of her mouth was, "Whaat?" Angelica proudly continued, "You are smart, beautiful and seem like a lot of fun. So can you help me with my science project?" Valerie was confused, "You had plenty of time in class, why didn't you finish?"

Angelica hung her head, "All my boyfriend thinks about is wood, he eats wood, sleeps wood, and poops wood. He loves wood! All he talks about is wood. Maple, birch, oak, pine, mahogany, cedar, balsam, walnut, cherry, wood, and more wood. Bottom line we didn't do our research paper that is due on Tuesday." Valerie was fascinated, "What is your research paper on?"

She smiled, "I changed it, the other stuff made no sense. Now it's everything that is good with the world, everything that is beautiful in the world, everything that is worth living for in the world. I am talking gold. Gold rings, gold coins, gold necklaces, gold earrings, gold watches, gold bracelets and gold bricks. Bling, bling, and more bling!" Valerie smiled knowing how simple and fast this would be, "I will give you the information and you will be on your way before lunch."

Angelica was sad, "Nobody is home at my house, I told them I was spending the long weekend working on the research paper. My mom was ecstatic, you have such a good reputation with all of our parents. Everyone thinks you are so smart. Wouldn't it be fun to have a girl's weekend?"

Valerie did not answer, she was too busy thinking about the letter from her mom. Six years until she was 18. Six years until she could break the curse. Six more years of bad luck. Six more years of accidents, misfortune, and unfortunate events. Six more years of being the laughingstock in middle school and high school. Six more years of her sister finding money on the ground. Six more years of embarrassment. This had to end, the sooner the better.

Angelica waited for an answer, but there was nothing. "Valerie! Valerie! A girl's weekend?" Valerie was too busy thinking about the letter from her mom. Uncle Bruce noticed Valerie's rudeness and quickly got her attention, "Valerie, don't be rude to your guest!" Upset, Valerie ran to her room crying hysterically.

"You really need to chill!" Angelica scolded Uncle Bruce, "don't you see she's going through an emotional trauma? She's a teenage girl playing hockey with tennis rackets. Her hormones are racing through her body 5000 miles per hour, she's a Yugo competing in the Daytona 500. Have you ever been a teenage girl? I didn't think so. Our bodies are confused. It's like playing football, wearing dance shoes, throwing a basketball trying to make home runs. It's bumfuzzling!

Speechless, Uncle Bruce stood there quietly realizing his niece was growing up. He was embarrassed and memories of his puberty days blurted across his mind. He thought of his first crush, his sixth-grade teacher, Ms. Craswell. How embarrassing! He realized how timid he was on his first date with Jennifer. How embarrassing! He remembered how determined he was to travel through a snowstorm to a college party. How embarrassing! He stood there unable to move or speak.

Angelica stared at Uncle Bruce, hoping he would say something, but he didn't. Angelica huffed, puffed, and stomped her foot in protest. Finally running out of patience, she herself went upstairs to console her new friend Valerie, leaving Uncle Bruce standing there with only his thoughts.

Upstairs, Angelica slowly entered Valerie's room. She noticed Valerie sitting on the bed crying and softly asked her, "Is there anything I could do to help?" Valerie quickly replied, "NO". Angelica approached Valerie cautiously, "do you want to talk about it?" Valerie quickly replied "NO!" Realizing Valerie was in no mood to talk, Angelica decided to change her strategy.

Looking around Valerie's room, Angelica was impressed with the vast array of anatomy books. "that's really cool you know what you want to do when you are older. Most of us can't figure out what to have for breakfast, let alone decide on a career. A solid career, nursing, no wonder everyone wants to be like you," Valerie smiled.

Angelica smiled back and said, "Whatever it is it will pass." Angrily, Valerie declared, "A curse does not pass, I have six more years of bad luck, six more years, do you hear me? Six more years before I can attempt to break the curse. I need to get the diamond necklace back to my family." Angelica was bumfuzzled.

"What curse? What diamond? What bad luck?" asked a very bumfuzzled Angelica. Surprisingly Valerie decided to finally open up to Angelica. Briefly she told the story of the infamous Papadopolus and Hernandez family camping trip, she confided with Angelica about the curse and Valerie told her that her mom said she had to be

18 before she could try and solve the riddle and bring the diamond back to the rightful owners, the Hernandez family.

But she also told her of the many first-born daughters who didn't make it back trying to break the curse. Did they guess wrong on one of the clues and get put in a black hole? Were they kidnapped by the Papadopolus family while solving the riddle? Were they caught red handed taking the diamond necklace back and sent to the salt mines? Nobody will ever know, what we do know is they have never been found.

Valerie handed Angelica the letter from her mom, "you don't want me as your friend, I am nothing but trouble, my uncle calls me NBT. If something could go wrong, it does wrong, if you handed me a set of 100 keys to a locked door, it would be the last key I tried, if I bought a goldfish and there was a 99% chance of survival past the first week, you know my goldfish would have passed before I left the store!" Mt. St. Valerie was getting ready to explode.

Angelica quickly realized what was about to happen. Did she call the National Emergency hotline? Did she evacuate the city? Or did she run and hide, hoping to outrun the explosion from the deadly blast? Valerie kept spewing hot ash.

"Six years of bad luck! Six years of not winning any prizes. Six years of accidentally tripping over curbs. Six years of toilet paper stuck to my shoes. Six years of mismatched socks!" Watch out! Mt. St. Valerie was getting close to exploding. Angelica read the letter as fast as she could, trying to save the world.

Mt. St. Valerie continued spewing ashes of complaints out of her mouth, "Six years of burning toast, six years of being last, six years of…" "Hold on!" exclaimed Angelica. "It says you have to solve the riddle; it doesn't say when, based on the letter, your mom doesn't want you to try and solve the riddle and break the curse until you are 18." Valerie was speechless, Angelica was a hero, she saved the world and stopped Mt. St. Valerie from exploding.

With the air finally clear and the world safe, Valerie took a deep breath and asked "Whaat?" There was an awkward silence that seemed to last for an eternity, but in reality, lasted only a few seconds. Smiling from ear to ear, Angelica happily replied, "it's your mom that wants you to wait, not the curse, you will always be the oldest daughter so you can do it anytime."

"Anytime? Explain anytime" replied Valerie. "You are the honor roll student; you are the straight A student. You could solve the riddle when you are 5, 10, 40, 50, or 95, or NOW!" proudly exclaimed Angelica. All Valerie could say was "Whaat?" Angelica shook her head in disbelief and whispered to herself, "sometimes smart people are pretty dumb".

Ideas were coming into her mind at 100 miles per hour. Ideas and thoughts were racing through her brain. Electrons were burning bright, neutrons were electrified, Angelica's mind was alive. "We can do it NOW! This is the PERFECT time! A long weekend, your parents are gone and best of all, I am here all weekend, and I can help you to break the curse of the diamond necklace!

Valerie was appalled, "I always listen to my parents, they will never let me go." They don't have to know; we will be back by Monday night. Next reason?" Valerie thought for a moment, "you have to do your chemistry paper on gold, I will not be a reason you fail." Angelica quickly responded, it had been done, turned in. I lied, I just wanted to spend some time with you!" "I know" sadly answered Valerie, "Uncle Bruce!"

Angelica was stunned, caught off guard, mystified, "What is an Uncle Bruce?" Valerie thought for a minute and surprisingly answered, "It's something you've never experienced before, he's unique one-of-a kind. He tries his best, but sometimes fails dramatically, he's loving and protective. He can be your best friend or your worst enemy. He breaks the rules a lot, but always for a good reason. He's stern, but gentle, proud, but humble, funny, but serious."

"Sounds terrible!" trembled Angelica. "Quite contrary!" smiled Valerie, "He's the best and he is all mine! But getting him to let us go, will take a miracle." Excited, Angelica put her index finger in the air and proudly declared "Challenge Accepted!"

Valerie laughed hysterically. "I live by what can go wrong does go wrong motto" I don't step on cracks to avoid cracking my mom's back. I would never get a black cat, walk under a ladder, pick up a tails up penny or leave my house on Friday the13th. I ask myself every day, "Why, why do I have such bad luck?

THE THINGAMAJIG

(Something that's name is forgotten or unknown)

Uncle Bruce was quite the character, ever since he was a young man, he beat his drum to a different tune. He never hurt or was mean to anyone, but he never buckled to peer pressure or the pressures of the social media. When the world went west, he went east, when the world loved sardines dipped in chocolate syrup and made them a national fad, he was honest and said they were disgusting. When the first itty bitty smart car came into the world, he said it was a dumb car, too small, too dangerous, too unrealistic. He was honest.

Uncle Bruce loved children, although he came from a big family, he still had three of his own. But they are grown now. There was something so innocent in a child, so beautiful, he always felt the unconditional love they gave was magical. Valerie was no different, he loved her like she was his own. They had a bond like no other, so whenever he had the chance to watch her, he did.

He knew everything, Valerie's temper when she got mad, her obsession to become a nurse, her unbelievable streak of bad luck and yes, he knew all about the curse that Wendy Papadopolus put on the eldest daughter in each generation so many years ago. Mt. St. Valerie didn't scare him, her obsession didn't scare him, and the curse didn't scare him.

For whatever the reason Uncle Bruce was a believer in underdogs. Maybe because he was a shy, skinny kid growing up, he watched Cinderella too many times, he just wanted to make it fair for everyone. In the Super Bowl he always supported the underdog, he supported the children who didn't have any friends, he supported and loved his cursed niece, Valerie.

Before going downstairs, Valerie asked Angelica how they were going to convince Uncle Bruce to let them go so they could solve the riddle to break the curse of the diamond necklace. Angelica wasn't sure, but said she would "wing it", Valerie didn't like this plan. Uncle Bruce was always good to her, so she didn't want to lie or deceive him in any way. Honesty was the best policy.

Angelica disagreed, whatever trouble they got into would be easy to explain. They were both in seventh grade, both had raging hormones, and both were in the same self-entitlement generation. Chances are, if they were caught, they would lecture the two troubled teens and at the most, make them do community service. Angelica felt it was a risk worth taking.

Valerie disagreed; she didn't break the rules, she followed the rules, she always followed the rules. Angelica felt she had to get to Uncle Bruce first, she looked at Valerie, Valerie looked at Angelica, first one down would get to ask Uncle Bruce their way.

Angelica darted first, Valerie quickly followed and grabbed Angelica's arm in an attempt to slow her down. Angelica tried shaking her off, but Valerie held on for dear life. Valerie finally slowed her down enough so she could spin her to one side and take a small lead. As she spun recklessly, Angelica's foot hit the corner of the brown dresser and down she went along with Valerie.

Determined to get downstairs first, Valerie struggled to get up quickly, however Angelica never gave up either, grabbing Valerie's red shoe with gusto. Kicking and screaming, Valerie relentlessly kicked to release her from Angelica's deadly grip. Miraculously, Valerie released herself, got herself up, and ran out the small entrance to the bedroom.

Aggravated, but driven to beat Valerie, Angelica quickly recovered and followed her out the door to the top of the staircase. Gently pushing her against the wall, Angelica laughed and proclaimed an early victory. Valerie dropped to the ground completely exhausted, she was no match for her much stronger new friend Angelica.

Out of breath, out of time and out of patience, Angelica looked for Uncle Bruce. She ran to the kitchen, no Uncle Bruce, she ran through the living room, no Uncle Bruce, she ran downstairs, but there was no Uncle Bruce. Frustrated, she called out to him, "Uncle Bruce, Uncle Bruce, where are you?" Nobody answered.

Valerie laughed, she looked outside the big front window and saw Uncle Bruce talking to Mr. Dulany. "Unbelievable!" cried Valerie. "Why is my uncle talking to my neighbor?" Angelica smirked, "Your uncle seems like a nice guy, he likes to talk, and he seems to give advice, what's wrong with the two talking?" Valerie hung her head in disbelief, "sounds just like Mr. Dulany. If I didn't know better, I would think they were the same person!" Finally, Mr. Dulany and Uncle Bruce shook hands saying goodbye to each other. Mr. Dulany went back to his gardening while Uncle Bruce headed towards the front door to Valerie's house.

The two girls stood patiently in the small living room waiting to talk to Valerie's uncle. Unaware of the girl's presence as he entered the house, he was startled when he noticed them. "Hello girls, what is going on here?" Valerie tried to talk but was quickly taken over by the very vocal and boisterous Angelica, "We need to go to the mall for equipment for our chemistry project. Is it okay if we go? we should be back in a few hours." Valerie was stunned by the big fat lie.

Uncle Bruce knew more than he was letting on, "So, exactly what do you need?" Angelica was quick with a response, "We need some beakers, some flasks, a microscope, a distiller and a Bunsen burner" proudly responded Angelica. Valerie stood there mortified. Uncle Bruce quickly responded, "I thought this was a research paper? If I remember right, aren't you researching gold?"

Angelica was mystified, most adults believed her, who was this masked man? Who dared to care enough to question her motives? Who was going to outwit a seventh grader? Thinking quickly,

Angelica knew she had to pull out all of the stops if they were going to solve the riddle. Rule number one, get an attitude. She took a deep breath and pretended to get mad.

She huffed, she puffed, and she blew the house down. "Why don't you believe me? You adults hate teenagers! You think we are all liars! You think we are still babies!" Valerie was flabbergasted. She wanted to give Angelica a standing ovation for her performance. Waiting for a response, Angelica was ready for a battle.

Uncle Bruce stood there very impressed with Angelica's determination. Quickly thinking on her feet, Angelica went in for the final blow, "we are adding a science experiment to my research paper, we are doing extra credit." Uncle Bruce just stood there speechless.

"So exactly what are you experimenting with gold? Why do you need the beakers, the flasks, the microscope?" asked a very curious Uncle Bruce. Valerie was embarrassed and ready to fly the proverbial white flag, not Angelica. She was relentless in her pursuit of trying to deceive Uncle Bruce.

Thinking back to her brief moments in chemistry class when she did pay attention, she bravely answered Uncle Bruce. Not knowing what she was saying, but trying to sound knowledgeable, Angelica began to rant "Trying to prove Raoul's Law, we will use activated charcoal as a catalyst to bring beta particles and anions to absolute zero thus using the reversible back titration data if Kelvin is not reached within an experimental amount of proper filtration, dissection and combustibility!"

Uncle Bruce was impressed with her attempt to fool him, but little did she know he took many science classes in his school days and quickly realized that Angelica was giving him a line of nonsense but decided to play along. "Sounds interesting, sounds exciting, sounds educational. Lucky for you, your neighbor, Mr. Dulany, has plenty of chemistry equipment. I am sure he will let you borrow them for your experiment."

Angelica smiled, but knew she was busted, "that's great!" she sadly proclaimed. Valerie stood motionless not paying attention, her mind was on something different, Grant. Grant was handsome, he was smart, he made her smile. Thinking of Grant gave her goosebumps. Valerie couldn't wait to see him again on Tuesday. Angelica elbowed Valerie, "that's great!" repeated Valerie.

Round 1, Uncle Bruce 1 the girls 0. Angelica and Valerie conceded victory and headed back upstairs to rethink their strategy. Valerie wanted to be honest, but Angelica needed another plan to fool an adult. Everybody knew seventh graders were smarter than adults. Angelica thought and thought about it, but nothing came. Valerie tried to explain to Angelica that Uncle Bruce was not your average adult.

Angelica paced back and forth, nothing. She tapped her finger, nothing. Valerie suggested they go shopping, Angelica told her to be quiet, she was thinking. Valerie remained quiet. Back and forth she paced, stopping occasionally claiming she had an idea, but nothing came out. Valerie tried to suggest another idea but was quickly shushed and had Angelica's hand shoved in her face.

Valerie had never met anyone like Angelica. Despite her relentless attempt to outwit Uncle Bruce, Valerie liked Angelica. Despite her rough exterior, Valerie liked Angelica. Despite her domineering personality, Valerie liked Angelica. She was different, she was unique, she was going to put a much-needed spark in Valerie's life.

Determined to find a reason to get out of the house, Angelica continued to think and pace, and pace, and think and pace, Valerie thought she would need a new rug soon. Then like lightening hitting, she suddenly stopped and started talking rapidly, "we should tell him we are volunteering; we could tell him with are raising money for the school, we could tell him we are walking dogs, or mowing grass, or raking leaves." Then she smiled, raised her finger, and proudly stated, "By George, I think I've finally got it!"

Valerie rolled her eyes, this new friend of hers was quite the character. Fun yes, but full of drama, something Valerie was not used to. Angelica liked to be the center of attention and let the world know when she entered the room, Valerie was quite the opposite, quiet, shy, and very reserved, for years she has been the "invisible girl."

Waiting patiently, Valerie waited eagerly for Angelica's idea. She wondered to herself how crazy Angelica was going to get. Would she say she needed to go to Pluto? Would she say she needed to go to the North Pole to help Santa? Or would she say she needed to go to the bottom of the ocean and find a thingamajig? Valerie snickered to herself as she waited patiently for Angelica to present her creative idea. Valerie sat on the edge of the bed in eager anticipation of Angelica's announcement. This was going to be good.

As predicted, Angelica turned around and got into character. She brushed her hair, straightened her shirt, cleared her throat, and smiled. Finally, she turned around, took a couple of steps forward, raised her hands and declared, "Let's go shopping! We need a thingamajig, don't we?" Valerie smiled and asked, "What a great idea, why didn't I think of that?"

Feeling confident, the girls raced downstairs to convince Uncle Bruce to let them go "shopping." As they ran downstairs, Valerie suggested that they slowly bring the idea up and butter Uncle Bruce up. Angelica shook her head in agreement as they whisked down the staircase.

Uncle Bruce was in the kitchen preparing his specialty, frozen pizza. He didn't like to cook; he didn't know how to cook and when he did try to cook, it was terrible. Thank goodness for frozen pizzas. He heard the elephant stampede and wondered how many girls Valerie had invited over. Startling him, Angelica and Valerie appeared suddenly in the kitchen.

Not heeding Valerie's advice, Angelica blurted out, "It's Saturday morning, we want to go to the mall, we need a thingamajig!" Valerie looked at Angelica with a sense of wonder, "what happened to slow?"

Angelica ignored Valerie as they waited patiently for an answer. Uncle Bruce checked the pizza in the oven and said, "I thought you had a research paper to write, and I thought you wanted to study the human skeletal system? Do you even need a thingamajig?"

Angelica told Uncle Bruce she was done with her paper on gold and Valerie insisted she knew the human body system inside and out. Uncle Bruce got out his phone and searched for information about the human body. Forgetting his reading glasses at his house, he squinted as his large fingers tapped on the keyboard of his tiny cell phone.

"Okay young lady, first question on average how tall can a human grow?" Valerie smiled and quickly replied, "6 feet." Uncle Bruce quickly responded, "wrong 24 feet!" Valerie was confused. "Next question how long is a human tongue?" "5 inches?" "Wrong 20 inches!" Valerie was flabbergasted. "Third question, how fast can a human run?" "10 miles per hour?" "Wrong 30 miles per hour!" Valerie was mystified.

Continuing his barrage of questions, Uncle Bruce asked, "how big is the human heart?" Valerie was proud she knew, "females are 8 ounces, males are 10 ounces!" "Wrong, the heart is 25 pounds!" "Looks like you need to study some more, final question, when can a baby walk?" "Usually between 12-15 months!" "Wrong, a baby can walk usually within 10 minutes! That's 0 for 5, looks like you need to stay home and study. No shopping for a thingamajig for you!"

Valerie was devastated, not so much about shopping for a thingamajig but the fact that she got all the questions wrong. She questioned her ability to become a good nurse in the future. She immediately hung her head and began to feel sorry for herself asking herself, "Why, why do I have such bad luck?"

CHAPTER 8

BAMBOOZLE

(To deceive or trick someone)

Angelica was not the brightest girl in class, nor was she the most motivated girl in class, but something did not sit right with her. As she thought about Valerie's answers, she realized Valerie was right and Uncle Bruce was trying to bamboozle them. Trying not to be rude or disrespectful, she slowly walked towards Uncle Bruce, and surprisingly grabbed his cell phone from his unexpectant hands. She demanded to know why he was trying to bamboozle Valerie. Valerie was flabbergasted, Uncle Bruce was shocked, and Angelica was being rude and disrespectful.

Valerie's friend quickly ran to the corner of the room to explore Uncle Bruce's phone. Working quickly and efficiently, she swiftly retraced his footprints on the technological device. Trying to stall for time she quickly yelled, "Aha!" Uncle Bruce was furious demanding his phone back and worked his way towards the thief. Valerie was embarrassed.

Having no other option, Angelica casually mentioned to Uncle Bruce that if he moved any closer, she would scream. A scream so loud that the neighbors would call the police immediately. A scream so loud that every cat within 100 miles would begin to howl. A scream so loud that every stoplight in the city would malfunction, causing massive confusion and unbelievable delays. She was not trying to bamboozle him.

Uncle Bruce froze but repeated his demand for his phone back. Angelica rolled her eyes and ignored the request. She held his phone tightly as she began to scroll through his latest history, "Just what I thought," she whispered as she continued to scroll. Valerie stood there at her new friend embarrassed how disrespectful to an adult she was being. "Unbelievable!" she stated as she stared at the phone.

Mystified with this young lady, Uncle Bruce moved slightly forward, Angelica quickly warned him, "I would stop right there, or I will tell everyone about the Thomas the Train underwear you ordered or tell everyone about the…" "Please stop, I am not moving" stated Uncle Bruce. Angelica went back to the phone as she kept repeating, "Just what I thought, unbelievable."

Valerie was stunned at Angelica's behavior. Uncle Bruce stood there quietly hoping no one would find out he ordered the Star Wars fighter jet action playset, for himself. Finally, and with no fanfare, and with no bamboozling, Angelica told Valerie she had found out something very interesting. Uncle Bruce wanted to hide in the corner, under a rock, or better yet, run away. Valerie was curious and stood there in anticipation of breaking news.

Angelica was being very dramatic, she smiled, she paced back and forth, and she cleared her throat knowing the world was waiting for her and watching every move she made. Both Valerie and Uncle Bruce were flabbergasted as to what was coming next. Continuing her Tony winning performance Angelica started her monologue, "A woman's heart is 8 ounces, a man's 10 ounces, not 25 pounds," Valerie gasped. "A human baby usually walks around 18 months, not 10 minutes," Uncle Bruce gasped. Angelica smiled.

"You see, Uncle Bruce, your history on your search engine shows you "accidently" were searching for interesting facts on giraffes, you were trying to bamboozle us." There was a long awkward pause as Valerie stared at Uncle Bruce and Angelica. Thinking the world was against her, Mt. St. Valerie began to rumble, her face began to turn red. Then suddenly it exploded, "Not only is my class against me, now the one person I could always count on is against me! Thank You Uncle Bruce, thanks for trying to bamboozle me!"

The damage was done, Uncle Bruce's heart was ripped out, torn apart, and smashed beyond recognition. He loved Valerie more than anything in the world, more than she would ever know. She was everything to him. It was an accident, he insisted he did not bamboozle anyone. Uncle Bruce and technology was like mixing oil and water, like having a pet tiger and pet dog, or a snowball on a hot July day, the two didn't mix.

Valerie, who was extremely upset and crying, ran hysterically upstairs leaving her once favorite uncle devastated. Angelica didn't realize what she had done and decided to follow Valerie back upstairs, but before leaving told Uncle Bruce he needed to let her and Valerie go shopping for the thingamajig, it was the least he could do to repair all the damage he had caused trying to bamboozle them.

Meanwhile, up in the Wisconsin Dells, Grant sat staring at the television which was turned off. His younger brother, George, asked him twice to get ready to for the waterpark, however Grant ignored him. Grant was thinking of Valerie's beautiful smile, the smell of her hair and her wonderful laugh.

Back in Glendale Heights, Uncle Bruce decided what to do. His one-of-a-kind plan to wait until Valerie was honest in asking to go on her quest had blown up in his face. This was a nightmare, he wanted to teach Valerie that honesty was the best policy, now the unthinkable happened, Valerie hated him.

He got out the letter that Valerie's mom had given to him before they left. He thought for a moment and decided that he needed to follow honesty is the best policy himself. He called Valerie over and over again asking her to come downstairs, she refused.

Not knowing what Uncle Bruce wanted, the girls consoled each other and bonded over the fact that Uncle Bruce was a scoundrel, a trickster, and a bamboozler. He was no good and could not be trusted. Angelica's last plan was simple, escape out the bedroom window, leave a note and hopefully with a little luck and a huge prayer they would be home by Monday night with the necklace and the curse broken. Or if they failed, they would go wherever all the past relatives had gone, whenever they made a mistake.

Valerie was a rule follower, she colored inside the lines, she dotted her I's, crossed her t's, unlike Uncle Bruce who colored outside the box and broke whatever rule was necessary to achieve his goal. Valerie thought she should go downstairs and tell her uncle that she was old enough to go on this quest, honesty was the best policy. Angelica shrugged her shoulders and plopped herself down on the bed.

Valerie wiped her tears and was determined to convince her uncle to let her go. She stormed out of the room and down the dark staircase. Uncle Bruce wiped his tears away and was determined to show his favorite niece the letter from her mom. He stormed up the dark staircase. Together they were two freight trains heading directly towards each other, destined for a head-on collision.

Focused on making things right, Uncle Bruce worried what he would say when he saw his niece, he barreled his body up the long dark staircase. Gravity pulled Valerie's body swiftly down the staircase. She was in seventh grade, she was responsible, she wanted to go on this quest. In the darkness Valerie increased her downward speed, while Uncle Bruce gave it everything he had, pushing his body swiftly up the staircase.

Then it happened, the unthinkable, the impossible, the crash heard around the world. KAPOW! Valerie hit her uncle with such velocity it knocked her backwards. Stunned and out of breath, Valerie sat on a stair confused and bewildered. Uncle Bruce lost his balance and rolled back down five steps. Although they both had bruised egos neither one was seriously injured.

"We have to quit meeting like this!" Uncle Bruce chuckled. Valerie laughed back. Angelica came running and turned on the light quickly accusing Uncle Bruce, "what else are you going to do to this poor girl?" Concerned only for Valerie's welfare she helped Valerie back up to her room telling her uncle, "Stay away from my friend, you have hurt her enough!" "But" replied Uncle Bruce. "But" replied Valerie. There will be no buts!" Angelica declared.

They left Uncle Bruce sitting alone on the stairway. To make things worse, Angelica turned off the lights in the staircase leaving Uncle Bruce in the darkness and slammed the bedroom door shut leaving him in the cold. This was not Valerie, this was all Angelica and not only did this little tactic fail, but it also inspired him even more.

Although getting up was difficult, he managed to use the walls to help him propel himself back into a standing position. Step by step he took up the stairs, focused on talking to Valerie. He approached the door with caution, Angelica was a feisty one. He knocked twice, no answer. He knocked again, somebody called, "GO AWAY!" Uncle Bruce knocked again and once again he heard "YOU ARE NOT WANTED HERE, GO AWAY!"

"I am not going anywhere until you hear me out, I am sorry about the giraffe answers, you know me and technology, we don't mix. I am not a bamboozler I know what you and Angelica are trying to do. I know about your curse. Your mother left me a note telling me she told you everything. She was worried you would want to solve the riddle and remove the curse before your 18th birthday. It looks like she was right. What you don't know is she wrote me a letter giving me permission to take you on this journey. She knew once you knew, stopping you would be impossible. Do you want me to read the letter?"

There was no go away, there was no I hate you, there was silence, stone cold silence. Uncle Bruce took this as a yes. He unfolded the short letter and began to read it:

DEAR UNCLE BRUCE,

THANK YOU SO MUCH FOR WATCHING VALERIE THIS WEEKEND. I WILL MAKE THIS SHORT, I FINALLY TOLD VALERIE ABOUT THE CURSE, SHE HAS BEEN GOING THROUGH A

LOT LATELY AND I HONESTLY THOUGHT SHE DESERVED TO KNOW THE TRUTH. HOWEVER, MY FEAR IS SHE WILL NOT WAIT UNTIL HER 18TH BIRTHDAY. SHE WILL WANT TO GO AS SOON AS SHE CAN. I CAN'T WATCH HER GO THROUGH THIS, THE LESS I KNOW THE BETTER.

IF SHE DECIDES TO TAKE THIS ON, I GIVE YOU FULL PERMISSION TO GO WITH HER AND HELP HER THROUGH THIS JOURNEY. SHE TRUSTS AND LOVES YOU SO MUCH AND I KNOW HOW MUCH YOU LOVE HER. TOGETHER YOU WILL MAKE AN UNSTOPPABLE TEAM. I KNOW YOU WOULD NEVER LET HER GO IN ANY DANGEROUS SITUATION. IF YOU DECIDE IT WOULD BE BETTER TO WAIT, I UNDERSTAND. GOOD LUCK WITH WHATEVER YOU DECIDE.

LOVE YOU,
YOUR SISTER ARIA.

Uncle Bruce folded up the note and put it back in his pocket. He waited patiently for any sign of life, any sign of forgiveness or even a sign of resentment, but there was nothing. It was so quiet you could hear a pin drop, so quiet you could hear your heart beating, so quiet you could hear Uncle Bruce's tear fall from his cheek.

He waited for what seemed an eternity, nothing stirred, not even a mouse. Another tear rolled down his cheek, he turned around and started to walk toward the staircase, the beautiful relationship he had with Valerie was over, caput, finite. Suddenly he heard the door open, but no one came out, he continued towards the staircase, hopelessly defeated.

With his broken heart on his shoulder, the accused bamboozler went downstairs, then he heard it. It was like the wilder beasts running through the gorge, it was loud and scary. Quickly he turned around and he saw Valerie running straight down the stairs directly at him. Coming at full force, she opened her arms ready to give him one of her signature hugs.

KAPOW! Direct hit! Knocking him across the living room into the couch. The couch moved slightly to the right, slightly tapping her mom's favorite antique reading light which she received as a wedding gift 25 years ago, it was priceless, it was rare, it held memories from so long ago. They held their breaths as they watched the light sway to the right, then to the left, then to the right and again to the left, they let out their breaths and felt comfortable they were safe.

Then Angelica violently slammed the door upstairs, shaking the whole house. The antique light fell off the table slamming into the ground into a thousand pieces. Mom would be mad, mom would be disappointed, mom would ground Valerie and Uncle Bruce for a very long time. Valerie looked at Uncle Bruce and asked, "Why, why do I have such bad luck?"

CHAPTER 9

FOOFARAW

*(A great fuss or disturbance about
something very insignificant)*

"Thank you so much!" screamed Valerie as they got up from the floor. Angelica came downstairs mad as hornet thinking Uncle Bruce was being mean to Valerie, "You leave her alone! Don't you see what a sensitive wall flower she is?" Valerie was confused, Uncle Bruce was confused, "What?" they both asked. Angelica continued her rampage, "Valerie step away from the mean man! You need to walk away from troublemakers like him! You…." Uncle Bruce tried saying something, but Angelica was on a roll, "Don't you have any manners? Why do you interrupt me when I talk?"

Uncle Bruce was speechless, he just stared at Valerie's new friend. "Now you have nothing to say?" rudely asked Angelica. Valerie walked over to Angelica and whispered in her ear. Angelica quickly composed herself, smiled and politely asked, "Can I go?"

Valerie immediately said "Yes!", Uncle Bruce immediately said "NO!" Angelica was stunned but was quick with an answer, "You have to bring me, I know things that most people don't know. I am an encyclopedia of useless knowledge. Besides good looking I am brave, and I am good with people." Uncle Bruce was not swayed by this information.

Angelica was mortified; besides school and her family and friends she was never treated like this before. Valerie knew the feeling of being left to the side, unwanted and being excluded.

Once again, she whispered into her friend's ear. Thinking, Angelica started spitting out some unusual information, "Did you the first person convicted of speeding was going 8 miles per hour? Did you know, when a woman is pregnant her hair and nails grow faster than normal? The large stone heads mysteriously left on Easter Island have bodies, some as big as 33 feet deep." Uncle Bruce was fascinated but was not swayed by this information.

Valerie desperately wanted Angelica to help her find the diamond necklace, so she encouraged Angelica to continue with more trivia. Digging deep into her mind, Angelica started spewing out information again, "Goosebumps are a way of warding off predators. Humans are the only animals that blush. The wood frog can hold its pee for up to eight months. The hottest place on earth is Libya. Your nostrils work one at a time." Uncle Bruce was intrigued but was not swayed by this information.

Although very impressed, Uncle Bruce still said no, reminding the two how important this journey was, and any mistake might cost Valerie her life. They had to stay focused, this was too high of a price to pay for failure and Uncle Bruce was not going to pay, he loved and adored Valerie way too much. Uncle Bruce was going to call Angelica's mom, wherever she was. Angelica was devastated and ran back upstairs crying. Uncle Bruce was still not swayed by her foofaraw.

Valerie was devastated, but what could she do? Valerie didn't think Angelica was throwing a foofaraw. Valerie hadn't had a good friend for what seemed an eternity. Many people used the word friend very loosely, sure they were acquaintances, but not friends. But she was in the seventh grade, what could she do? Should she have Mt. St. Valerie explode? That wouldn't work, Uncle Bruce was too smart for Mt. St. Valerie. She rubbed her chin, thinking. She thought, she pondered, she speculated, she imagined but nothing came.

Then she remembered what one of her favorite teachers at Hallsberry School had taught her, Mrs. Marino her fifth-grade teacher taught her about every body's Achilles heel. This was their weak spot, the thing they couldn't say no to. For some people it was a Frappuccino, for others it was M&M's, no matter what it was, everybody had at least one.

Uncle Bruce was no different, he had many. Fresh nachos smothered in queso cheese, freshly made guacamole, and chili, cheesy lasagna, Bavarian cream donuts. These were great but she needed something now. She pondered some more, ice-cold glass of Pepsi, M&M's, watching Beauty and the Beast, these were some of Uncle Bruce's favorite things, but would they work?

She thought some more, knowing time was not on her side. This needed more than a small foofaraw. Valerie needed something quick, something powerful, something Uncle Bruce had no power over. She rubbed her chin once again, she pondered, she paced, she speculated, she sat, she wondered, she paced some more. Valerie needed a miracle, not a foofaraw.

Then like a bolt of lightning appearing suddenly during a storm, it hit her, something Uncle Bruce could not resist, something so special, something so rare. Valerie was confident Uncle Bruce would finally be swayed. She rushed to find him.

Uncle Bruce was in the living room working on his computer. He wanted to become a writer and was working on his story. He talked about a beanstalk, a hospital and a young girl growing up in a difficult world. Everybody thought this was a crazy idea and nobody thought he would follow through. Valerie believed in him and encouraged her Uncle Bruce, "Did you think of a title for your book yet?" she sweetly asked.

There wasn't much to say, all he had on the paper was his name and the words chapter one typed. "What's the girl's name?" Valerie asked. "I don't know" replied Uncle Bruce. Valerie quickly replied, "Maybe Aria? Camilla? Maria? Xxlayna?" then there was an awkward silence, and then she shyly suggested, "Maybe Valerie?"

He smiled for a second, raised his head and as quickly as he lifted his head, he lowered his head and sadly replied, "No, that would never work." Peppy and full of energy, Valerie told him he needed some inspiration. Uncle Bruce didn't react. "I know what you need, you, me and Angelica need to break this curse of mine."

Uncle Bruce didn't say a word, he just looked at Valerie with those baby blue eyes of his, that said it all. Valerie knew this was the time, the opportunity, the chance of a lifetime to break down his Achilles heel. Without regard for her own safety, she slowly went closer to her uncle. He was oblivious and didn't see what was coming, he was doomed. Suddenly, Valerie raised her hands and went in for the biggest hug possible. He was shocked, he was mystified, he was under attack. Valerie squeezed him with everything she had.

Completely paralyzed by the power of love, Uncle Bruce was powerless. Valerie kept hugging her uncle with everything she had virtually melting his backbone. "Can Angelica please go on this journey with us?" Whatever she did she did not want to cause a foofaraw, this was important. Uncle Bruce remained strong, and he remained quiet. Valerie began to worry, was her power wearing off?

Valerie hugged a little harder, but there was still no answer. Valerie knew she had to pull out the big idea, the big guns, the no you didn't idea. She knew this was not fair, she knew it was illegal in 49 states and the Virgin Islands, but she also knew she wanted her new friend to join them on their journey.

As she hugged her uncle, she decided it was time, in a swift and delicate motion she gave it to him. The one, the only sad puppy dog look. It had worked when she was five and wanted a new princess bike with a horn and pink tassels, it had worked when she was eight and her second-grade class needed a chaperone for the trip downtown to the field museum, it had to work now. She had the sad brown eyes; she had the frown, and she had the stiff upper lip as she looked at her unexpecting uncle.

Uncle Bruce knew he was in trouble, he was losing his backbone, he was becoming butter in her hands. He resisted the irresistible face with every ounce of strength he had left. Aggravated at what was happening he cursed, annoyed at losing to a 12-year-old, he cursed, disappointed he didn't foresee the future, he cursed once again . Things were not going his way.

As she hugged Uncle Bruce with every ounce of love she had in her tiny body, Valerie sweetly asked him once again, "Can Angelica please go with us?" He held his breath, he bit his lip, he avoided eye contact, but the sweetness was overflowing. He squirmed, he fidgeted, he wiggled but Valerie's power was too much, way too much for this young man.

She waited for a reply, but he was fighting with every ounce of his soul, he was determined to say no, but the determined young girl they called Valerie was too much for the big man they called Uncle Bruce. Finally, out of pure exhaustion, he whispered faintly, "Fine, she can go!"

Valerie released her tight grip on her uncle, he went down to the floor like a wet noodle exclaiming, "That wasn't fair!" Valerie smiled and proclaimed, "All's fair in love and war!" She then went upstairs to get ready for her adventure of a lifetime. "I will be back with Angelica in a few minutes." In a pile of twisted limbs and body parts Uncle Bruce laid on the floor trying to get his body functioning again.

Soon Angelica and Valerie came happily down the stairs chit chatting about school. Angelica teased Valerie about her new crush Grant. Valerie denied that he was a crush, let alone the fact that she liked him. Angelica started by ordering Uncle Bruce to get ready, it was time to leave, then she handed Valerie the very heavy fully stocked backpack proclaiming, "It's your journey. it's your backpack so you carry it!" Valerie could barely lift it, let alone put it on her back. But you have your Canon f-5 sports camera in here, your Nike steel toed boots, a folding garden shovel, and your sixth-grade advanced algebra book in there!" Angelica rudely replied, "Well your solar flashlight is in there! You carry it!"

Valerie quickly replied, "No, you carry it!" Back and forth they went arguing about who was going to carry it. Neither one wanted to carry the unusually heavy backpack. Fed up with the never-ending bickering and arguing, Uncle Bruce had one word for the two amigas, "STOP!" He demanded.

Silence broke out, beautiful silence, Uncle Bruce just sat there enjoying the silence. Then he told the girls "Flip a coin! Loser carries the backpack!" Both ladies thought it was a great idea, however neither one had a coin. Uncle Bruce grabbed a shiny 2018 nickel from his lint filled front pocket and handed it to Valerie.

Valerie tried handing the coin to Angelica, but she insisted Valerie throw the coin in the air. Valerie agreed but told Angelica to call it. Valerie threw the shiny coin high into the air, Angelica called heads as the coin dropped down to earth. The coin rolled for a few feet and then spun and spun and spun. The girls held their breath as the coin spun, neither one's eyes blinked as the shiny nickel started to slow down, still spinning clockwise.

Taking forever to stop spinning, Angelica stared intently yelling over and over again, heads, heads, heads! Valerie begged the coin gods, tails, tails, tails. Uncle Bruce really didn't care as long as he didn't have to carry it with his bad back. Finally, the coin dropped flat on the ground. Angelica bent down quickly to see the outcome, Valerie bent down quickly to see the outcome to, they gently bumped heads in anticipation of the winner.

Angelica saw it first and excitedly yelled "HEADS!" Angelica was ecstatic, Valerie was disappointed, but that was Valerie's life. Unexpectantly, she asked her uncle, "Why, why do I have such bad luck?"

CHAPTER 10

DUMBFOUNDED

(Speechless with amazement)

Begrudgingly, Valerie picked up the heavy black backpack and ordered her followers, "let's go!" Angelica quickly followed behind her, Uncle Bruce remained steadfast, not moving anywhere. Rudely Angelica ordered him too, "Come on old man let's get those legs moving!" Disrespect was one thing Uncle Bruce did not tolerate, "If you want to continue on this journey, I suggest you watch your tongue!"

Angelica smiled knowing she crossed the line, but quickly answered, "Only kidding!" Uncle Bruce was not happy, Angelica knew so she decided to throw a joke in the mix, "I can't watch my tongue, my nose is in the way." Valerie rolled her eyes, Angelica laughed, and Uncle Bruce was dumbfounded.

After an awkward silence, Uncle Bruce told the two eager beavers they hadn't even discussed the first clue. "We don't have to, I figured it out already!" proudly stated Valerie. Agreeing with her new best friend Angelica got very defensive, "Valerie is the smartest girl in the seventh grade. Don't you believe in her? You never believed in her, you think Aaliyah is smarter than Valerie. What kind of uncle are you?"

Quickly realizing all Angelica wanted to do was argue, Uncle Bruce changed the conversation, "If you remember many of your first-born relatives never came back from their journey, are you willing to risk Valerie's life on this epic journey? Valerie quickly responded, "Definitely not!" Uncle Bruce vehemently declared, "I'm not!"

But good old Angelica had to be a rebel, "It depends on so many things, "Is she buying lunch?" Nobody laughed. Once again Angelica apologized, "Only kidding!". Uncle Bruce wished he never said yes to Valerie's demand. Valerie was embarrassed and wished she never pressured her uncle to let Angelica come on this journey.

Trying to stay positive, Uncle Bruce asked what the clue was, Angelica didn't have any idea, Valerie pulled the piece of paper out of her back pocket and read it, "General Store, Tick tock, tic tock." Uncle Bruce was confused and quickly asked, "Whaat?" Angelica rolled her eyes and instead of repeating herself just handed Uncle Bruce the paper. He stared at it intently:

GENERAL STORE- TICK TOCK- TICK TOCK

He rubbed his chin, he paced back and forth, he scratched his head, but nothing came to his one-of-a-kind mind. He looked up, he looked down, but nothing came. Flabbergasted, he looked at the girls asking them what they were thinking. The bold and brash Angelica promptly answered, "Well, the clue clearly means that in the watch section in Target."

Valerie was dumbfounded, she thought the next clue would be found by the time clock in the Jewel grocery store. She argued that Jewel sells everything from fruits and vegetables to canned beans to paper towels and bathroom tissue to pencils and markers to oil and brake fluid, a true general store.

She even commented that they had a fresh bakery. Angelica quickly interjected that she loved the fresh bakery, it was the best. She loved to put cream cheese on the fresh baked bagels, her favorite were the cinnamon raisin bagels, slightly toasted. Angelica also loved it when her mother made her famous sausage, egg and cheese breakfast sandwiches using the delicious treats. Her mother also made the best chicken salad and when put on a fresh croissant were to die for.

Angelica also loved her birthday cakes, which also always came from Jewel. Whether it was Dad's birthday and the chocolate butter creme with strawberries, or her brother's birthday with the marble cake, whipped cream frosting, sugar roses and an insane amount of rainbow sprinkles scattered across the top of the fabulous creation it was always, I mean always excellent.

But even better, better than excellent, better than awesome, better than awesomeicious, yes, it's a word, was Angelica's birthday cake, it was awesomeiciousest. The professional bakers at the Jewel bakery made it perfect year after year, they were the God's of the bakery world. It was a confetti cake with fresh chocolate buttercream frosting decorated with Angelica's favorite theme, one year it was Barbie themed, another year Molly and the Big comfy couch, the Teletubbies, Disney Princess's and this year would be the Seventies, no matter what the theme was they always did a great job.

Valerie was satisfied with her answer and told everybody that the tick tock clue was in reference to a clock somewhere in the store, whether it was the time clock, the clock that hung by the customer service booth or another clock somewhere in the store. Finding it wouldn't be that hard. Angelica disagreed despite loving Jewel's bakery she thought Target was the right store.

As they decided Valerie's fate, Uncle Bruce made some lunch for him and the girls. He grilled some hamburgers and put some frozen fries into the oven. The girls continue to discuss where the first clue was. Angelica got a Sprite and sat down again ready to defend her reason the first clue would be in Target

"Have you ever been in the clock aisle?" she rhetorically asked. "The clue has to be somewhere down aisle 32B. They have big clocks, small clocks, metal clocks, plastic clocks, wooden clocks, plain clocks, designer clocks, analog clocks, digital clocks, clocks with numbers, clocks with roman numerals, clocks with no numbers, wall clocks, table clocks, lighted clocks, glow in the dark clocks, solar clocks, clocks with batteries, electric clocks......" suddenly Uncle Bruce interrupted Angelica declaring "Lunch is ready!"

"How rude!" Angelica said. "Where was I?" Valerie didn't answer. Angelica couldn't remember where she left off, so she started from the beginning. Both girls ignored Uncle Bruce. He was dumbfounded. "They have big clocks, small clocks, metal clocks, plastic clocks, wooden clocks, plain clocks, designer clocks.........". Suddenly Uncle Bruce interrupted yet again. "Let me repeat myself, "lunch is ready!" Both girls didn't move a muscle. Angelica continued, "analog clock, digital clocks, clocks with numbers...."

Uncle Bruce was getting frustrated with the girls, "I didn't make it hot for you to eat it cold!" The girls quickly got to the kitchen table where they had cheeseburgers and crinkle cut fries for lunch before going on their journey. Angelica gave up listing the clocks and insisted that Target was the perfect general store for this journey.

Skipping breakfast, the girls chowed down on the cheeseburgers. Valerie put ketchup on her burger and put a small pond of ketchup on her plate for the crispy French fries. Angelica put lettuce, tomato, and ketchup on her cheeseburger, then put a large lake of ketchup on her plate for her fries. As Uncle Bruce slowly ate his double cheeseburger he intently listened to the girls.

Angelica finished her cheeseburger and fries but left most of the ketchup lake on her plate. As she threw away her paper plate, she asked everyone if they were ready to head to Target to find the first clue. Valerie was mystified, although Target was by far her favorite one stop shop, she thought the first clue would be found at the Jewel grocery store.

Angelica thought she was right, Valerie thought she was right. Not backing down Angelica huffed, crossed her arms, and turned herself around, in response Valerie huffed, crossed her arms, and turned herself around, and if you were wondering neither one did the hokey pokey. Uncle Bruce continued to eat his double cheeseburger; he was an incredibly slow eater.

Not to be outdone by Valerie, Angelica continued her relentless attempt to be correct. It was like turning on a faucet, tears of sadness rolled down Angelica's cheeks like Niagara Falls, this always worked at home, it had to work here. Valerie was not impressed, influenced, or swayed by this desperate attempt to get her way, she too had tear glands. Matching her tear for tear Valerie turned on her waterfall, Kaieteur Falls in Guyana, the world's tallest. Uncle Bruce remained dumbfounded as he dipped his lightly salted fries in the delicious ketchup.

"Touché" Angelica said to Valerie. This was getting serious, the stubborn Angelica realized that she had to pull out her best weapon, the optimum weapon, the unsurpassed weapon, the piece de resistance. It was unfair, it was dangerous, it was unique. In a split-second Angelica pulled out Mt. St. Angelica. Suddenly ashes of insults, manipulative words and sounds came spewing out of the crater of Mt. St. Angelica, there were no survivors.

Valerie laughed; Angelica was flabbergasted. She thought Valerie had no answer, she thought Valerie had no match for this high-tech weapon of mass devastation. Valerie would be going down like an ice cube on a 100-degree day in July. It was hopeless. Then it happened, out of nowhere, without any warning completely surprising everyone, Mt. St Valerie erupted spewing ashes of bad attitude, insults, and meanness. Between the two eruptions, nothing would survive.

Uncle Bruce didn't flinch, didn't respond, or didn't react to any of this nonsense. He finally finished his fries and threw away his paper plate. The girls continued arguing, each one determined to get their own way, little did they know what Uncle Bruce was going to say. Simultaneously, they hollered, "Where are we going?" Then they waited for the answer.

Nonchalantly, Uncle Bruce looked at Angelica, then he looked at his sweet niece Valerie not saying a word, then he got up and poured himself another ice-cold Pepsi. He took a long gulp and put down his glass. "Girls" he said quietly. Angelica stomped her foot and quickly replied, "Blood is thicker than water, I didn't have a chance." Valerie began to wonder about her friendship with Angelica.

"Let me repeat, girls neither one of you is correct." Both girls acted like their pet goldfish had just died. Their Broadway performance was very dramatic, award-winning, and almost very convincing. Uncle Bruce gave them a slow clap and sarcastically suggested the two girls make it a musical and take their show on the road, neither one of the girls laughed.

"But why?" asked Valerie, "I thought either one was a good idea. Angelica had a good choice." And so did you!" quickly replied Angelica. Suddenly, the two were best friends again. Uncle Bruce praised the girls for their excellent choices but informed them of their mistake, "Both of you forgot these clues were written in the 1850's, neither of these stores were around back then."

Valerie was intrigued, "Really?" I know all about the human body, but nothing about the history of Glendale Heights." Angelica was dumbfounded, "Just think what would have happened to Valerie. She would have been gone, you would have been toast, gone but not forgotten, it would have been adios amigos. Thank goodness you listened to me."

Both Valerie and Uncle Bruce looked at each other and said, "UHH?" Uncle Bruce loved history and looked for his book, "The History of Glendale Heights". He started giving the girls a little knowledge, "This town was originally farmland owned by families working the land including the Redding family, the Papadopolus family, and the Hernandez family. Army Trail Road was a simply known as Army Trail and was an east to west passage for homesteaders trying to build a new life for themselves. Thousands of stagecoaches used the trail."

Valerie was intrigued and listened intently, Angelica hated learning and headed to the refrigerator for three cans of Pepsi, one for each one of them. She took the three cans and placed them temporarily on the counter unaware she knocked Kiara's leash off the counter. Uncle Bruce continued talking, "Many towns popped up surrounding the Redding farm. Glen Ellyn was incorporated in 1892, Bloomingdale in 1833 and Lombard in 1837. Carol Stream while still unincorporated in the 1850's had a thriving local market".

Angelica came back to the group carrying the three sodas, hearing their conversation, rudely replied, "Why are we talking about Carol Stream? Wasn't this curse thing in Glendale Heights?" Then she tripped on the dog leash she had previously knocked off the counter dropping all of three cans of Pepsi. Uncle Bruce continued, "they had a barber shop, a hotel, a dining room, a blacksmith and a general store."

Valerie was thankful she had an uncle like Uncle Bruce, he was smart, he was nice and according to him, very handsome. Angelica gave Uncle Bruce a can, Valerie a can and kept one for herself. Uncle Bruce continued, "The general store closed in 1978, however it is now a 24-hour gym called Taylor's Fitness, however, before remodeling the historical society had the building declared an historical landmark, meaning they had to preserve most of the interior, including the old, wait for it, antique handcrafted Swiss grandfather clock."

Excited, Angelica opened up her can and took a sip of the soda, she commented how refreshing it was and suggested they have a toast in celebration. Uncle Bruce agreed and opened his can thinking of an appropriate toast. Knowing what could happen, Valerie was hesitant to open her can. Angelica told her he would have, could have, and should have. Uncle Bruce waited for Valerie to open her can so he could start his toast.

Valerie knew she was scared, Valerie knew the chances, Valerie knew what a mess it would make. However, neither can had done anything so far and Angelica put a lot of peer pressure on Valerie, giving her no choice, she had to do it. Putting a smile on her face, she grabbed her can of Pepsi and closed her eyes, hoping she would have the same good luck as Angelica and Uncle Bruce.

In one swift motion she grabbed the tab and popped it opened. KAPOW! The Pepsi shot up like Old Faithful at Yellowstone National Park, getting soda all over poor little Valerie and the floor. Angelica was dumbfounded, Uncle Bruce was dumbfounded. She didn't beat the odds, she didn't have the same good luck, she didn't like this whole situation. Finally, after the laughter and the explosion of Pepsi, Valerie asked herself, "Why, why do I have such bad luck?"

CHAPTER 11

ULTRACREPIDARIAN

(One who gives opinions on matters they know nothing about)

Valerie ran upstairs to change her Pepsi covered clothes. Although she admitted to herself that getting the can that exploded was comical, she thought it was rude when Angelica and Uncle Bruce laughed at her, they deserved to clean up the mess in the kitchen. There was sticky film on the counter, sticky film on the floor and a sticky film on the cabinets.

Once Valerie got upstairs, she looked in her closet, she had nothing to wear, she looked in her dresser drawers, she had nothing to wear and she looked in the hope chest, she had nothing nice to wear while she was searching to break the curse of the diamond necklace. Valerie was getting older and liked to dress nicely, she was turning into a fashionista.

Downstairs Uncle Bruce and Angelica waited patiently, well to be honest Angelica waited patiently, she listened to some new age music wearing her ear pods. Still hungry she got up, went into the refrigerator, grabbed a Sprite, some guacamole, the tortilla chips on the counter and sprawled herself on the big comfy couch. She knew this was not going to be quick for Valerie.

Uncle Bruce was not a patient person, when growing up his parents taught him to always keep busy, idol hands are the devil's workshop. First, he emptied the dishwasher, the plates came first, then the silverware, then the glasses. Next, he cleaned the pots and pans, scrubbing, rinsing, drying, and putting each one away in its

82

proper place. Still waiting, he swept the hardwood floor and then used the Swiffer on it. He thought this was going to be quick for Valerie.

Upstairs Valerie sat on the edge of her bed in deep thought. "What would look good on this journey? If she happened to run into Grant, would he think she was pretty? What would be the proper code of dress on this journey? Would Grant notice her? Should she wear a casual outfit? Does Grant like the casual look? Should she wear more of a sporty look? Does Grant like the sporty look?" Valerie sat frozen on the corner of the bed contemplating her next move.

Determined to wear the correct outfit she stared blankly into her vast array of clothes in her closet. She asked herself, "Do I wear the blue blouse with my designer jeans? Or do I wear a casual T-shirt with the jeans. Maybe skip the jeans, wear a nice pair of black pants with a white blouse and my red shoes. Too fancy, more casual, sweatpants, a t-shirt, and the red gym shoes. Too casual, a nice summer dress and my nice comfortable brown sandals, quickly telling herself summer was over." Not happy with any of her choices, thinking she herself was becoming an ultracrepidarian she told herself, "Think Valerie, Think!"

With Saturday afternoon quickly fading away, Uncle Bruce was losing the little patience he did have. He paced, he looked out the front window, he paced, he looked at the weather report, he paced some more, he checked the sports scores, he finally lost his patience. He called out, "Valerie, are you almost done?"

"What are you doing? When a girl is picking out an outfit, she is in a special zone, it's a state of mind, it's hard to explain. It's a girl thing, but you never bother her, you could destroy her life, picking the right outfit is a matter of life and death, yes, it's an incredibly important decision. So, Uncle Bruce shush, be quiet, hush, keep silent, mums the word and most important SHUT YOUR PIE HOLE!" Uncle Bruce was shocked Angelica was talking to him this way, especially since she was such an ultracrepidarian.

Several hours went by as Valerie thought about her unlimited choices. With 20 pairs of dress slacks, 5 pairs of designer jeans, 5 pairs of sweatpants, 15 blouses, 20 t-shirts, 10 sweatshirts and 25 pairs of shoes, 5 hats, the possibilities were endless, or to be exact 187,500,000 choices. Then it hit her, no hat, her beautiful lime green blouse, her designer blue jeans from world class designer Carisa Van T and her light blue Nike gym shoes. She joyfully screamed.

Thinking she was almost finished, Uncle Bruce timidly asked, "Does that mean she is done?" Angelica quickly replied, "Yes and No, she is done picking out the outfit, now she has to do her nails and hair, sit down, relax, it's going to be awhile. Being a fashionista takes time." Uncle Bruce was out of patience, out of tea and out of daylight."

Upstairs, Valerie looked at her messy hair and told herself something needed to be done. She also looked at her fingernails and wondered if she should change the color, Valerie always wore her classic white nail polish. Today she should surprise the world and make them fire engines red, emerald, green, or cobalt blue. She should paint a rainbow, a patriotic theme, a black and white checkerboard, or she should keep them classic white.

Her hair was a completely different issue. Now it was dirty and messy, now it was a hat day, now she needed to get to work. To change things, first she needed to wash it three times with TRESemme shampoo, then she needed to use the TRESemme conditioner. When her hair was done drying, she would use the TRESemme hair maximizer and finish off with the TRESemme hair spray, she was going on into the world and needed to look good.

Downstairs Uncle Bruce was getting ready to call this journey off, it was 10:00 at night and he was getting tired, it was way past his bedtime. Angelica was perplexed, "Do not be so old, for us "YOUNG" people the day is just starting!" Uncle Bruce was very insulted, he always thought of himself as a young man, "I am young, I only took one nap yesterday." Angelica laughed and said, "Okay!" Then she went upstairs to get Valerie.

When she walked in the door, her mouth dropped open, Valerie was absolutely gorgeous, beautiful, perfectly pretty. "We have to go; your uncle wants to go to bed" she warned. "But I have still need to do my makeup, brush my teeth and put on new eyelashes." Angelica was stunned, like a true ultracrepidarian she looked at all the beauty products and told Valerie," You are beautiful without makeup, you are a wonderful fashionista, but you are turning into a diva!"

Valerie looked into the mirror, really looked. She was stunned. Valerie looked at the clock, where did the time go? She was stunned. Valerie thought about Grant. She was stunned. Being a fashionista was one thing, but being a diva was another. She promised Angelica she would finish quickly and head downstairs to begin their journey.

Meanwhile in the Wisconsin Dells, Grant and his family were getting ready for a late dinner. They had spent the evening sliding down water slides, shooting water guns, and getting soaked by the gigantic unpredictable bucket of water at the top of the play area. Grant was always lucky enough to know when the bucket would spill.

Then Grant's family went to the arcade. Grant's younger brother, George, used his tokens quickly playing Whack a mole, Deal or No Deal and Ms. Pacman. He could not whack any moles, he didn't make any deals and the four ghosts Blinky, Inky, Pinky and Clyde found him quickly and devoured him. George did not have a good time, George didn't win any tickets, George didn't win any prizes.

Grant on the other hand, as usual was very lucky that night. He did extremely well in Whack a Mole, hitting the mole an unprecedented 122 times in two minutes, a record earning him 5,000 bonus tickets. In Deal or No Deal, he picked the million-ticket case and followed it through till the final offer, earning him an unprecedented one million bonus tickets. Blinky, Inky, Pinky and Clyde never touched Grant giving him the opportunity to get to level 35, giving him an unprecedented award of 250,000 bonus ticket.

George was happy for his lucky brother. However, Grant, the best big brother ever, surprised George by exchanging the bonus tickets for a big teddy bear, a spaceship model, a gift certificate for the apparel store and a gift card to the snack shop, all for George.

For a late dinner they would have a pizza party, but they needed to change clothes and freshen up. Mom and dad were exhausted, Grant was excited and little George was just getting started. Finally, mom was ready, dad was ready, and George was ready. Grant took forever to shower, shave and changed clothes. He thought about Valerie, hoping she would miraculously follow him up to Wisconsin. After an eternity, his dad went to get Grant. Not realizing the time, Grant finished quickly so they could enjoy a very late dinner together.

Back in Glendale Heights, Valerie finally came downstairs. Apologetic, but looking very nice, Valerie hustled to the car with Angelica and Uncle Bruce following. Prepared for adventuring into the great unknown, Uncle Bruce started his 2020 red Jeep Cherokee, it purred like a kitten when you scratch its chin. He slowly pulled out of the driveway, thinking it was clear and continued backward gently accelerating. Out of nowhere, Angelica screamed, "Wait!"

Uncle Bruce slammed on the brakes, hurling everyone forward. Thinking the worst, thinking it was over, thinking he hit someone he automatically pulled forward and shut off the car. He rushed out of the Jeep and checked behind his vehicle, there was nada, rein, absolutely nothing. Mystified, Uncle Bruce reluctantly asked Angelica why she dramatically demanded him to stop the car.

With a burst of attitude, Angelica proudly replied that she needed her gum. Uncle Bruce told her that she either could have just asked like a normal person, or they could have stopped at 7-11 and bought a package. Still carrying her bag of attitude, Angelica vehemently told Uncle Bruce, "I am not a normal person, nor will I ever be," Valerie smiled knowing she too would never be a "normal" person. Angelica proudly continued, "besides, I only chew Orbit's tutti fruiti long lasting extra flavored calorie free gum!"

Uncle Bruce was speechless, Angelica patiently waited for an answer. Out of desperation, out of respect, out of a desire not to be a "adult" all Uncle Bruce could say was "OVEY!" Trying to avoid World War 3 between the two, Valerie quickly told her that her special gum was in the backpack. Then it was Valerie's turn to scream, "The Backpack! I forgot the backpack!"

Darting quickly out of the Jeep, Valerie ran swiftly back into the house, almost tripping on a small branch left on the front sidewalk from last Tuesday's storm. Composing herself expeditiously, she ran into the house pushing the front door open. She rummaged through the house searching for the elusive backpack. It was not in her bedroom, it wasn't in her parent's bedroom, it wasn't in the upstairs bathroom or the utility closet.

Frantically, she continued the mad search. Completely out of patience, Uncle Bruce honked the horn three times, HONK! HONK! HONK! Valerie did not know where to look next. Downstairs she promptly perused the kitchen, living room and dining room, nothing. HONK! HONK! HONK! Valerie had no idea, Valerie had no time, Valerie had no backpack. Discouraged and accepting failure, Valerie decided to go back out to the car.

Being late October, there was a chill in the air, Valerie decided to grab her jacket from the coat rack behind the door. "Unbelievable!" she said to herself. She tried to pick up the backpack, but it was too heavy. HONK! HONK! HONK!

Feeling rushed, she opened up the bulky backpack and took out the huge hammer, the heavy flashlight, and the large bundle of rope. Valerie took the cumbersome algebra book thinking anytime is a good time to practice math, the peanut butter sandwiches, the bottled water and of course the tutti fruiti gum. Easily grabbing the backpack and under the mist of darkness, she ran to the Jeep.

Uncle Bruce started driving. Angelica started chewing her gum and Valerie smiled, hoping, praying, wishing that this could be the end of her life of bad luck. "So, where are we going?" asked Angelica. "We are going to Taylor's Gym on Geneva Road." This is where the general store in the 1850's was. It is open 24 hours" stoically replied Uncle Bruce. Right away Angelica pulled out her sassy attitude and promptly said, "Whaat?"

Seeing the look in her Uncle Bruce's eyes, Valerie knew he had had enough of Angelica's fiery attitude. Before the fire spread and innocent people got burned, Valerie knew she had to react and react quickly. Pulling out her proverbial fire extinguisher Valerie started dropping knowledge bombs on them.

"The Historical Society had the property declared a historical landmark in 1978. Any remodeling could only be done if anything related to the original general store was incorporated, displayed, or remained in storage. So, this clock we are looking for has to be there" calmly instructed Valerie.

Angelica calmed down; Valerie saved the day with her quick-thinking firefighting skills, her proverbial fire extinguisher put Angelica's burning attitude out. Uncle Bruce was proud of his niece and smiled, knowing what a special young lady she was. Words could not express how much he loved and adored her. He knew she was destined for greatness.

Suddenly, a loud noise came from the back seat. Uncle Bruce knew this loud rumbling noise was not anything his Jeep would make. The horrific noise came again, even louder, and scarier. "Is everything okay back there?" asked a concerned Uncle Bruce. The noise came again scaring everyone in the Jeep. Then it came again and again and again. Not wanting any attention Angelica defiantly replied, "Not me!"

With the only other person in the backseat being Valerie, Uncle Bruce was concerned, "What's wrong honey?" he sweetly asked. All was quiet, nobody said a word. Then it came again, was it a tyrannosaurus rex, was it a diesel truck starting, or was it a volcano exploding? Valerie sat quietly with the eyes of the world staring at her.

Under intense pressure and scrutiny, she finally broke down, "It's my stomach, I haven't eaten anything all day, I'm hungry!" Concerned, Uncle Bruce stopped at the 24-hour gas station and bought Valerie two egg salad sandwiches, that is all they had left, and an orange juice. He told her to eat them quickly because they were just minutes away from the gym. Valerie tried to say something, but Uncle Bruce insisted she eat them and would never take "NO" for an answer.

'Thinking only of removing the curse, Valerie ate the two egg salad sandwiches quickly and quietly, forgetting about her allergies to eggs. Uncle Bruce pulled into the empty gym parking lot. Determined to find success, the three detectives got out of the Jeep and headed towards the front door. Valerie felt a sharp pain in her side but continued.

Inside was a young girl mopping the floor, nobody was working out. "Hello folks, sorry we are about to close, can't get enough overnight help, but we open back up at 6:00 am." Uncle Bruce got goosebumps. A very pale Valerie suddenly held her side again fighting immense pain, she was crushed. Then it happened, BLAAAAH! The biggest vomit bomb ever produced on the planet exploded, Valerie threw up the egg salad sandwiches all over the young girls freshly mopped floor.

There was vomit to the left, puke to the right, there was puke in front and puke behind them. The vomit was disgusting, the puke smelled, the puke burned their eyes. Angelica was embarrassed behind belief; Valerie wanted to leave and forget about the quest. As she stood back up, she asked everybody, "Why, why do I have such bad luck?"

CHAPTER 12

STROOPWAFEL

(A wafer cookie with a caramel filling made by the Dutch)

The young lady mopping the floor reacted quickly. She dropped the mop, escorted Valerie over to a table and a chair where she could sit down and grabbed a nice cold water from the cooler behind the counter and a couple of freshly folded towels. This angel from heaven opened the water bottle and helped Valerie take a sip. She gently wiped her face and the few spots of vomit that splattered on her designer jeans and blue gym shoes.

Then Taylor went to her backpack under the counter and got a small, wrapped package, unwrapped it and handed it to Valerie. Confused and slightly lightheaded, Valerie asked Taylor what it was, Taylor gleefully replied, "It's a stroopwafel!" Valerie looked at Taylor strangely. Keeping a positive attitude, Taylor smiled at Valerie and replied, "A stroopwafel is a Danish treat. It is a waffle cookie made from two thin layers of baked dough joined by a caramel filling. It is absolutely delicious! Try it!"

Trying not to be rude, Valerie reluctantly took a small bite of the stroopwafel, she smiled, the stroopwafel was delicious, the stroopwafel was scrumptious, the stroopwafel was appetizing. Valerie took another bite of the stroopwafel, then another bite, then another bite of the stroopwafel. Soon the stroopwafel was gone, but her stomach stopped hurting.

With Valerie starting to feel better, and with those nasty sandwiches out of her body her color returned to her face, she was no longer in pain. Uncle Bruce stood frozen in amazement, in today's world very few people were this nice. He wondered who this angel was. He wondered where she came from. He asked himself why she was here. He wondered where he could get a stroopwafel. The angel quickly returned to her mop and began mopping once again.

Still in a state of shock and disbelief, Uncle Bruce bent down on one knee and made sure Valerie was okay. Uncle Bruce wondered who he was dealing with, Was she the Lone Ranger? Robinhood? Could she be Florence Nightingale? Maybe Mother Theresa? Who was this pretty redheaded young lady? With Valerie feeling much better, Uncle Bruce decided to find out who this young lady of few words was.

Without wasting any more time, Uncle Bruce went into action. Where was she? The vomit was gone, the mop was gone, the young lady was gone. The stroopwafel was gone. Everything he knew about angels was coming true. They come out of nowhere, help the lost, the sick, the needy, then they disappear on to their next assignment. Valerie's helper disappeared. A true angel wants no credit for what they do, this young lady wanted no attention.

Finally, Uncle Bruce read once that a true angel from heaven has a special aura that surrounds and protects them. This young lady gave off a vibe that made you feel comfortable and at ease. As soon as he entered the gym, he had goosebumps, now he knew she was an angel sent from the mighty God from above. Now, if possible, he needed to find this angel and thank her.

He looked everywhere for Valerie's angel. Uncle Bruce looked north, nothing, he looked south, nothing, east, nothing, and finally west nothing. Like a miracle from heaven, a door in the back opened and a very bright light shined. Out of a mist of brightness walked the young lady carrying a basket full of towels. Overtaken with emotion, Uncle Bruce got down on his knees and began crying.

Humored by her uncle, and feeling much better, she got up from her chair and asked him, "What are you doing?" Uncle Bruce wiped the tears from his cheeks and quietly whispered, "She's an angel, an angel sent from the heavens above to help us!" Valerie laughed hysterically. The young lady brought her small green hand towels to the counter and asked Valerie why she was laughing.

Still laughing Valerie sweetly replied, "He thinks you are an angel!" Valerie continued laughing, the young lady stood silent, starting to fold her towels. Valerie asked her what was wrong, the young mysterious lady seriously replied, "I am!". Then there came the awkward silence. The young lady looked at Uncle Bruce, Valerie looked at the young lady, Uncle Bruce looked at the young lady, Valerie looked at Uncle Bruce, the young lady looked at Valerie. There was stone cold faces, there was stone cold smiles and stone-cold silence.

Then the lights flickered, papers blew off the black granite counter and the door opened up. The young lady was unphased and continued folding her towels. Like a precision machine, she took one at a time, flattened the towel, folded it in half, smoothed it, then tri-folded each side. Each one was perfect, each one was a work of art, each one was put away under the counter. Valerie and Uncle Bruce just stared in amazement as she methodically folded each towel into a perfect square.

Finally able to speak, Uncle Bruce calmly asked, "Who are you?" "Oh sorry," replied the red headed young lady, "I'm Taylor!" Uncle Bruce introduced themselves and told Taylor, Angelica was outside. Uncle Bruce shook Taylor's tiny hand and said, "Thank you." Although big in politeness and helpfulness, she was a small young lady, around five feet tall. All she did was give a thumbs up.

Not wanting to be left out, Valerie reached over to shake Taylor's hand and say thank you and apologize for the whole vomit situation. Taylor reached over but, in a surprise move Valerie suddenly pulled her hand back, hoping no one else saw what had just happened. Unfortunately, the very observant but unusually quiet Taylor saw the whole thing, and loudly shrieked, "WHAAT?"

Hearing the scream heard around the world, Angelica came barging in from outside. Uncle Bruce, who was walking around the gym, was amazed how much equipment was in the gym, they had rows and rows of stair climbers, treadmills, rowing machines, elliptical machines, bicep curls, leg presses and countless other workout equipment that he had no idea did, this was the first time he was in a gym, he came running. Embarrassed, scared, and nervous, Valerie started to cry. Uncle Bruce gave her a big hug and held her tight.

Not knowing what was happening and assuming the worst, Angelica came running to save her new friend, she grabbed Uncle Bruce's arm, pulled him away from Valerie and flipped him over on his back. "What did you do now? You are a bad, bad man!" proclaimed Angelica. Taylor went over to help Uncle Bruce and told Angelica that he had done nothing wrong.

As Taylor helped Uncle Bruce back to his feet, she stared intensely at Valerie. Valerie stared back hoping Taylor would say nothing about what she had seen. It was too weird, too unusual, too odd for Taylor to ignore. It could be dangerous, it could be hazardous, it could be treacherous for Taylor to ignore. It could be too scary, too ghoulish, too sinister for Taylor to ignore.

"So, what's with the flashing hand?" asked Taylor. "Whaat?" asked Angelica, "Whaat?" asked Uncle Bruce and "Whaat?" asked Valerie as she hid her hand. "Don't hide it, don't lie about it, what is wrong with you?" quickly responded Taylor. Always taught to tell the truth, Valerie burst out in tears, "I don't know, I don't know, please for heaven's sake please help because I really don't know."

Valerie pulled up her sleeve to show everyone her hand, one second it was there, next it was invisible. Everyone was scared, everyone stared, everyone had ideas. Angelica thought it was an infection spread from an alien spacecraft, Uncle Bruce thought it was from new tech gadget from Best Buy, Taylor thought it was a gadget to wear when you try to take over the world. Valerie was scared and started blubbering, "All I wanted to do was find the clues to find the diamond necklace to break the curse. I am so tired of my bad luck!"

Taylor's ears came to attention, she had heard that somewhere before, but where? "What did you say?" asked a very curious Taylor. Valerie kept crying thinking her quest was over. Uncle Bruce stepped into help, "she, said, "she needs to find the clues to find the diamond necklace to break the curse!" Taylor repeated, clues, diamond, curse, bad luck, clues, diamond, curse, bad luck". Nothing came to her, she yelled at herself, "Think Taylor, Think!"

Taylor paced back and forth; nothing came to her. Taylor drank some Mountain Dew Baja Blast; nothing came to her. Taylor started tapping her fingers on the black granite counter, nothing came to her. Aggravated she could not remember; Taylor angrily clapped her hands together in last ditch attempt to remember. Then like lighting hitting a tall oak tree during a spring thunderstorm, it hit, KAPOW! BOOM! SNAP! CRACKLE AND POP! Taylor remembered, yes, Taylor remembered.

"I need to find the book, the book that has been in my family for generations. The book tells all about your curse, but I have not seen it for years. It is called The Cursible, it's here somewhere, I know it. She started in the back room 1, nothing, room 2, nothing. 3,4,5, nothing. Room 6,7, nothing, leaving only the small breakroom.

Taylor and an older gentlemen had cleaned the breakroom a few months prior, together they had cleaned it and removed any supplies that actually belonged in the storage room. She looked on the shelf, nothing, she looked under the table, nothing, on top by the People magazine stack, nothing. She looked through the stack of books on the table, nothing, then she saw it, under the poor dry cacti plant, the Cursible.

Almost knocking the sad-looking plant off the table, she firmly grabbed the large purple book and went running back to her guests. She tried reading it but could not. Finally, back at the counter, she scanned the book quickly, Valerie's hand was more invisible than visible. She found a chapter on figuring out each clue, she found a chapter on things you cannot do while figuring out a clue. Then she found a chapter on time limits.

Taylor scanned each paragraph quickly hoping to find an answer. Angelica demanded she read faster; Uncle Bruce held his poor niece praying this was not the end. Valerie began to realize that this was no joke, this was real, and now realized why her mom did not want her to go on this journey. Valerie wondered if this is what happened to all her past relatives that went missing so many years ago.

Everybody stared at Taylor as she looked for an answer. Sweating profusely, Taylor read as fast as she could, then she looked up, smiled, and gave the group a welcoming thumbs up, the group cheered, however Valerie hand becoming invisible, now moved up to her arm, how long before it was all invisible? How long before the end? How long before the lights went out?

"Read it! Read it!" Demanded Angelica. Taylor put on her glasses and started to read aloud, "As in all cases where there is a clue driven opportunity to break the curse, to keep it fair for both parties involved, once the quest to break the curse is started you have twelve hours to find the first clue and twelve hours between each clue to find the next clue. As a reminder that time is running out, the fore mentioned cursed person will slowly start to vanish with one hour remaining, when the hour is over, the cursed person will cease to exist, unless you have figured out the clue, whereas the person will return to normal. "

Uncle Bruce quickly looked at his watch, 10:45 pm, "This started what ten minutes ago?" Valerie sadly replied "Yes." Angelica argued it was more like eight minutes ago, Uncle Bruce said nothing but rolled his eyes. Taylor had heard rumors of a curse, but nobody ever said anything. This gym was owned by her family for generations. They originally kept the book the Cursible as more as a conversation starter, eventually no one thought about or cared about it, that is how it ended up under the plant.

Reacting quickly, Uncle Bruce stated the ugly truth, "We have until 11:35 to find the clue. Angelica stay back and care for Valerie, Taylor you come with me." Angelica was not happy, "First we have until 11:37, second don't you think I'm good enough to find the next clue?" Uncle Bruce said nothing. Valerie insisted she could help and insisted she help find the clue; she was the cursed individual. Uncle Bruce looked at his watch

50 minutes left

Knowing time was not on their side, Uncle Bruce decided to let Valerie and Angelica search for the next clue. Taking command, Uncle Bruce commanded the two to search the storage room for the antique clock, Taylor and himself would search the grandfather clock on the big mirrored back wall. Angelica defiantly replied, "You are not my boss of me, don't tell me what to do, we are taking the grandfather clock, you and Taylor take the storage room."

Flabbergasted, Uncle Bruce angrily replied, "It doesn't matter, just look for the clue!" Valerie, with one arm, and Angelica started searching the big dusty old antique grandfather clock. They opened up the cabinet, they opened the front of the clock, they looked underneath, they looked behind the clock and they looked, on top of the clock. There was nothing, nothing, nothing, nothing, and nothing.

Taylor and Uncle Bruce hustled to the big black double doors to the backroom, unfortunately it was locked, fortunately Taylor had the keys in her tan khaki pants. Pulling her purple T-shirt up she swiftly dug into her right-side pocket, pulling out a set of ten keys. Uncle Bruce watched as Taylor nervously tried several of the keys. After what seemed like an eternity, Taylor found the key and the door opened.

Not wasting any time, they ran around the storage room determined to find any evidence of the four-mentioned clock.

Taylor ran to the left; Uncle Bruce ran to the right. Uncle Bruce looked at his watch.

40 minutes left

Despite the fact that time was ticking, despite the fact that Valerie was disappearing, despite the fact nobody knew where the next clue was, Angelica wanted a stroopwafel. The caramel packed between the two layers of thin dough looked absolutely scrumptious and Angelica could not keep her mind off of it. To avoid any more delay in time, Valerie rushed back to the counter, opened the drawer, and was pleasantly surprised, it was full of stroopwafels.

Trying to be swift, Valerie looked at the drawer and tried deciding. How could she? There were strawberry stroopwafels, chocolate stroopwafels, M&M stroopwafels, sprinkle stroopwafels, vanilla stroopwafels, sweet and sour stroopwafels, peanut butter stroopwafels, marshmallow stroopwafels, smore stroopwafels, low calorie stroopwafels, gluten free stroopwafels and countless other stroopwafels. Taylor obviously loved her stroopwafels. She grabbed Angelica, a strawberry stroopwafel and headed back to the storage room.

"Here is your stroopwafel!" Valerie said as Valerie handed her the unique treat from the Netherlands. Angelica did not say anything, not even a Thank you. Looking like she lost her best friend, Angelica put her head down. "What's wrong?" asked a concerned Valerie.

With absolutely no remorse or any concern for the real problem at hand, Angelica sobbed, "I wanted a caramel stroopwafel!" With her right arm completely invisible, Valerie sarcastically replied, "Really?' Despite her handicap, despite the time, despite her thoughts she grabbed the strawberry stroopwafel and ran back to the counter to find Angelica a caramel stroopwafel.

Meanwhile in the cold, dark storage room Taylor and Uncle Bruce found nothing to resemble any antiques, let alone a clock of any type. The saw a pallet of water bottles, used pieces of exercise equipment, some old signs and boxes and boxes full of old receipts, but no clock. Uncle Bruce looked at his watch.

30 minutes left

After Angelica finally finished the caramel stroopwafel, the two decided it would be best to help, or at the least find Taylor and Uncle Bruce in the storage room. Angelica wanted another stroopwafel, preferably a strawberry stroopwafel. Valerie looked at her watch and sternly replied, "Absolutely not!" Without further delay, they headed towards the storage room.

The backpack remained on the floor, Angelica looked at Valerie, Valerie looked at Angelica. Finally, Angelica broke the silence, "Don't look at me, you lost the challenge, it's your responsibility to carry it." Despite having only one arm now, Valerie hoisted the backpack onto her back, and they headed into the storage room. Uncle Bruce looked at his watch

20 minutes left

Taylor and Uncle Bruce were an incredible team. Watching the clock closely, the two stayed focused like hungry lions on a hunt for dinner. Uncle Bruce watched the clock closely and kept telling Taylor how much time they had left to help his niece, Valerie. Suddenly, Uncle Bruce heard noises. Taylor told him she thought the gym was haunted by ghosts for years. Uncle Bruce did not want to hear that, he shivered and got goosebumps. Taylor laughed at the big, tall man.

The noises continued; Uncle Bruce was uneasy. Taylor took the lead, Uncle Bruce followed closely behind the petite young lady. Unable to find anything in the dim light they were ready to give up on this junk-filled storage room. "Shh!" exclaimed Taylor, "I hear footsteps!" Uncle Bruce's heart began to race rapidly, his breathing became short and difficult, and his body started to sweat profusely. The footsteps sounded like they were coming closer and closer.

Uncle Bruce thought he felt somebody behind him. He felt the breathing on his neck, the cold brush against his back, the hairs on the back of his neck stood tall. Bravely he looked back, there was nothing, he shivered once again. Taylor had gotten ahead of him a few feet, he rushed to catch up to the fearless young lady and grabbed hold of her tiny hand.

They heard voices again; Uncle Bruce held her hand even tighter. Taylor assured him she would protect him, but the ghosts had been around since she was a young lady and never hurt anyone. The footsteps were getting closer and closer, Uncle Bruce took a deep breath and continued to hold onto Taylor's hand.

Mysteriously in the dark, someone, something, somebody stepped on the back of his shoe. Without thinking he turned around, he screamed, "OOOOOHHHHHHH!" The other thing screamed, "OOOOOHHHHHH!", grabbed Uncle Bruce's arm and flipped him on his back. Uncle Bruce curiously asked, "Angelica?"

Angelica defensively replied, "You shouldn't sneak up on a girl like that!" Valerie's whole body started to flash invisible, everyone was scared, everyone worried, everyone shed a tear. Uncle Bruce looked at his watch.

10 minutes left

Taylor looked up as she helped Uncle Bruce up and saw something, "It's a staircase" We have to look down there." Everyone agreed, "I have never seen it before, I wonder what is down there. With the dim light from the cracked floorboards overhead. Valerie struggled down the rickety old staircase, but Taylor gently helped her down. Uncle Bruce now knew for sure Taylor was an angel sent from above. He tried complimenting her, but all she did was give a thumbs up.

The clock ticked, they all went downstairs and started searching. Angelica kept running into cobwebs and complaining about her deathly fear of the eight-legged monsters from Hades and the underworld. Taylor stayed focused on finding the antique clock that held the clue. Uncle Bruce could not help but stare at his pretty niece, this could be the end for her.

Although she was flashing on and off more rapidly, he hugged her and held her tight. With tears in her pretty brown eyes, she hugged him back tightly. Then she saw something, Valerie wiped her eyes and screamed "OVER THERE, TAYLOR TO YOUR RIGHT." Taylor reacted immediately and moved to her right, Valerie screamed, "Your other right!" Taylor went to her other right and looked, she saw nothing.

"Under the blanket! Under the blanket!" Valerie desperately screamed. Taylor hustled over to the old white blanket as fast as she could scraping her leg on assorted old wood planks and leftover junk of years gone by. Without fanfare, without hesitation, without fear she intensely grabbed the blanket and pulled with everything she had. Uncle Bruce looked at his watch.

Five minutes left

The old blanket fell with a deep loud thud spreading dust and little particles everywhere and over everybody. Valerie suddenly found hope realizing they might have found the "clock". Uncle Bruce brushed the dust off his shirt, pants, and hair. Taylor was relentless in her search for anything that looked like a clue. Angelica started by cleaning her glasses.

Having the power to see now, she hand brushed her hair with her hand, brushed away the dirt on her pants and then took her hand and started brushing away the dirt with her hand. Unexpectedly she felt something crawl on her hand. Shaking nervously, she inched herself toward Valerie and asked her what it was, "Please don't tell me… please don't tell me…"

Stoically, Valerie quickly replied, "it's a spider, the eight-legged creature who we all know and love." Angelica quickly screamed, "A spider! Get it off me! Get it off me now!" Then she screamed "NO OOOOOOOOOOOOOOOOOOOOOOOOOOOOOOOOO" as she ran back upstairs swatting imaginary bugs off her arms and legs to civilization. Taylor continued to search the old grandfather clock for any clue to stop Valerie from vanishing, Uncle Bruce looked at his watch.

1 minute left

Uncle Bruce scanned the old clock searching for the clue, Taylor scanned the old clock searching for the clue and Valerie, sitting on the bench scanned the old clock searching for the clue. Without the clue, there would be no hope, no optimism and unfortunately, no Valerie.

Then without provocation Valerie saw a white paper peeking out from behind the big brass pendulum of the old grandfather clock. "The pendulum, the pendulum!" she screamed with every ounce of breath she had left. Taylor reacted quickly but was stopped by the glass case, Uncle Bruce told Valerie to take the hammer they packed in the backpack. Valerie took a deep breath and told him she took it out before she left the house, Uncle Bruce looked at his watch.

Thirty seconds left

"Push the glass in, push the glass in!" screamed Uncle Bruce. Taylor tried but could not. Uncle Bruce tried but could not push the glass in either. Surprisingly, Valerie crawled over to help. On/ off, on/off Valerie flickered. Like her cousin Gertrude, like her cousin Agatha and like her cousin Lilliana, Valerie realized there was little hope, what she needed was a miracle. Flashing faster and faster, Valerie knew it was now or never. Uncle Bruce looked at his watch.

Five seconds left

In one swift unexpected move, Valerie jumped at the antique grandfather clock. She pushed the glass into the clock, breaking it instantly. Unfortunately, the glass cut her arm and instantly the blood started gushing out of her small arm. Having no fear, no pain, and no regrets she gave it everything she had, reaching, and grabbing for the piece of paper. Uncle Bruce looked at his watch, there was no time left.

Valerie disappeared, Uncle Bruce cried, Taylor cried. "Uncle Bruce, asked himself, "How did this all go so wrong?" Taylor tried to console him but there was nothing anybody could do to fix the giant hole that was ripped from his heart. Despite not knowing what to do or say, Taylor held his hand as a sign of support. Sometimes actions speak louder than words.

Tap, tap, tap went fingers on Uncle Bruce's shoulder, he ignored them. Tap, tap, tap went the fingers again. "Go away!" he painfully answered. "Don't you want to see the next clue?" a voice asked. "Ecstatic, euphoric, and blissful, Uncle Bruce recognized the voice. He turned around and saw his niece holding the clue, she had both hands, both arms, both legs and her head. Valerie really was beautiful. He jumped up and gave her a giant hug, Taylor smiled and gave Valerie a thumbs up.

Fortunately, Valerie's cut was small, unfortunately, Valerie was a bleeder. They went to the sink, washed her bloody arm, put some hydrogen peroxide on the small wound, rubbed some Corizon-10 on the wound and put a Minnie Mouse bandage on her arm.

Speechless, all he could say was "Who, What? Where? How?" Valerie smiled and shrugged her shoulders but showed Uncle Bruce and Taylor the next clue. It read:

NORTHEAST-CORNER-ROCK-
CRASSULA-OVATA-GOLLIUM-STORE

"It is time to go, let's get out of here. Valerie put the note in her back pocket and went upstairs with the rest of the small group of warriors. As they went upstairs Taylor offered everyone a stroopwafel, she went to the drawer, but it was empty. Everyone looked at Angelica, "Don't look at me!" exclaimed Angelica.

Taylor invited everyone to her parent's house to stay the night. Valerie reminded Taylor according to the Cursible they only had twelve hours to solve the next clue or else. "So that would be 11:35 am," calmly stated a very tired Uncle Bruce. "But I am so tired!" exclaimed Angelica, "Maybe I will stay at your house?"

"That's fine," said Uncle Bruce, Taylor smiled. "Since she is not going, can I go and help break this curse?" Uncle Bruce liked Taylor, she was smart, and hardworking. She was sweet and personable; she was dedicated and fun to be with. "Uncle Bruce immediately answered, "Yes".

Angelica took Uncle Bruce and Valerie to the side, "Hold on whippersnapper" replied Angelica. "You barely know her, she barely talks, she barely whines or complains, how can you trust a person like that?"

Uncle Bruce expeditiously answered, "Easily, she's an angel!" Angelica laughed. "She is sweet, personable, smart, and hardworking, I can trust a person like that!" Uncle Bruce looked over at Taylor, she smiled and gave him a thumbs up. He smiled back at her. Valerie agreed with Uncle Bruce, "let her come, the more the merrier!"

Swiftly changing her mind, Angelica told everyone she was coming. Taylor offered her house once again, "We can wash up, have pizza, and figure out the next clue. We do not need to stay long, they abruptly got their things and left for Taylor's house. The ride in the Jeep Cherokee took less than ten minutes.

As they went into Taylor's overcrowded bedroom, Taylor asked to see the next all-important clue, again, she was extremely good with word search and crossword puzzles and wanted to start thinking about the solution. Valerie reached for her back pocket; it was not there. She checked her front pockets, they were not there, her shirt pockets, it wasn't there and her shoes, it wasn't there. She embarrassingly told everyone she inadvertently lost the clue,

Uncle Bruce said he had a memory like an elephant he said it said: Northeast crook- Crab Store

Taylor said she was young and smart and said it said: Northwest corner- Crabby Cakes

Valerie corrected everyone and said the note said: Northeast Corner- Rock- Crassula Ovata Gallium -store

Angelica who never saw the note said: Anybody got a Sprite?
Valerie could not believe this was happening, how could she do this? Where did she lose the clue? When did she lose the clue? How did she lose the second clue? Flabbergasted, she asked everyone, "Why, why do I have such bad luck?

CHAPTER 13

SCRUMDIDDLYUMPTIOUS

(Extremely delicious)

Uncle Bruce slept on the old lumpy living room couch, while the girls all had a sleepover in Taylor's tiny room. With everything Taylor had in her bedroom, there was not much room for Valerie and Angelica, but they made the sleepover work. The girls laughed, did their nails, talked about boy's, and ate goldfish cracker's, Taylor thought they were scrumdiddlyumptious. All three said they were friends with a certain boy and not girlfriend/ boyfriend. Valerie did start to blush once she started thinking about Grant. Once Uncle Bruce's head hit the pillow, he was out, however the girls stayed up a few more hours trying to figure out the second clue. Unfortunately, everybody had a different idea of where it was located.

Angelica had her opinion and stubbornly argued her case. "The rock meant diamond, Crassula Ovata Gallium was a new famous designer, the store meant Target. Putting it all together, Angelica told everyone, "It's in the diamond section, probably by the famous designer, Crassula Ovata Gollum section at the Target store on Army Trail Road!" the group snickered.

Eventually they fell asleep, but thankfully, Uncle Bruce only slept a few hours at a time. Like a well-oiled machine, Uncle Bruce's internal clock woke him up at 6:00 am every morning, it did not matter winter, spring, summer or fall. It did not matter what time he went to bed. It did not matter what was on his mind, he was the best alarm clock money could buy.

It was early, but everyone knew what was at stake, Valerie's life. Worried, Valerie barely slept, now she knew what happened to her cousin Agatha, her cousin Gertrude, and her cousin Lilliana. They made a grave mistake somewhere, did they run out of time? Did they turn right instead of left? Did they not think about 1850? Either way, Valerie knew every decision meant life or death for her.

Uncle Bruce reminded everyone to think like it was in 1850. He thought, whichever corner it was, it was by a rock in a store, he did not know what that other stuff even meant.

Afraid of public scrutiny, afraid of being wrong, and afraid of disappointing Uncle Bruce, Taylor gave a giant thumbs up to Uncle Bruce. She said nothing else and went to the kitchen to get a quick breakfast ready for everybody. Surprisingly, everyone woke up, surprisingly, Angelica was in a good mood, surprisingly Valerie did not take six hours to get ready.

Taylor put out a nice breakfast spread. She had found about half a dozen bagels, two blueberry muffins, half a box of Lucky Charms cereal and four slices of pumpkin bread. With this odd assortment of breakfast treats she put out the carton of Tropicana orange juice and the gallon of 2% low fat milk. Everyone ate, thankful for Taylor's hospitality and thankful the food was scrumdiddlyumptious.

*   *   *

After one blueberry bagel.one blueberry muffin, two slices of pumpkin bread Uncle Bruce wiped his mouth with his sleeve and bravely asked, "so what did we decide on the clue?" Angelica quickly answered, "Don't you listen? I said…" Valerie quickly shut her down.

Nobody knows what got into her that day, but it was out with the shy, timid girl and in with the bold, confident young lady. Was it a new hormone racing through her body or was it something in the air, either way, Valerie felt good about herself. With a commanding voice, she quickly stepped forward and told everybody to gather round.

Uncle Bruce was impressed, he had waited for this moment for years, no more pity party, no more feeling sorry for herself, no more the world is against me. With Angelica eating a blueberry bagel smothered in cream cheese, which was scrumdiddlyumptious, Taylor eating a banana, absolutely scrumdiddlyumptious, and Uncle Bruce sipping his scrumdiddlyumptious hot cup of peppermint tea, Valerie took charge.

"Okay team, todays mission will be tough, tougher than yesterday, so if anyone wants to back out, now is the time, nobody will hold it against you." As always Uncle Bruce tried to be funny and told everyone he needed to walk his goldfish, as always nobody laughed, however Taylor was not sure she should go, she told the team, it was up to them, whatever was easier, whatever worked, whatever the team decided, but she didn't want to make the difficult decision.

Valerie was stunned, Angelica was confused, Uncle Bruce was mystified. In a unanimous show of love and support the three started shouting words of encouragement, "Of course we want you to go, without you we are nothing, you're the best. The more the merrier." Hesitantly, Taylor smiled and agreed to go.

Uncle Bruce got up and poured another cup of his scrumdiddlyumptious tea and grabbed another scrumdiddlyumptious blueberry muffin. Valerie continued, "I could not sleep last night so I got on the internet and did some research. Crassula ovata gallium is a plant, it is origin is Africa, northeast is the area where the clue will be found, rock is a rock, and store means store."

Angelica was confused and quickly was mean and sarcastic, "So we have to go to the northeast part of Africa, find a rock, buy a plant at a store, and return home?" Valerie had had it with Angelica, "Look you will stop being mean and start treating everybody with kindness and respect or you can go back home."

Valerie continued, "You cannot just pick up a plant from Africa anywhere, I am assuming that this plant was from a store, a plant store, specifically a nursery, and the clue will be underneath a rock in the northeast corner of the nursery. The problem is there are no nursery's in town. I looked for nursery is on the history page for Glendale Heights and all I found was this black and white picture of Uncle Bob's nursery. It does not say where it is or was, so I am not sure what to do."

Taylor asked to see the picture, there was a clue. Valerie insisted she looked at the photo at least one hundred times but handed her phone with the old black and white photo to Taylor anyway. Trying to get herself involved once again, Angelica rudely took the phone away from Taylor, almost dropping it on the ground.

Valerie was getting tired of Angelica's antics; Didn't Angelica realize this was a matter of life and death for her? Didn't Angelica realize the clock was ticking? Didn't Angelica realize this was not some story somebody made up? Frustrated, Valerie boldly asked Angelica, "Don't you realize how important this mission is? I would appreciate it if you would start being part of the group!" Taylor gave a thumbs up in agreement.

Angelica just stared down at the phone. Valerie was once invisible, but not today, she was not going to tolerate being ignored, "Angelica!" she hollered. Angelica was completely memorized by the phone and continued to ignore Valerie. Angelica pushed buttons, dragged icons, downloaded programs never once looking up.

Valerie was getting impatient, "It is 6:30! We do not have time for playing video games or for listening to music! "Still ignoring Valerie, Angelica started to sweat profusely as her fingers raced across the screen, dragging squeezing, enlarging, and shrinking whatever was on the screen. "Angelica!" screamed Valerie.

Startled, Uncle Bruce dropped his cup of hot coffee, Taylor's thumbs up turned into a thumbs down. Mt. St. Valerie had exploded. Valerie stormed over to Angelica, like Pompeii so many years ago, Mt. St. Valerie was going to destroy everything in its sight, buildings would be destroyed, cities would be covered in hot lava, families would lose their homes.

As Mt. St. Valerie quickly carved a devastating path through the house, frightened people took cover. Uncle Bruce instinctively hid underneath the kitchen table, grabbing two more scrumdiddlyumptious blueberry bagels hoping he would survive. He closed his blue eyes praying his time was not over yet. Sensing danger, Taylor also took quick notice of Mt. St. Valerie and her destructive ways, Taylor ran to the bathroom for cover, she abruptly locked the small thin bathroom door, and cowered in the tub. She closed her big brown eyes hoping she would survive.

Angelica stood solid, concentrating on her fast-moving fingers, unaware of Mt. St. Valerie's lava flowing directly towards her. Steaming with anger Mt St. Valerie was unstoppable and continued on her destructive path. Angelica was oblivious and continued to stare at the screen. Mt. St. Valerie inched closer and closer. Angelica stood bravely and quickly tapped the screen.

Mt. St. Valerie, and Pompeii, destructive forces of nature, it neared Angelica with a thunderous noise and immense heat. Angelica never looked up, her palms became sweaty, her forehead perspired heavily, and goosebumps appeared on her arms and legs. Closer, closer, steam began to appear. Ready to end this situation, Mt. St. Valerie came barreling within inches of Angelica.

Clouds covered the sun; darkness covered the earth. It was all but over for Angelica. Then in a last second surprise move, Angelica miraculously spun around and held up the phone, "Look, look what I found!" she proudly stated. Valerie stared at the phone in amazement. Suddenly, the dark heavy clouds disappeared, the sun shone, Taylor opened her eyes, and Uncle Bruce opened his eyes. Mt. St. Valerie began to dissipate.

Smiling from ear to ear, Valerie grabbed Angelica and gave her an enormous hug. Uncle Bruce came from under the table completely confused and bewildered, he did not understand what was happening. Taylor came from the bathroom mystified and flabbergasted; she did not understand what was happening. Valerie started jumping up and down, thanking Angelica what she had done in record time.

Never being shy about asking a question, Uncle Bruce asked, "What happened?" Angelica just stood there basking in the glory of being a hero. Not wanting to waste any more time, Valerie tried to explain what Angelica had accomplished. Proudly she explained, "Angelica brilliantly took the old photo sent it to Walgreens where they quickly restored it, and sent it back where she downloaded a pixel correcting app, then she enlarged each section of the old photo, looking for anything unusual or unique, dividing the photo into individual fragments…"

Angelica quickly interrupted, "In one of the pixel corrected, high resolution fragments there's two old oak trees marked with giant X's." Angelica jokingly continued, "Wait for it." The awkward silence seemed to last forever. Finally, Angelica continued, "Those old oak trees are over 150 years old," once again there was a long pause, "And we know where the trees are today!"

Now everybody was smiling, now everyone was happy, now everyone started to celebrate. As the celebration subsided, Uncle Bruce asked, "Where?" Valerie quickly responded, "It's near the school, near the corner of First and Main." Uncle Bruce quickly asked, "Isn't that near the Great Western Trail?"

The usually quiet Taylor was confused, "isn't that the bike and jogging trail that runs between Villa Park and West Chicago? What does a bicycle trail have to do with you finding the next clue? How much time do we have?"

Valerie looked at her classic Timex watch from Target, "OMG! It is 8:30, we need to get moving!" Angelica quickly chimed in, "it is really close, six minutes away. We know it is under a rock in the northeast corner. What could go wrong?" Everybody laughed knowing anything, something, or everything could go wrong, this was the life of Valerie.

As they packed, Taylor's curiosity about the Great Western Trail peaked. Taylor always loved learning about history, it was always her favorite. Learning about dates, facts and places was fun and exciting, but learning why leaders acted in a certain way or made decisions fascinated her. She asked Uncle Bruce, but he was honest and admitted he knew very little about the trail. So, while everyone else packed, Taylor googled the Great Western Trail.

Uncle Bruce got in the driver's seat of his red Jeep Cherokee while Valerie claimed the passenger seat, Taylor and Angelica piled into the back seat, everyone buckled up. While Angelica and Valerie showed Uncle Bruce how to find the two specially marked oak trees, Taylor started reading an article on Google about the Great Western Trail.

Realizing she had six minutes, okay 10 minutes, Uncle Bruce was driving, Taylor read the one-page article quickly and quietly. According to the Google article, the Great Western Trail was used by the early settlers as early as 1832 to find their piece of freedom in America. In their wooden stagecoaches desperate families searching for a better way of life packed everything they owned and picked up the Great Western Trail.

Traveling for months at end, the journey was painstakingly long, extremely difficult, unbelievably dangerous. Some homesteaders took the trail north to Minneapolis, others east to Chicago, some went south to Kansas City, while others went to Omaha to begin their new life. It was an easy and safe trail for many years until the summer of 1852, that is when a gang of thieves took over the trail. While they were never able to prove it, they think it was a nasty old lady named Ma Papadopolus and her children. They were mean, angry and to be honest very stinky.

"This is it! See the trees!" Uncle Bruce pulled up between the two oak trees. However, there was no nursery, the old sign was covered by overgrown grasses, weeds, and small bushes, so, they really had no idea what was here. "It's a rescue for abandoned pets!" exclaimed Taylor. "See the scue on the top and pe on the bottom?"

Uncle Bruce did not see it, Valerie didn't see it and Angelica didn't see it. Taylor ran out of the Jeep and quickly brushed the weeds away from the sign, it read,

GLENDALE HEIGHTS
ANIMAL RESCUE

Taylor got back in the car and quickly said, "Told you!" Uncle Bruce was puzzled and asked how she figured the sign out so quickly. She told him that a new older gentlemen at the gym liked to make word search puzzles and offered prizes for employees who entered. She won many of the word searches that she entered. Uncle Bruce pulled the Jeep up the long driveway and parked.

As they slowly got themselves out of the car, Valerie noticed a young lady working in the large fenced in yard with her back turned to the four. She had long black hair, jeans and a pair of green rubber boots on. After grabbing the black backpack, the group started heading towards the mysterious lady working in the field. Angelica was going to call to the lady, but the lady with her back still towards the group firmly yelled, "This is private property. Unless you have business here, I strongly suggest you get off my property. I do not hear any pets, so I will kindly ask you to leave, or I will be forced to call the sheriff."

The group was stunned by the unusually rude welcome and on any other day they would have quickly turned away, but they were on a mission, a mission to save Valerie from a life of misery, misfortune, and mischance. The small young lady Taylor stepped up first, "We are here . . ." The young lady quickly cut off Taylor, warning, "I'm not kidding, I'm going to call the sheriff!" Taylor liked to follow the rules, so she wisely backed off.

The unusually brash and bold Angelica came next with her strong attitude, "That was rude, all we wanted to do was . . ." Once again, the lady interrupted, "This is private property, I do not like people, I don't like visitors and I certainly don't like you. However,

I do like the sheriff, shall I call him?" Angelica thought about meeting the sheriff very briefly, but quickly backed off.

Uncle Bruce quickly realized this young lady did not want their company and decided they needed to regroup. With under three hours to find the second clue, he encouraged Taylor, Angelica, and Valerie to return to the Jeep. Hesitantly, cautiously, reluctantly the three young ladies followed Uncle Bruce. Valerie respected her uncle but thought he should have tried harder with the young lady.

It seemed like they were walking twenty miles back to the Jeep, it seemed to take forever. Valerie's mind raced with every footstep she took. Will we find the next clue in time? What will happen to me if I do turn invisible forever? Will I end up in heaven? Will my family miss me? What will my sister Vivian do with my personal stuff? Will my dog Kiara find somebody else to love? Valerie did not have any answers, just questions.

With each step of her tiny size eight red Nike tennis shoes, her emotions built. Mt. St. Valerie was starting to build pressure again with every step she took. As the group continued to walk, nobody noticed Mt. St. Valerie coming back to life. At a level 5 danger, she was still controllable, but she continued thinking and walking. Step, level 6, another step, level 7 danger. She thought about the rude lady, step, level 8 danger level.

Somebody should have noticed, warning signs began flashing, danger, danger, but nobody did. Another step, level 9, sirens began blaring, people should have evacuated, but nobody was paying attention. Then as the thinking continued, Valerie took another step, level 10, Mt. St. Valerie exploded. BOOM! BOOM! BOOM!

Mt. St. Valerie violently turned around and ran straight back to the fence where the young lady stood in her boots. This was no ordinary Mt. St. Valerie, the ashes, the lava the incredible heat all were directed at the young lady in green boots. The massive volcano started to erupt, "How dare you do not help us! How dare you ignore us! How dare you not even ask what is wrong! How dare you be so rude!" Mt. St. Valerie took a well-deserved breather.

The young lady turned around in response to the angry return of Valerie. Uncle Bruce was speechless, he could not believe who the young lady was, eventually he stood frozen saying "OMG, is it really you?" over and over again. Taylor and Angelica quickly followed but were mystified who the young lady was. Valerie was shocked, astonished, angry as she saw her long-lost cousin Nicole standing there.

Valerie and Nicole did not get along, Valerie and Nicole hated each other, Valerie and Nicole hoped when they split so many years ago, they would never see each other again. Now Valerie's life depended on her long -lost cousin. Valerie asked herself, "Why, why do I have such bad luck?"

CHAPTER 14

SHENANIGANS

(High spirited or mischievous activity)

"Well, well, well, look who it is," said Nicole. "Where have you been?" she calmly asked. The truth was she really did not care about her or her shenanigans. Nicole Hernandez hated Valerie Hernandez, Nicole Hernandez despised Valerie Hernandez, Nicole Hernandez never wanted to see her slightly older cousin Valerie Hernandez.

Their dislike, distrust, distain for each other did not happen overnight, it took years in the making for the hatred to grow and manifest into the terrible monster it is today. The hatred, like a weed in the garden, grew uncontrollably with the aid of several ingredients, lies, mistrust, and shenanigans. Years of running from the problem could of easily be averted with a little love, some trust, and a little admiration.

To be honest, it all started on January 1, 2012, this was Valerie's Birthday, her parents were excited as well as the entire Hernandez family, she was the first grandbaby in the family. Everyone knew about the curse, but nobody believed it. Everybody was at Parkview hospital. Uncle Bruce sent one hundred balloons celebrating the birth. Nana and Papa set up a $10,000 college fund for Valerie. Aunt Jolie remodeled the extra bedroom and gave Valerie the coolest nursey to start a new life, it even included a live-in nanny for a year. Uncle Roger built a three-room tree house for the families first grandchild. The Hernandez family was excited.

Then on January 3, 2012, Nicole Alexandra Hernandez was born, this was Nicole's Birthday. Her parents were excited, but being the second born, the Hernandez family was ambivalent. Nobody but her parents came to Parkview hospital. Uncle Bruce sent one hundred balloons celebrating her birth. Nana and Papa gave her a $100 savings bond for college. Aunt Jolie vacuumed the storage room where Nicole would sleep. Uncle Roger fixed the garbage disposal for the families second grandchild. The Hernandez family was busy.

Nicole and Valerie's parents lived near each other. The girls went to the same elementary school, Hallsberry School, but despite being the same age, always had different teachers. In Kindergarten, Valerie had Ms. Paturini for a teacher, she was young, sweet, and very kind to each one of the young students. Nicole had Ms. Lichenstein for a teacher, she was not so young, not so sweet, and not so nice.

The two cousins even had different friends in their classes. Valerie had Mia and Jose' in her kindergarten class, Mia was quiet and shy, but still encouraged everyone to do their best, Jose' was a neat freak and did not go home until all the supplies were neat and organized. The scissors had to be put neatly in the cup, the pencils all erasers up, the papers all aligned perfectly, the markers all caps on blue with blue, red with red, everything had its place and there was a place for everything. Valerie's class had plenty of nice supplies.

Nicole had Mathew and Mark, two very ambitious boys, two very energetic boys, two very mischievous boys who loved shenanigans, in her kindergarten class. Mathew was a nice boy when alone, Mark was a nice boy when alone, but together they were compared to Tom and Jerry, Chip and Dale and Laurel and Hardy. Mathew loved to eat crayons; Mark never put the caps on markers. Mathew loved to draw and wasted many sheets of paper, Mark tried making paper airplanes but never had success in flying them, each attempt resulted in an immediate nosedive. Mathew left scissors wherever he used them, Mark liked to break pencils, Mathew liked to play basketball with his garbage, but he was no

Michael Jordan, Mark loved to use the stapler, but after stapling Sarah's braids to the message board, he was no longer allowed to use them. Nicole's class had few supplies. The shenanigans never stopped.

Despite the evil curse that Valerie had upon her, she managed to live a decent life, compared to Nicole. It was the fact she had a curse that her family spoiled her a little more, favored her a little more and loved her a little more. She was on the pity party train, but nobody deserved to have the bad luck that she seemed to have.

Although Valerie managed to get the better of the classrooms, Valerie and Nicole still remained tight as friends throughout their early years spending time at recess and lunch talking and building their friendship. Unfortunately, Valerie started having moments of bad luck early in life.

Some say they were moments of any young girl growing up, her family knew there were too many incidents, it was too consequential to think anything else, Valerie was indeed cursed. The red crayons she ate, pooping red for a week, was it the curse? The piece of apple stuck in her nose, was it the curse? Johnny peeing down the slide and her immediately following, was it the curse?

The incidents kept occurring, so many unusual incidents, so many situations, so many shenanigans. At one point her parents thought about hiring a security guard for her protection. They also looked into buying a giant bubble suit for her protection. After watching the movie Rapunzel, her dad even thought of locking her in a tower until she turned eighteen. They decided against all of them in hopes Valerie would grow up to be a normal person.

However, the perplexing predicaments persisted, the confusing circumstances continued, the surreal shenanigans sustained. Valerie spent time playing with kids in the neighborhood, she wandered away into the nearby forest preserve, lost for hours, was it the curse? Valerie was hungry one day, she ate half a grasshopper, was it the curse? Valerie entered a raffle at school, the prize, a Holiday Barbie, she bought ninety-nine tickets, she used all her allowance, nobody else entered the raffle except a young girl named Ariana, she bought one ticket, Valerie lost, was it the curse?

Second grade came, Valerie and Nicole continued to make their friendship work despite being in different classrooms. Valerie had Ms. Stafford who was fun, and exciting. Nicole had Mrs. Ardmore, very serious and dry. Ms. Stafford went on field trips to learn, Mrs. Ardmore studied books for learning. Ms. Stafford never used quizzes or tests in her class, every Friday Mrs. Ardmore tested her students. For indoor recess, Ms. Stafford played heads up seven -up and Uno, Mrs. Ardmore used the extra time to practice math facts. Despite the differences the girls friendship thrived.

The breaking point came in November 2019, Thanksgiving Day. After Valerie's family and Nicole's family ate a fabulous meal, a delicious turkey, done the Hernandez way with special Peruvian seasonings, sweet potatoes, homemade mashed potatoes and turkey gravy, green bean casserole, the Hernandez homemade butter twist rolls and the salad. Dessert included pumpkin cheesecake, pumpkin muffins, and pumpkin pie.

After cleaning up the many dishes from the Thanksgiving dinner, the men retreated to the basement for the much-anticipated matchup between the Chicago Bears and the Detroit Lions. After dinner, the women cleaned up and sat down at the kitchen table, made themselves a cup of coffee and grabbed all the advertisements for the Black Friday sales.

The stack was thick, everyone had huge Black Friday sales. The Hernandez women enjoyed the pumpkin cheesecake as they went through the ads from Best Buy, Michaels, Walmart, GameStop, Target, Meijer, Ashley Furniture, BCD Discount Electronics, The Great Escape, Macy's, and Kohl's. The mission was daunting, the ads were thick, but the Hernandez women had plenty of coffee, plenty of pumpkin cheesecake and plenty of time.

While the Hernandez men focused on the big football game, the Hernandez women focused on the sales for Black Friday, Valerie and Nicole played nicely in the playroom next to the kitchen. Both

Vivian, Valerie's younger sister and Daniela, Nicole's younger sister, went with their dads to watch the colossal football game.

The two young ladies loved to play with their dolls, Valerie had one of the biggest Barbie Doll collections and Nicole had one of the most complete Care Bear collections. Valerie was proud of her collection, she had Nurse Barbie, Doctor Barbie, Stay at Home Barbie, Camping Barbie, Astronaut Barbie, she had them all and kept them in pristine condition. Nicole's Care Bear collection included Friend Bear, Wish Bear, Bedtime Bear, Cheer Bear, Funshine Bear and Love-a- lot bear. It was beautiful how they brought the two different worlds together.

There was no plan for the Hernandez women to go shopping that night but once Aria Hernandez saw the ad for BCD Discount Electronics everything changed. BCD Discount Electronics was the area's biggest, best, and cheapest electronic store in the Glendale Heights area. They had all the newest and coolest electronics including the latest cell phones, ear buds, headphones, video games, televisions and more.

Valerie's mom needed a new television set badly. The old twenty-five-inch television had so many problems, Aria wanted a new television so badly, but new televisions were so expensive and after the mortgage, the car payment, the water bill, the phone bill, groceries, and clothing for her two beautiful girls there simply was not enough money left. For now, until the prices of new televisions dropped drastically Aria would be watching the Hallmark channel with the funny line down the middle of her screen, the volume not working and the poor reception.

The advertisement from BCD Discount Electronics was like a message from God. It spoke directly at Aria, it was the perfect television, it was the perfect price. The only problem was the price would only be good Thanksgiving night from 7:00 pm till 11:00 pm while supplies last. It was 6:30, Aria Hernandez decided it was best she did not go, for now she would deal with the terrible line, poor volume, and poor reception. The normally priced $1899 television, now priced at an unbelievable $499, would have to wait.

She could afford $499. She could deal with a flat screen television with Wi-Fi capabilities. It was 6:35, she thought the television could wait. Aaliyah encouraged Aria to go, she could go with her, they would be back in no time, BCD Discount Electronics was right down the road. Aria struggled with deciding what to do, in her brilliant mind she went over the benefits of having a new television.

Nonchalantly she read the advertisement more closely, it was an Insignia premium sixty-five" 4k flat screen television, Wi-Fi capable, surround sound stereo, Netflix and Disney Plus were included. Exclusive 5-year guarantee. She thought of her old clunker of a television, the line, the poor volume, and the poor reception. Aria looked sad. Aaliyah, Nicole's mom, got their coats, called downstairs they were leaving and asked Valerie and Nicole if they wanted to go. They declined; they were having too much fun teaching all the Barbies about having good character from the Care Bears.

Before leaving they reminded the girls to be good, no shenanigans, get their dad's if there was any trouble, and do not leave or let anybody in. This was not going to be a problem, both Nicole and Valerie were good girls and followed the rules wherever they went. Very rarely did they involve themselves with any shenanigans. The girls went back to playing in the playroom at the back of the house.

As they played, The Friend Care Bear taught the camping Barbie how to be a better friend by keeping secrets, Valerie was insulted, Nicole smiled. The Love-A-Lot Care Bear taught the Office Secretary Barbie about loving unconditionally, Valerie was insulted, Nicole smiled. The rainbow Care Bear gave advice to the Stay at Home Barbie about being happy and staying positive. Valerie was insulted, Nicole smiled. Valerie needed a break, so she offered to go to the kitchen and make some peach iced tea.

Nicole continued playing with her Care Bears and Valerie's Barbie's. Nicole set the room up just like a classroom and could not wait to show Valerie. Nicole felt all the Barbies needed a lesson in being a little less arrogant, a little less makeup and a little less, "it's all about me." Things were going well when Nicole heard a knock on the screen door to the playroom. She looked up and saw it was the new kid in school, he waved and motioned to Nicole to let him in. Nicole shook her head no, the new kid shrugged his shoulders and asked why.

He was a handsome young man and Nicole really did not have a reason why, it was cold out, so she let him in. He introduced himself very fast as Jeffery Grant Papadopolus, Nicole was too nervous to hear his name. "Listen very carefully sweetheart," he spoke. Nicole did not like to be called sweetheart; she was getting nervous. But he continued, "In my last school I ran things, in this school I intend to do the same thing, I am in charge, you do nothing without my approval, Got It?"

Nicole laughed, "We do not allow bullies in our school. All I have to do is tell an adult and you will be done!" Valerie was taking too long. Nicole was starting to get scared. "Fine have it your way!" the boy declared. "Would you like some peach iced tea?" Nicole asked as she headed to the kitchen. The boy mysteriously disappeared.

As Valerie and Nicole returned to the playroom, Nicole promised Valerie a surprise she would never forget. "I did something with your Barbie's that really needed to be done!" Nicole boasted. Valerie was mystified but played along carrying the two cups of Lipton peach iced tea. Turning backwards, thinking how she signed the Barbies up for school, Nicole boasted how they needed to be taught this lesson. Finally coming to the large playroom, Nicole let Valerie lead the way. "Surprise!" yelled Nicole.

Poor Valerie, she stood frozen seeing the destruction, the decimation, the devastation. What had happened with Nicole, why the shenanigans? Then in an instant, no warning, no prelude, no alert, Mt. St. Valerie blew. She dropped the Lipton peach iced tea, spilling it all over the floor, she screamed hysterically. Both Hernandez men came running, both younger sisters came running and both Hernandez women who had just gotten home came running to see what all the fuss was about.

Valerie's family was astonished at what they saw, wondering what evil creature did this. Why would they do this? They hugged Valerie in support of her massive loss. At last, Valerie quit crying hysterically and asked Nicole, "Why?" Nicole was just as surprised as everybody else.

Vehemently denying any involvement in the dismemberment of Valerie's dolls, Nicole insisted she had nothing to do with the crime. Valerie cried, "Mentirosa!" To Nicole. There was an awkward silence as everyone looked around at the headless, armless, legless bodies of once successful, prosperous hard-working Barbie's. Nicole's family looked disappointingly at her, mystified why she would partake in such bad shenanigans. This was the last time these two families spent any time together.

As Nicole and her family quickly left, Valerie looked at her mother and asked, "Why, why do I have such bad luck?

CHAPTER 15

MENTIROSA

(Spanish, a compulsive liar)

Nicole stood there just staring at Valerie. Valerie stood there just staring at Nicole. Angelica, Taylor, and Uncle Bruce stood back not knowing what was going on. After a long stalemate Nicole finally yelled, "Mentirosa!" Valerie was shocked. "That's the last thing you said to me before my life changed forever." Everybody remained frozen. "Compulsive Liar!" Nicole calmly stated.

Nicole continued, "Mentirosa!" That is what I was labeled. My mother thought I was a Mentirosa, my father thought I was a Mentirosa, my sister thought I was a Mentirosa, even my dog Luna thought I was a Mentirosa. I did not do that to your dolls, honestly!"

Valerie quickly replied, "nobody else was in the house, nobody. Who else could have done it? Have you been getting help? Mental health is a serious problem." Nicole took a deep breath and angrily stated, "it must have been that new kid." Valerie snapped back, "What new kid?" Nicole thought for a minute, she had put this whole episode of her life behind her, "it was Gary? No Geoff? No Gifford? Oh, I cannot remember, but it must have been him."

Taylor did not say a word but thought she was a mentirosa, Angelica didn't say a word but thought she was a mentirosa, Valerie didn't say a word but thought she was a mentirosa. Uncle Bruce missed his niece so much, he was so happy to see her again and she was happy to see him again, they ran and gave each other the biggest longest hugs imaginable.

Surprisingly, Nicole's mom called out the door, "Breakfast is ready!" Not knowing who it was, she offered breakfast for everyone., I have plenty of chicken and waffles, bring your friends in". Taylor quickly replied, "I could eat!" So together they headed in for a special breakfast of chicken and waffles. Nicole's mom yelled one more time again, "Do not forget your final appointment with Dr. Trongwatarangasig is this afternoon.

Valerie reminded her entourage that they did not have time to eat, they had two and half hours to find the clue, otherwise it was lights out for Valerie. Taylor thought they had plenty of time, Angelica agreed, repeating it is under a rock in the northeast corner of the property. "How hard can it be?" Innocently asked a very hungry Taylor.

Everybody swiftly went in, leaving Uncle Bruce and Nicole by themselves. Valerie hung back long enough to watch the two. Uncle Bruce was hers; it had been years since Valerie had to share her uncle with anybody, especially a mentirosa. Nicole thought Uncle Bruce was the coolest, nicest person that ever existed, he was the one person she missed dearly during their travels of trying to escape the label of being a Mentirosa. Like a bolt of lightning, it hit them at the same time, together they looked into each other's eyes and said,

What are we going to do with each other?
With or without, either way
Without, have a sad heart
With, have a heart full of love

Valerie wanted to vomit; she remembered them always saying the verse whenever they saw each other. She was glad when Nicole and her family disappeared, no more annoying Nicole, no more special verse, no more mentirosa. Seeing the two together made Valerie jealous, she had to get "her" uncle back. As the two turned towards the front door Valerie ran swiftly to the breakfast table. Strategically she sat where the two could not sit together.

Nicole's Mom was ecstatic that Valerie and Uncle Bruce found them. Family was everything to her and coming back to Glendale Heights was just the beginning of helping her daughter Nicole recover from being a mentirosa. Dr. Trongwatarangasig was the world's leading specialist in dealing with chronic mentirosa cases.

For years since the destruction of Valerie's Barbie collection, Nicole had been seeing Dr. Trongwatarangasig for her severe case of mentirosa, never before had he seen such a terrible case. Nicole's case was so severe that Dr. Trongwatarangasig dedicated his life in helping this poor confused child. Everywhere Nicole went, Dr. Trongwatarangasig followed documenting the poor girl with a severe case of mentirosa.

Hoping to find a cure for mentirosa, Dr. Trongwatarangasig took Nicole on a nationwide tour depicting the unusual young girl from Glendale Heights, struggling to survive, and be accepted in this cruel world. Dr. Trongwatarangasig wrote books explaining being a Mentirosa, it made it to the New York best seller list. He even wrote a country song, called "I can live without my pickup truck, but I can't live without my Mentirosa!", it made it to number 4 on the Billboard hot 100.

In his attempt to help others with Mentirosa, Dr. Trongwatarangasig took Nicole on the talk show circuit. They visited Good Morning America and the Today Show, they visited the Drew Show, the Kelly Clarkson show, and even the famous Joey show, bringing awareness to the very unusual disease of Mentirosa. Despite Nicole's medical progress, Dr. Trongwatarangasig's plan backfired.

Everywhere Nicole and Dr. Trongwatarangasig went, the world mocked and made fun of her. Nicole was the first poster child for Mentirosa. They traveled to Indiana, Wisconsin and Ohio trying to find a new home, but they mocked her. They tried settling in Pennsylvania, Tennessee, and Georgia, but the girl was a Mentirosa. Nobody wanted to be friends with the chronic liar. They tried

Florida, New York, and Kentucky, but the world was not ready to accept a Mentirosa. She was a social outcast.

Nicole and Uncle Bruce walked hand in hand, both had huge smiles. Nicole's mom saw this and was happy for her daughter and happy she made the right choice in moving back home where her family was. Taylor saw the two and without hesitation, without reservation, without any fanfare moved over one seat so they could sit together and talk, Taylor wished she had an Uncle Bruce.

Valerie was furious, Valerie was confused, Valerie was jealous. Uncle Bruce belonged to her, Uncle Bruce spoiled her, Uncle Bruce loved her. Valerie ate her chicken and waffles very quickly, hoping everybody else followed, so they would be able to get on with their journey. Uncle Bruce and Nicole barely touched their plates, they were too busy talking about the past, present and the future.

Finally, Nicole grabbed the bottle of maple syrup and began pouring massive amounts on her chicken and waffles. Uncle Bruce thought the chicken was drowning, and wanted to call a lifeguard, Nicole chuckled, but nobody else said a word. Before taking a bite, Nicole calmly asked, "So what brings my favorite uncle and you to our house?" Valerie was hesitant and wanted to think about what she was going to say, she remained quiet. Thinking Valerie did not know, didn't care, or didn't answer, Angelica loudly proclaimed, "We are on a mission, three clues any mistake any error any delay and Valerie is history, goes vamoose, turns invisible forever! You are clue two, we have until 11:35 to find clue two.

Nicole chuckled, "So, if I understand, somehow, some way, sometime, you need to find a clue by 11:35 on my families property, or my sweet lovable, adorable, irresistible cousin goes POOF!" What time is it? 10:00? That would be a shame. Tick tock tick tock" Uncle Bruce was appalled. Valerie did not mince words this time, "Not only are you a Mentirosa you are a monstruo loco salvaje!" Nicole chuckled at the thought of being called a wild crazy monster by her cousin, she did not care about Valerie, she didn't destroy her Barbie collection and she hated being chastised every day for a crime she didn't commit.

The green-eyed monster devoured Valerie that warm October day. Uncle Bruce complimented Nicole on her choice of a breakfast entrée, Nicole smiled. Valerie reminded Uncle Bruce that her mother always has extra raspberry pop tarts whenever he came over. People just stared, embarrassed for Valerie. Nicole told Uncle Bruce how handsome he looked, Valerie quickly added, "You should see him in the morning, hair messy, eyes closed, drool on his cheek.

People just stared, embarrassed for Valerie. Finally, everybody finished their delicious breakfast of chicken and waffles. Nicole gracefully offered to take Uncle Bruce's plate, Valerie rushed over insisting she could and should help him. She firmly grabbed the syrup covered plate and pulled it out of Nicole's hand. The syrup covered plate slipped and landed on Uncle Bruce's lap. Nicole started yelling at Valerie.

Nicole's mom heard everything and scolded Nicole for being a bitter, angry, pessimist. Over the last few years, Dr. Trongwatarangasig had worked closely with Nicole and encouraged her to forget about the past, move on and think positive thoughts. He thought she was doing better, despite the fact that Nicole continued her tall tale of a young man destroying Valerie's Barbie collection, Dr. Trongwatarangasig felt Nicole was ready to come back home.

Under the intense pressure of her mother and the gentle reminder of Dr. Trongwatarangasig's commitment, Nicole changed her attitude very quickly. Instead of hearing the top one hundred sad song, "Poor, poor, pitiful me" or the famous popular ballad, "I lost my goldfish, missed the bus, and owe the phone company", she now was humming the melody to, "Sunshine, Rainbows and Lollipops."

Reluctantly, Nicole cleared her throat, swallowed her pride, and announced, "Fine, go ahead, search for your stupid clue." She raised her hand to point to the infamous rock on the northeast corner of the property. In a flash, Uncle Bruce, Taylor, Angelica, and Valerie headed briskly out the small brown door.

All that remained was a cloud of dust caused by the quick departure of the small group of warriors trying to save Valerie. As Nicole lowered her hand, she immediately thought how special it was that Valerie had special friends willing to help solve the riddle. Valerie was not that bad. Valerie did not know who Gary, Grant or George was. Valerie missed their special friendship, Nicole chuckled, was she crazy? She should call Dr. Trongwatarangasig?

10:02 am
1 hour 23 minutes left for Valerie

Trying to save time, they cut across the property, staying off the main paths jumping over the walls of a huge backyard playpen, the small group of inexperienced adventurers rushed towards chosen destination. Nicole slowly followed the rag tag group.

Squish! Squish! Squash! Went their shoes as they walked through the playpen. "Gross!" yelled Angelica. "Disgusting!" hollered Taylor. "OOHH!" exclaimed Valerie. "What is this stuff?" exclaimed Uncle Bruce, "It Stinks!" Nobody knew as they stepped carefully through the muck. All you heard was, "EWW! AHHH! GADZOOKS! AHHH!" Uncle Bruce rhetorically asked, "What is this stuff?"

Suddenly a voice stoically answered, "it is puppy pooh! I did not get to clean the pen yet today." "What?" asked Valerie. "It's Puppy pooh, we run an animal shelter here. My dog Luna had nine puppies, Petunia, Poppy, Cheeseburger, Oreo, Max, Maxfield, Toby, Dali, and Charlie. Valerie was disgusted, Angelica wanted a puppy, Taylor had already started to clean her shoes and Uncle Bruce, well nothing was going to stop him, he continued on his journey towards the rock.

After they quickly cleaned the muck, dirt and pooh off their shoes, Uncle Bruce and the small group of adventurers continued marching forward. Taylor remained strong, Angelica pushed forward, Valerie blazed forward, however Uncle Bruce's legs became heavy as he continued walking, slowly falling behind further and further with his steps.

Valerie and Angelica continued moving forward at an incredible pace. Taylor, that sweet angel, stayed back and made sure Uncle Bruce would be okay. Exhausted, Valerie and Angelica stopped and waited for advice from Nicole. "So, where is this rock?" asked Valerie.

10:47am

48 minutes left for Valerie

"You will know it when you see the rock, it's very obvious" replied Nicole. Valerie was confused, they should have found the rock by now, but now this giant boulder stood in their way. Angelica sat down on a piece of granite, both looked at the map trying to figure out where the rock was, Valerie started to weep, this could not happen again.

As the two lost explorers waited patiently for Nicole, Uncle Bruce and Taylor, Valerie's mind began to wander mostly at the thought of everything she would miss if she disappeared. She would never be married, graduate from high school or college, get a driver's license, go to prom, or never see Grant again. How terrible!

Up in the Wisconsin Dells Grant was playing miniature golf with his brother George, however he kept calling him Valerie. He was not sure why, but he couldn't get his mind off of Valerie. She was unique, she was phenomenal, she was exceptional, she was the one and only Valerie. On the eighth hole, the hole with the giant windmill that goes round and round, George had a hole in one. Grant came over gave him a high five and said, "Congratulations Valerie!" George did not like being called Valerie; George went back to the hotel room.

10:55 am
40 minutes left for Valerie

Nicole helped Taylor with Uncle Bruce, he was tired and weak, so they encouraged him to sit on the large stone. Valerie started vanishing again, this time it started with her left hand slowly fading in and out, she tried not to panic. Taylor saw the hand vanishing and held her new friends right hand, trying to comfort her. Uncle Bruce sat there exhausted. Angelica saw all this and got mad.

"What is wrong with you people? We have less than 40 minutes left before Valerie disappears into the great unknown!" She paused to control her emotional instability. "Are you people going to sit here blubbering feeling sorry for yourselves or we going to fight and try and find the last clue?" Nobody moved, nobody said a word, Angelica got up very frustrated, "Well I am going to find this rock and the clue!" She started to walk away. Uncle Bruce followed as well as Valerie and Taylor. Nicole watched as they walked away.

Almost feeling guilty, almost caring about Valerie's fate, almost taking the "chip" off her shoulder, Nicole screamed out, "Wait!" Nobody knew what to expect. Unexpectedly, she picked up a black water bottle and asked, "Did someone forget this?" Angelica came over, looked Nicole straight in the eye and swiftly swiped the water bottle from Nicole's cold hands. "Thank you!" she replied as she started to walk away.

Angelica knew what she did, she kept her back turned as she sauntered away. Nicole did not know what hit her, but something inside her had changed. The chip on her shoulder disappeared, she smiled for the first time in a while and there was a spring in her step. "Wait!" she hollered, "please wait!"

With a tear in his eye Uncle Bruce came over and took control, with anger in his voice he told Nicole, "I love you so much, but Valerie's life is on the line here, I love her too, I don't want to lose her, so no more games, we have to find the rock and then look under it." Nicole started crying, her first meaningful cry since the great Barbie incident.

11:10 am

25 minutes until Valerie disappears

Wiping the tears from her cheeks, Nicole smiled from ear to ear. For the first time in a long time, she felt good about herself. For the first time in a long time, she felt like a giant weight had been lifted off her shoulders. For the first time in a long time, her heart was happy. Valerie's left arm now began to disappear, everybody knew what that meant.

Taylor reminded everybody about the clock ticking and reminded everyone to find the rock. They needed to find the clue as soon as possible, it was a matter of life and death. Once again, they began to disperse hoping to save the life of their special friend Valerie.

Despite her reputation for having a bad attitude, Nicole bravely stood up quickly and ask them to stop. They refused knowing the clock was ticking. "Please stop looking for the rock. This is the rock you are looking for."

Uncle Bruce was confused, Angelica was flabbergasted. "This giant rock we are sitting on? this giant rock that is the size of a house? This giant rock that we will never be able to move?" Everyone was in shock, Taylor was baffled, "The clue is under here?" Uncle Bruce got lightheaded as the thought of moving this gigantic rock in under 25 minutes worried him. Evil thoughts swirled around his head. Worried, Taylor escorted Uncle Bruce to a chair to relax and got him a big bottle of water.

Nicole continued, "Ever since we bought this house there have been rumors about a message chiseled into the face of this rock. It is believed to be carved from the ancient Indian tribe that lived here years ago, known as the Hitocholi tribe. The problem is I have never seen it, I've never read it, I've never encountered it.

11:22 am

13 minutes to go

Suddenly, Valerie fell to the ground, her legs were disappearing faster than ice cream on a hot summer day. What went wrong? Where did the time go? Who knew where the clue was? Uncle Bruce looked at his watch, 13 minutes until his niece disappeared into the great unknown, 13 minutes until the story ended, 13 minutes until his world would be crushed.

Without being told, everybody spread out and scanned the rock for any messages on the huge rock. Valerie sat calmly not being able to help much without any legs, Taylor found a lot of heart messages on the east side, JK + GH, AD +SD, and WY+ MK. She wondered who these people were and if there love survived, but no message. Uncle Bruce had the north side of the huge rock but with just a steep flat surface there was only one message written on his side of the rock, it read NAH and BCD Best Friends Forever.

11:25 am

10 minutes left for Valerie

Angelica had the west side of the rock, a side which was very accessible because of smaller rocks available for stepping on. Valerie's whole body began flashing on and off, everybody knew this was the beginning of the end. Everybody desperately searched their wall side for the message in a final effort to save Valerie. Was this the end for Valerie? Could they save Valerie? Where was this clue for Valerie?

The west side was covered in drawings and notes telling the world what people thought. Make-shift artists used the wall to tell the world STOP the VIOLENCE, RECYCLE, and The BEARS ROCK. There was no messages like the other ones. Valerie kept flashing; Angelica wondered if it was painful, but realized she had to focus. Message after message, My Mom is the Best! I Hate YOU!

132

Tacos are the BEST! Everybody had something to say, but there was no message. Angelica was frustrated.

11:30 am

5 minutes left for Valerie

Nicole was given the south side. It was dark, cold, and wet, the sun never appeared on this side. Nobody ever came on this side, the rocks were slippery, the wind howled, and strange noises came from the rocks. Nicole kept both eyes opened and focused on the wall for anything that might jump out at her, claw at her, or slither towards her. Nicole scanned the wall desperate to find any message, but there was nothing, not I Love You, not a Best Friend, not a Heavy Metal Music is Great! Nicole turned on her phone's flashlight in a final effort to find anything.

Suddenly a gust of wind blew, knocking Nicole's phone out of her hands, Nicole was upset. She bent down on the jagged rocks and searched for her phone, unfortunately she ripped her jeans in many places. Undaunted by bad omens, she saw the phone on a hidden ledge about four feet below her. She got down on her belly and reached for her phone.

Her arm was too short, she extended her shoulder, not enough, she extended her arm, not enough, she extended her fingers, not enough. Frustrated she looked down at the phone, that is when she saw it, no not a long -legged bug-eyed mosquito, no not a long slippery snake and no not a big hairy eight-legged poisonous spider, but it was the clue.

Very swiftly Nicole stood up and called for help. Valerie was more invisible than visible at this point and every second counted.

11:33 am
Two-minute warning

Uncle Bruce came running, Taylor came running, Angelica came running. Everyone knew how much time was left, everyone knew Valerie's life was in danger, everyone knew they could not fail. Without wasting any time Nicole got back on her belly and instructed Uncle Bruce to hold her feet. Uncle Bruce was confused and asked, "What?"

Knowing time was not on their side, Taylor frantically ordered Uncle Bruce, "Do what she says, NOW!" Uncle Bruce grabbed Nicole's feet and lowered her where she could see her phone and the clue that was clearly carved on the rock. Valerie kept flashing on and off, faster, and faster. Nicole had to read the clue quickly in order to save Valerie.

11:34 am
One minute left

Uncle Bruce lowered Nicole so she could get the phone and most importantly read the clue. Frantically, she called up Uncle Bruce, "Lower! Lower! Keep going!" Uncle Bruce tried but he just could not hold on anymore, he begged Angelica and Taylor to help. They were more than willing to help lower Nicole into the deep passageway.

11:34:30 am
30 seconds left

Together, they were able to hold Nicole upside down in order to read the clue. Quickly, she adjusted her eyes to read the carved message, it read:

TILICEMEN CARAROR,
DEWANE, POT 2252

Taylor laughed, remarking that what Nicole said made no sense. In a desperate race against time, Nicole squinted her big brown eyes and read the secret message again:

HILLCREST CEMETERY,
DULANY, PLOT 252

As soon as they read the second clue the sky began to change. The heavy black clouds suddenly rolled in like a bowling ball being thrown at the pins, instantly `covering the bright fall sun. Darkness loomed onto the property. BOOM! Lightning suddenly lit up the daytime sky with force, an energy that was unmatched by any other. SNAP! CRACKLE! POP!

Valerie stopped flashing on and off and returned to her normal beautiful self. Before pulling Nicole up, Nicole grabbed her tattered cell phone. It did not survive the steep fall, the cover was shattered, the case was cracked, and the corner was bent. It was time to say goodbye, time to say adios, time to say auf wiedersehen to this phone. Nicole held onto her cousin firmly and they pulled her up onto solid ground.

Within seconds Valerie came running, "Thanks you guys, that was close." Valerie paused for a second and saw Nicole's ripped pants. "Always the fashionista, ripped jeans could be the next fashion fad." Everyone loved them except Uncle Bruce, he thought they looked raggedy. "Here Nicole, here's your cell phone, you left it on a rock over there, has anyone seen mine?"

Nicole took her cell phone from Valerie, she smiled and timidly said "thank you". Then in a rare return to sadness and remorse, Nicole handed the phone that she thought was hers to Valerie. The phone that looked like it was stepped on by an elephant, the phone that looked like a train ran over it, the phone that was never going to ever work again. Valerie laughed, and asked, "Why, why do I have such bad luck?"

CHAPTER 16

SNOWMAGEDDON

(An unusually quick snowstorm)

The change in weather was unexpected, the wind howled sending papers flying, flags flapping in the wind, and people struggling to hold onto to their hats. The rain was cold as ice, eventually turning into snow pounding on roofs, tables, and peoples backs, it was snowmageddon! Everyone ran for cover, Taylor ran to the small tool shed and took shelter, Valerie and Angelica ran to the big old barn to avoid the snowmageddon. Nicole dove into the house, so the wet snow did not soak her.

Uncle Bruce made sure all the girls were inside before running for shelter. The skies became darker, the chilling wind blew stronger than ever before, and the torrential snow poured relentlessly down on him soaking him to the bone. Valerie called to her uncle, "Over here! Come into the barn! I will save you from snowmageddon!" Not to be outdone by her cousin, Nicole called out, "Over here, over here, Uncle Bruce! I will save you from snowmageddon!" He darted to the left, then he darted to the right.

Despite the heavy downpour from the unpredicted snowmageddon, he could hear everything the two girls were yelling, "You know, I'm your favorite, pick me, over here!" Uncle Bruce was so conflicted, Uncle Bruce was so confused, Uncle Bruce was getting soaked. Finally deciding neither one was a good choice and deciding Taylor's barn was too small, Angelica was the choice.

Without further ado, he ran splishing and splashing through the numerous snow piles.

Surprisingly enough she would not let him in, there was only enough space left for her cat Winston. Uncle Bruce was appalled but respected her decision. With his nieces still yelling, "over here, over here," he decided to go in the house, but use a different door. This was definitely too early in the season for snowmageddon. Suddenly, lightening filled the sky with bright lights and loud claps of thunder, BOOM! CRACK! SNAP!

Trying desperately to get out of the snowmageddon, Uncle Bruce ran faster and faster, somehow managing to hit every snow pile large and small, within fifty yards as he did so. Soaking wet and firmly exhausted, he thought he saw a light brown door and ran frantically towards it, hoping for a warm crackling fire, hoping for a dry spot, hoping for the smallest of miracles.

All he heard was, "No! Do not go that way!" Uncle Bruce thought it was his niece Valerie or his niece Nicole playing games again, so he decided to ignore their cries. Despite the warnings, despite the thought of the unknown, despite the snowmageddon, he headed straight towards the "door."

In the Wisconsin Dells, Grant was having a great time with his family. During the course of the weekend, he discovered two of his good friends, Joey, and Justin, were also staying at the same waterpark as his family. How lucky? Over the weekend, his father received a phone call telling him he was promoted and would be receiving a large pay raise. How lucky? Over the weekend, his family received notification because of a small leak in the bathroom, their bill for their stay at the resort would be refunded in full. How lucky?

On the edge of Glendale Heights, right on the border with Lombard and Glen Ellyn, sat the old forgotten Hillcrest Cemetery. Sitting on what is now land owned by the Forest Preserve district, this quaint historic cemetery was officially closed the same year it opened. It is not something they are proud of, it's not on the website, it's not something they brag about, but it is part of their history.

Way back in 1855 there was the little known Covid-7 pandemic. The little isolated town of Glendale Heights was usually immune from the crime of the world, the drama of the world and most important the diseases of the world. It was a small farming community of hard-working people just trying to make ends meet.

Not this time, the little town 20 miles northwest of Chicago was thrust into the spotlight by being the epicenter of the pandemic of 1853. Joceline and Luis met while working the winter of 1848 on the thriving Stoner farm. It was love at first sight. Every day they worked together in the cold winter weather. Every day they spent time talking to each other. Every day they fell deeper and deeper in love.

In the spring of 1851 they both turned eighteen, they could now vote, they could now own a horse and they could now both get married. They wanted their parents blessing, neither one approved, they felt the two lovebirds were too young.

Their love was too strong, so they left the only town they ever knew and headed to the next big metropolis, Misty Meadows. Misty Meadows was a thriving fast growing city, too fast. Big business moved in; people flocked from all over for good paying jobs. Soon, the small town was overcrowded causing many people to sleep in the street. Litter filled the streets, toilets overflowed, and the extra horses and carriages brought extra poop.

Extra candy is good, extra money is good or extra cheeseburgers is good. However extra poop, human or horse poop, is not good. Instead of just picking it up and not making a mountain out of a molehill, nobody in Misty Meadows picked up the poop. This one blamed that one, he blamed her, they blamed them. Nobody took responsibility.

So, the stinky slimy, smelly, bug infested poop sat in the streets of Misty Meadows for days on end. Flies and mosquitos came to feast on the leftover poop, they in turn spread disease to the human population. Thus, Covid-7 was born, thus Covid-7 spread quickly and rapidly.

Joceline and Luis missed their families. Although their marriage of four years was as strong as ever, working in the cold was taking a toll on them. The sickness and disease spreading throughout Misty Meadows was devastating. The once beautiful town was filthy, and unattractive. Homeless people were scattered across the once beautiful sidewalks. With no work, no money and no food, crime was a way of life.

Having no other option, Joceline and Luis packed their bags and headed back to their home in Glendale Heights. They came back home and were greeted with open arms. Unfortunately, before leaving they were robbed of all their possessions. They came back home with basically only the clothes on their backs. What they brought back with them will forever be written in the history books.

Little did they know, they were carriers of the disease and brought back the Covid-7 virus. The young town of Glendale Heights did not know what hit them. Fever, achy muscles, coughing, sneezing were just a few of the symptoms of this terrible disease. The disease was relentless, most victims did not last more than a day or two before passing on. The town was quickly labeled and put under a strict quarantine warning, nobody came, nobody left.

Everyone in this small town knew where this virus came from. A town meeting was held to discuss the disease. Because of her immense wealth and streak of good luck, Wendy Papadopolus was easily elected to the town council where her and her colleagues banished the couple once the pandemic was over. Unfortunately, as the pandemic ended, Luis and Joceline contracted the disease. The mean-spirited Wendy Papadopolos would not let them perish in peace. Wendy contacted her friend the witch and the two quickly devised a devious plan to punish the couple forever for what they did to their town.

Today in the Cemetery

"Wake up honey! An alarm has gone off!" Luis told his lovely wife Joceline. She did not move. "Come on! If we ever want to leave this after life, we need to get up and figure out what is going on" Luis earnestly stated. Joceline was not a morning person and quietly whispered, "What year is it? I feel like I have been sleeping forever!" Luis looked at the calendar on the wall, October 2022. His head began to spin.

Unbelieving, he quickly told his beautiful wife Joceline, "It's October 2022!" Joceline laughed in disbelief, "So we have been sleeping for over 170 years?" All Luis did was smile and shake his head in agreement. Still groggy and needing a cup of coffee, Joceline asked, "What happened?"

Flabbergasted, Luis paced back and forth trying to remember. Then he saw it, covered in cobwebs, dust and dirt, a note gently placed on the table with their names on it. Luis grabbed the note and began reading hoping for some answers:

JOCELINE and LUIS:

WELCOME TO YOUR PUNISHMENT. YOU TWO LOVEBIRDS DESTROYED OUR TOWN SO MANY YEARS AGO BECAUSE OF YOUR SELFISH ACT OF COMING BACK TO TOWN CARRYING THE DEADLY COVID-7 VIRUS. YOUR THOUGHTLESS ACTION CAUSED SO MANY OF THE RESIDENTS HERE TO PERISH, INCLUDING YOU. RIGHT NOW, YOU ARE STUCK BETWEEN HERE AND THERE. YOUR JOB NOW IS TO PROTECT THE LAST CLUE AT ALL COSTS. IF ANYONE GETS THIS FAR IT IS YOUR JOB TO DO EVERYTHING IN YOUR POWER TO STOP THEM. IF AFTER 200 YEARS NOBODY HAS GOTTEN THROUGH YOU WILL BE SET FREE. IF ANYBODY GETS PAST YOU AND GETS THE CLUE YOU WILL

FACE IMMEDIATE AND QUICK ELIMINATION.
SO, PROTECT THE CLUE BY THE TOMBSTONE
ON PLOT 252 MARKED DULANY- GOOD LUCK
WENDY PAPADOPULOUS

Joceline finally got her cup of coffee and sat up in bed, "So, we are dead?" Luis shook his head in agreement. They looked at each other hopelessly. "What is this clue about? Where are we?" Joceline asked. "I don't know" replied Luis, "But we must be in a cemetery, and we need to protect plot 252 if we ever want to get out of here."

Snowmageddon was out of control, the fast-moving storm quickly dumped several inches of slippery white snow in just a few minutes, making travel impossible. The visibility was poor. Uncle Bruce was soaked to the bone, his hands were numb as well as every bone in his body, he desperately wanted and needed to get out of this rare snowmageddon.

Uncle Bruce was relentless in his attempt to get to the golden-brown door, it was so close yet so far away. He pushed his heavy legs to a breaking point he had never seen or felt before as he came closer and closer to that door. "NO!" cried Valerie. "No!" cried Nicole. With the snowmageddon bearing down, their cries went unheard.

Nobody knows why he chose to run toward the door, it was getting too cold, he was getting too wet, he was too impatient, but that is what he did. In the blinding snow he swiftly ran towards the door, unfortunately there was no door. It was a staircase going down, the door was a reflection.

Uncle Bruce never knew what hit him as he flew down the stairs. A concerned Valerie ran to his aide trying to help and a concerned Nicole ran to his aide trying to help. As the snowmageddon started to dissipate they both found their Uncle Bruce laughing/crying at the bottom of the staircase. Although he was conscious and alert, there was no way he could continue this journey.

With a bruised wrist, bruised ankle, and a bruised ego, Uncle Bruce was quickly brought to Parkview Hospital. Should the journey be cancelled? Angelica was upset! Taylor was annoyed! Nicole was aggravated! And Valerie was more determined than ever to solve the clue. But how could they do it without Uncle Bruce?

There was only seven hours left. Valerie was determined more than ever to get the last clue before time ran out. However, with her smart uncle unable to help her, she wondered if she and the group could find the last clue. She just laughed and wondered, "Why, why do I have such bad luck?"

CHAPTER 17

DOOHICKEY

(a gadget)

Before leaving for the hospital, Uncle Bruce made a phone call, the most important phone call of his life. He loved Valerie more than life itself and could not just abandon her in a crisis, just because of a few superficial injuries. He had to find a replacement, somebody special, somebody unique, somebody he could trust. He knew many people, but he needed someone who was brave, smart, and clever. Who could fit this list of rare qualifications? There was only one person of whom he could think.

No, it was not David, no it wasn't Stephen and no it wasn't Sammy. The list was narrow, the list was short, the list was exclusive. No, it was not Ilda, no, it wasn't Angela, no, it wasn't Cathy, no it was not Anna, . All good candidates for the ordinary, but this was no ordinary job. He searched his brain one more time looking for that certain someone, that someone who you know is perfect, that someone is simply the best. No, it was not Sal, no, it wasn't Vanessa, Penny or Howard, excellent characters for maybe substituting for the Fantastic Four, but not for replacing Uncle Bruce.

Legend has it Uncle Bruce cannot be replaced. He is one of a kind and God definitely broke the mold after he was born. He is different, when the world goes right, he goes left, when all hope is lost, he sees a ray of sunshine, when the world hands him a lemon, he makes lemonade. Trust me, he drinks a lot of lemonade.

As he sat painfully on the stretcher, one name came to him, one name good enough to replace him, one name he could trust, one name who was brave enough, one name that was clever enough, one name that was smart enough to take over for him. One name that stood out above the rest. She was awesome, awesomer, she was awesomest, she was the one the only Princess Emily.

"Quick, give me my doohickey!" commanded Uncle Bruce. Both Valerie and Nicole wondered what a doohickey was but started picking up things to figure out exactly what a doohickey was. Valerie handed him a can of Pepsi, Nicole handed him a screwdriver, neither one understood what a doohickey was. Trying again, Valerie grabbed a can of Baja Blast Mt. Dew, Nicole gave him a bag of cool ranch Doritos. "No!" Uncle Bruce cried, "A doohickey!" Both Valerie and Nicole were confused and thought Uncle Bruce hit his head too hard, "Carumba! So young yet he is losing his mind!" Both girls laughed.

Seeing the two girls struggle made Taylor laugh, without saying a word she walked over to the table, grabbed his cell phone, and proudly handed it to Uncle Bruce. "That my friend is a doohickey!" Valerie and Nicole were both embarrassed. Taylor said nothing else but grabbed the can of Baja Blast and the bag of cool ranch Doritos and walked away. Uncle Bruce got on his cell phone and called Princess Emily. The conversation was short and sweet, Uncle Bruce quickly hung up.

"Sorry we must go" exclaimed Ariana, the ambulance driver. We have already taken too long; the doctor is waiting. "I told Dr. Deramos about your fall and the quest you are on." Uncle Bruce knew this was not going to be good. Ariana held her laughter back as she continued, "He wants to know if you saw any unicorns, rainbows, or fairies on your journey, so far?" Uncle Bruce knew he had to escape. Suddenly, Ariana pushed a button, and a set of belts came out and encircled him, locking him on the gurney, he was trapped.

He was quickly taken to Parkview hospital where he was immediately checked for any head wounds, leaving the girls alone and scared. Angelica was shocked, Taylor was mystified, Nicole was surprised, and Valerie was disheartened. They all looked at each other confused and bewildered. Simultaneously, they looked at each other and asked, "What do we do now?" Nobody knew.

Then from high above the sky came a thunderous roar. Was it a rocket? Was it lightning? Was it a solar flare exploding? A sonic boom? Nobody knew for sure; they did know they were upset, confused, and bewildered.

"Look, Uncle Bruce forgot his doohickey!" screamed Taylor. Both Valerie and Nicole still wondered what a doohickey was but decided to sit down to figure things out. Valerie bravely took the lead fearing that this was indeed the final chapter in her book of life. She wondered what to do next, should she even try, or should she just lay down and wither away? Solemnly, she gathered her small group of friends.

Back in the cemetery, Joceline and Luis wondered what protecting Dulany 252 meant. After sleeping for over 170 years their minds were groggy. Luis had so many questions: Who was Wendy Papadopolus? Why did they have to protect Dulany 252? What were they protecting? Joceline also had some questions: How would they protect Dulany 252? Where was Dulany 252? What happens to them if they do not protect 252?

Both Joceline and Luis liked to look good wherever they went, so they both showered and got into a fresh sheet. Luis always got out of the shower first, after getting dressed first, he combed his hair and went in front of the mirror. 'Honey, come here please."

Joceline thought her handsome husband just wanted some attention. He had been working out in the barn every day before going to work. Luis was being impatient, "Honey, come here please. Is this doohickey working?" Joceline reminded Luis it was a mirror and laughed when he did not think it was working. She stepped in front of the giant mirror, "OMG! What is happening?" Luis insisted this doohickey was not working, Joceline just stood there frozen, she knew what this meant but didn't want to say it, afraid it was true. Luis stepped out and back in, nothing, not a shadow, not an overcast, nothing. Joceline waved at herself, nothing. Luis took a deep breath and knew the truth.

Joceline refused to accept the truth, she did not want to think or tell the truth. Joceline begged her husband not to speak the truth. This could not be happening. Joceline stepped in front of the mirror again, nothing, she danced, nothing, she brushed her teeth, nothing. She sat down realizing the truth, Luis hugged his beautiful bride telling her there was nothing that would make him not think she was the most beautiful girl on the planet.

"So, the mirror thinks we are invisible. But you can see me, right? Can't be that bad, can it?" asked Luis. Joceline was quiet, she was upset, she didn't want to be invisible; she did not want to be a defender of Dulany 252, she didn't want to be over 170 years old. Luis did not say a word, he just came over and gave her a huge hug, assuring her they would get through this ordeal together. They bravely decided to explore their surroundings.

Valerie felt like she lost the battle, she had lost her Uncle Bruce. He was supposed to help her remove this curse, unfortunately Valerie now realized that bad luck was her life. She would now end up with her old cousins that disappeared so many years ago. Valerie wondered if the final moments would be painful. She sat on the bench throwing herself a pity party.

Nicole came over to the pity party, in a deep angry voice she said "I thought you were strong? Get up! Quit feeling sorry for yourself! Get yourself, your doohickey and start looking! You have plenty of time to solve the last clue!" Angelica wondered why Nicole was yelling at her good friend Valerie. The usually quiet Taylor was appalled at what she saw and heard. Taylor avoided conflict, but she could not let Nicole be a bully.

The petite young lady carried her big voice to the circle of friends. Taylor yelled at Nicole for treating Valerie poorly. Angelica thought Valerie was her friend and yelled at Taylor. Nicole defended herself and scolded Taylor for getting involved. Valerie got mad at Taylor for getting involved. Nicole fought with Angelica saying she had a bad attitude. The stress, the pressure, the tension was too much, the girls were beginning to crack under the heavy pressure.

Uncle Bruce would have been very disappointed. Instead of staying focused and concentrating on helping Valerie, they took out their attitudes. Then out of nowhere came a very pretty lady dressed in all pink. Pink jeans, a pink blouse, pink shoes, a pink jacket, and a very cute pink hat. Her nails were pink, her lips were pink, and she had several pink hair extensions.

She called out "Excuse me ladies!" Nobody noticed her. She called again, "Ladies?" The four ladies did not hear the lady in pink call out. The lady in pink did not tolerate being ignored, but Angelica was yelling at Taylor, Nicole was yelling at Valerie, Taylor was yelling at Nicole and Valerie was yelling at Angelica. It was chaos. The lady in pink had enough.

She snapped her finger and a thick cloud of white smoke appeared. Suddenly, she was wearing a pink cape, suddenly the girls mouths could not open, suddenly a gust of wind guided them to their seats. Now the lady in pink was in control.

She decided to be nice and took the lock off one of their mouths, only with the promise they did not talk until she was done talking. Valerie sat quietly, Taylor sat quietly, Nicole sat quietly, not so much Angelica. As the lady in pink started, Angelica started yelling at the lady, strike one, three strikes and you are out. Angelica was quiet only momentarily, "I don't know who you are but," strike two.

The lady in pink tried starting over one more time, "I am . . ." "get out and out!" Angelica screamed. Strike three, suddenly a force that very strong sealed Angelica's mouth. The lady in pink smiled, crossed her arms, and stood ready for battle. "Hello," she looked over to Angelica making sure she stayed quiet, "My name is Princess Emily, fierce protector of everything that is good, destroyer of all that is evil.

Princess Emily continued, "I have been called here by my special friend Uncle Bruce." The girls were overwhelmed, Valerie wanted to get her doohickey to get an autograph. Nicole was just amazed that her Uncle Bruce knew Princess Emily. Taylor was so impressed she gave a rare thumbs up on a first meeting. Princess Emily continued, rhetorically asking, "Do you know why we are here?"

Like deer in a headlight, the girls sat staring at Princess Emily. Valerie thought Princess Emily was here to do something big, like save the city from a big monkey like King Kevin. Nicole thought Princess Emily was doing something big like saving the town from meteors. Taylor thought Princess Emily was here to stop Taco Bell from discontinuing Baja Blast. Angelica still could not speak.

Princess Emily started speaking again, "I am here to help you get the third clue. First and foremost, who is Valerie?" Valerie raised her hand. "Does everybody understand one thing? (She paused) We have until 11:35 tonight to find the last clue or according to my intelligence information, the young Valerie will no longer exist, the data strongly suggests she will disintegrate before our very eyes if we fail. "

Valerie sat there scared at her future. Nicole just stared, open mouthed, at Princess Emily. Taylor just stared, not realizing the importance of this mission until now, Angelica remained quiet. Princess Emily summed it up one more time, this mission is to get the diamond necklace back and save Valerie. Failure is not an option; due you understand me?" The girls both said "Yeah!" very meekly.

Princess Emily did not like that response and repeated, "Do you understand me?" A little louder a little bolder the girls all yelled, "YEAH!" Still trying to pump them up, Princess Emily wanted a little more energy, a little more power, a little more enthusiasm, "DO YOU UNDERSTAND ME?" screamed Princess Emily. Finally, all pumped up the girls hollered back, **"YES MA'AM!"**

Princess Emily was happy, now she had to figure out the clue, "Where is the clue?" asked Princess Emily. Valerie and Nicole both ran to get it from the backpack in the Jeep. Everything was now a contest, everything was a race, everything was a competition between the two cousins. Valerie got to the Jeep first, but Nicole found the backpack first.

There was no warning, sometimes with a calamitic event like this it is better that way. Mt. St Valerie erupted violently, Mt. St. Nicole blew its top, the earth shook. Nicole emptied the backpack searching for the clue, out of nowhere Valerie grabbed the backpack dumping the contents on the ground. Important papers flew randomly in the sky. Valerie wrestled Nicole in the dirt, Nicole pushed Valerie. They both held onto the backpack for dear life as they searched inside for the clue. It had a doohickey for this, and a doohickey for that.

Hearing the commotion, Angelica, Taylor, and Princess Emily headed towards the Jeep. They watched as Valerie rolled to the right; they watched as Nicole rolled to the left. They watched as the two circus clowns finally stopped because they were exhausted. Too tired to stand, too tired to breathe, too tired to move her, they just sat in the dusty dirt exhausted beyond words. Angelica chuckled as she walked over to them, pulled the paper out of their hands, and handed the clue to Princess Emily. Princess Emily read the note:

HILLCREST CEMETERY
DULANY PLOT 252

Angelica was the only one curious enough to keep the conversation alive, "What does it mean?" she asked with curiosity. Valerie still exhausted from her battle, lay quietly on the ground as well as Nicole who was just as exhausted. Princess Emily, surprised at the lack of focus with this young group, just stared into the eyes of these young warriors. Her loyalty and her promise to help Uncle Bruce is all that kept Princess Emily here. She did not tolerate this immature type of behavior.

Princess Emily looked at the clue and said, "Good news, bad news". The girls have not had any good news for a while, so they chose the good news first. Princess Emily was a little shocked. They chose the good news first, "Well, it is a pretty easy clue, it's in the Hillcrest Cemetery, plot 252, the headstone has the name Dulany engraved on the front. Should be pretty easy to find."

Valerie and Nicole stopped fighting long enough to be happy and give each other a huge hug. Princess Emily kept a serious smile despite the good news. Taylor was getting tired, and her patient level was quickly diminishing, she yawned and headed back to the house. Angelica was not sure what was going on but wanted to know why this information was bad. Princess Emily took a deep breath and reiterated that the clue was easy, because it was a setup.

"They build your confidence, you think you are the smartest, greatest, most successful treasure hunter that ever lived. You walk into this clue overconfident, under prepared, overzealous and BAM! The mousetrap snaps shut". Valerie was upset, "What do I do now?" she asked politely. "It's your choice, completely up to you," said Princess Emily.

"You have to know, whatever it is by plot 252 it will be dangerous, extremely dangerous. According to what I know this curse was started in 1852, whoever produced this curse was not only mean, but she was also smart and wanted revenge, we have to be prepared for anything, fires, floods, dragons, monsters, earthquakes, and even dangerous doohickeys flying randomly through the air at us. It will be a challenge to say the least!"

Nicole quickly replied, "Challenge accepted!" Angelica was not sure about going and thought about not going, asking if spiders were involved. Princess Emily replied, "Those curses back then were some of the best, todays curses are watered down not made to last. The curse could include anything from spiders to ghosts. How lucky do you feel?" Angelica stepped back realizing that this was not her battle either. Valerie looked at Princess Emily and asked her, "Why, why do I have such bad luck?"

CHAPTER 18

CATTYWAMPUS

(In Dissaray)
Hillcrest Cemetery

Luis was not sure he understood the seriousness of the situation. Joceline was hungry, which was surprising considering they were ghosts. Luis suggested they go out to get something since their room had no food in it. Joceline did not want to leave, everything was cattywampus, the bed was unmade, the room was dusty, and their clothes were spread all over the tiny room. Joceline was too proud of a women to leave a room cattywampus. Luis did not care; he thought nobody could see them anymore.

Despite the fact Joceline was a neat freak, her stomach cried for food. It had been 170 years since she last ate, the mess could wait. Luis tried to open the door, but it was locked. Luis tried again but the door would not budge. Luis tried to tell his wife the bad news, but the words would not come out. Joceline was getting impatient with her sweet husband and asked him why he had not opened the door yet.

He held her hands tightly and bravely looked into her deep brown eyes, "I'm sorry honey, the door is locked, we are stuck in here until someone lets us out." Luis liked to fix things, so he looked at it one more time in hopes he could show her how talented he was. He was overwhelmed with the door and its massive lock, but he continued to stare at it.

Not having a clue, he walked over to his pretty wife and began to "talk" shoppe. Talking very masculine, "If I take this contraption, discombulate it, then adjust the whatchamacallit, it must be nonfunctional, I should be able to fix this, however I need a thingamabob to fix the doohickey!"

He thought she would bust out crying, he thought she might start yelling, he thought she might just start throwing a thing or even maybe a doohickey. She did not, all she did was smile, grab his hand tightly and say, "Remember, we are ghosts!" Together, they gently walked through the big wooden door to a world they had never seen before.

A New Leader

This was a long weekend; the army of soldiers were cattywampus. Once this battalion of rag tag fighters were ready to battle the evil forces of this terrible curse, however there numbers were dwindling. Taylor was exhausted and did not think she could go on, she was now resting inside Nicole's house, her mind was spent, and her battery was out of energy, she felt lethargic and paralyzed.

Angelica, once a dominant force in helping Valerie, had arachnophobia, the fear of spiders, she was going nowhere near the cemetery. Angelica could deal with the ghosts and goblins, the spirits and everything else a cemetery could offer, but if there was even one teensy weensy spider going up a waterspout anywhere near the cemetery, she could not help any more. Angelica knew her mind was cattywampus, but there was nothing she could do, the fear of arachnophobia was too big.

Then there was Uncle Bruce falling down the stairs in that rare snowmageddon. He was resting comfortably in Parkview hospital; his injuries were not life threating but enough to keep him in the hospital overnight. The bruised wrist, bruised ankle and bruised ego would all heal in due time, but he felt terrible he couldn't be there to help his nieces solve the curse of the diamond necklace.

Uncle Bruce was proud of his quick thinking under pressure, but that is who he was. He always had a what if plan, a backup plan, a contingency plan. Uncle Bruce had known Princess Emily a long time, he not only knew how pretty she was, but how extremely talented she was.

Have you ever heard about the hostage situation with the King and Queen of Lechtenstein? Or have you heard about the massive oil spill off the coast of Menamark? Have you heard about the nuclear reactor problem they had in western Wanada? How about Mary's lost puppy, Toby in Glendale Heights? Maybe you read about the fight between the King of Laredo and his next-door neighbor the Queen of Vermasino, which almost started an international war? Of course not, all top-secret problems were handled quickly and quietly by Princess Emily.

For Princess Emily, failure was not an option. By 11:35 pm, they would know where the diamond necklace was and soon afterward, they would take back what was rightfully theirs and the curse would be removed, Valerie would be lucky. For good or bad, the team only included Valerie, Nicole, and Princess Emily.

Princess Emily handed each girl a bag, telling them to quickly put on their uniforms. Valerie complained, saying a uniform was not necessary, and for the first time since the great Barbie incident Nicole agreed with her cousin Valerie. Princess Emily just stood there amazed Valerie was giving her attitude, being short circuited. Thinking they were getting the upper hand, Nicole told Princess Emily that Uncle Bruce did not make them wear uniforms, he would never overload the system. Valerie unexpectantly agreed with Nicole. Princess Emily was not happy.

Trying to remain calm, Princess Emily looked at the two rebels with a very insincere smile if you could call it a smile. Valerie was scared, her body froze with fear as the hairs on the back of her neck electrified. Valerie decided she was going to put on the uniform. Nicole was fearless and was not going to back down, her ripped jean look was rad, there was definitely going to be no uniform in her future. Princess Emily came face to face with Nicole, so close their noses touched, Nicole did not budge. Princess Emily began barking, "I am Princess Emily!" spit flew wildly at Nicole as she reminded the two who she was.

Valerie was tired, this journey was harder than she ever expected, she wondered if she should give up and join her long lost cousins, Agatha, Gertrude, and Lilliana. Suddenly, Valerie began to cry. Nicole looked over at Valerie with a disappointing look, Valerie kept crying, Nicole called out, "you're such a weenie!" Valerie kept crying. Nicole could not handle one more tear, "Okay, Okay I will put on the uniform!" she exclaimed as she fell to her knees.

"Hurry up! It's 7:42 pm, that only leaves us four hours to find the clue." The girls were disappointed but did not argue, they walked towards the bathrooms worried how foolish they would look in a uniform. Valerie was thankful Grant was in the Wisconsin Dells, he would never see her in a terrible uniform, but on the other hand she thought Grant would look awful handsome in any uniform he was forced to wear.

Grant was spending the time of his life in the Wisconsin Dells with his wonderful generous family. They ate wherever they wanted, including the very exclusive Mickey's all you can eat buffet, money was no object. They went sightseeing wherever they wanted, including the very exclusive underwater river cars, money was no object. They bought an unlimited amount of souvenirs for family and friends, including an exclusive limited edition twenty-four carat ring for Aunt Cathy, price was no object.

However, he was clueless what to get that pretty new girl he recently met in chemistry class. He wanted something unique; he wanted something special; he wanted something that Valerie knew was from him and him only. Something that says Grant thinks you are a very special girl, something that says you fill the void in my heart, something that says I really like you. Would it be a sweatshirt? Jewelry? A key chain? A postcard? A Snow globe? Grant's mind was cattywampus, he had no idea what to bring Valerie, all he knew was price was no object.

Valerie opened up the garment bag and saw the uniform, she gasped. Nicole opened up her garment bag and gasped. Valerie put on the one-of-a-kind uniform and shrieked. Nicole put on her one-of-a-kind uniform and shrieked. Totally in shock, Valerie started to weep. Totally in shock, Nicole started to weep. Simultaneously they both ran out of the changing room, straight into the folds of Princess Emily.

Unprepared for the response of these two ladies Princess Emily bunkered down for the unprecedented attack on her. Praying for a miracle, adjusting her stance, and preparing her mind, Princess Emily prepared herself for the pain of what she was going to experience. Her mind quickly raced through the painful memories in her life.

Pain, what a terrible word. It is a four-letter word that should never be mentioned like cold and snow. Her mind wandered to fifth grade where after spending all night doing her nails, she broke one after tripping over her father's size thirteen over -sized black and white shoes he left in the middle of the living room. The pain was unbearable.

The pain of social exclusion. How about the year when Sara wore her $450 Johnny Aria designer blouse to school? She was the envy of every 6th, 7th, and 8th grade girl at the middle school. Princess Emily's father said no because it was too expensive, blouses at Walmart were $8.98. Princess Emily's mother did not like how the blouse was too risqué, no more needed to be said. They both said no to the blouse. The pain was unbearable.

Princess Emily imagined all the pain and suffering she had endured. All the embarrassment of not being normal. People picked on her because she was short, because her teeth were cattywampus, because she had short hair. One year, she volunteered to be the copy girl, meaning every time her teacher needed her to, she would run to the office and make copies. Her friends thought she was always in trouble and made fun of her. The pain was unbearable.

Was Princess Emily being to dramatic? Her sister's thought so, her mom thought so, her dad thought so, even the dog thought so. This is why Princess Emily joined the elite special forces, this is why Princess Emily had so much to prove, this is why Princess Emily is proud to be called Princess Emily. This was a title that very little, if any would have bestowed upon them, it was only given to the few, the proud, the Princess Emily's of the world.

Standing proud, for the last time, Princess Emily watched in horror as Valerie and Nicole rushed her. Thinking this could be the end for her Princess Emily smiled realizing she had led a good life. What would she be remembered for? The cattywampus of dirty dishes she left in the sink this morning? The clothes she left on the floor this morning? She would be remembered for leaving the empty milk container in the refrigerator. Princess Emily's mind began to ponder these overwhelming questions and much, much, more.

Princess Emily opened her eyes for a quick millisecond, all she saw was pink. Simultaneously, Valerie and Nicole reached her at the same time. BAM! KAPOW! BOOM! Were the sounds everyone heard! Princess Emily cried out, "NOOOOO!" "Thank you! Thank you!" The girls screamed as they hugged Princess Emily thanking her for supplying them with the best uniform ever. "Uncle Bruce never gets us stuff like this anymore, thank you so much!"

The uniforms were awesome, one-of-a- kind, and totally rad. The specially fitted customed tailored uniforms were fluorescent pink. The warm snuggly hoodies were fluorescent pink with their monogrammed names neatly written on the left chest. The pink leggings were unbelievingly comfortable and had silver and gold sparkles scattered randomly across the fabric. The outfit included pink Nike gym shoes that lit up and very stylish pink, fluorescent gloves. They were fashionista mini superheroes!

But what they did not know was how protective the suits were. Nothing could penetrate the special Kevlar fabric, nothing. The girls were safe from bugs, spiders, dog bites, fangs. Nothing could penetrate this newly designed protective wear designed by Dr. Irving Schagoondalop for the Nasa Space program. The newest feature included a special layer to keep out insults, curses, and evil spirits.

"If you are going to be a success you have to dress for success!" Princess Emily said proudly as she got herself up. "I am not only going to help you find the third clue, but I am also going show you how to do in style, with style and for style." Valerie and Nicole were all smiling.

"But, on a mission like this we need a plan, or everything leads to cattywampus. It took me hours but based on the data we secured from our undercover agent; we have put together two plans to get the necessary clue from the headstone where Dulany 252 is located. One plan is absolutely useless, wrong ideas, wrong concepts, inappropriate behavior, you get the idea, the other plan has the right plan of attack!"

Nicole was curious and asked, "Why two plans? Especially why waste your time on a bad plan?" Princess Emily quickly answered, "We at the department also like to teach our students so one day, you can fight your own battles. One plan is good, the other not so good, it is up to you which one you follow." "So, where are these plans?" asked a concerned Valerie.

Nicole quickly grabbed a piece of paper out of her pocket, "Mine was stuck inside the pair of pink gym shoes that were packed in the garment bag. I almost threw it away but did not. I opened it up and saw instructions, so I saved it." Valerie took a big breath and looked down. Princess Emily looked at Valerie and asked what she did with her plan. Valerie said she did not have it and remained solemn and quiet.

Princess Emily reminded Valerie the importance of a good plan. She told Valerie about the countless research, the countless meetings and the countless ideas that were given to insure the success of mission x-875789 . Valerie was embarrassed and remained quiet. Princess Emily asked Valerie to retrieve the well thought out plan,

Valerie refused. Princess Emily ordered Valerie to get the plan. Valerie started to cry and told her she could not. "But why?" gently asked Princess Emily, "because, I can't!" quietly said Valerie. Nicole began to laugh.

Princess Emily was flabbergasted at the stubbornness of this young lady, "You have five seconds to either get me that plan or tell me where it is!" barked Princess Emily. Valerie was frozen, crying her eyes out. Princess Emily began to count slowly, "5....................4...............3................2................1 and 3/4.....................1 and 1/2...............1 and 1/4......................1..........." Valerie very loudly yelled, "Stop! I will tell you!"

Princess Emily listened intently. "I had to use the bathroom when I changed, I had to go number 2, there was no toilet paper. I did not have a choice." Nicole began laughing. Princess Emily bit her lip trying to stop herself from laughing, it was no use. "Maybe just maybe we will be lucky, and Nicole will have the real rescue plan, Princess Emily told Nicole to open up her rescue plan and read what you should do in case of being lost, Nicole looked at the sheet and it read, "If lost, call your mommy!"

She told Nicole what she does in case of being bullied, Nicole quickly answered, "If you are being bullied call mommy." Nicole knew, Princess Emily knew, and Valerie definitely knew they had the wrong rescue copy. Valerie was overwhelmed and asked her cousin, "Why? why do I have such bad luck?"

CHAPTER 19

BASTION

(A Place That Is Well Defended)

Luis and Joceline went through the thick wooden door without an incident. They flew through the air free as a bird discovering the 21st century. Big, tarred street's instead of small dirt trails. Cars had replaced horses, big steel buildings instead of wooden buildings. Everyone was in a hurry, cars beeped, people yelled, trains whistled. This was not the small little farming town they had once known and loved. Glendale Heights was all grown up.

Joceline was fascinated with the mode of transportation which everyone was using. Out was the horse, the horse and buggy and the bulky stagecoach. In was the car, all different colors, and different sizes. Some went fast and some went slow. Joceline saw huge trucks . She saw bikes with motors on them. Suddenly the alarm started beeping again, meaning they needed to get back soon, headstone 252 would soon be under attack. Joceline thought they had plenty of time to get back, while Luis wanted to get some food.

Joceline saw people everywhere, she thought they were dressed funny, but were fascinated how they acted. Truck drivers yelling out their windows, "Move it!" Kids playing in the park chasing a Pokémon? But she wondered what were in these cars. In one swift motion she swooped down and went into the first car she saw, with a woman steering it and two small children crying in the back.

She immediately sat in the back with the children, instantly both children stopped crying and started laughing. The woman, mom, told the children, "See thinking about rainbows and unicorns is much better than thinking about how hungry you are." The children continued to laugh while Joceline played with them. Mom kept her eyes on the road while she said, "I have never seen you laugh like that what game are you playing?"

Neither one answered, they were having too much fun playing with Joceline. Stephen? Sammy? What game are you playing? Sammy answered first, "We are playing the stagecoach game mom!" mom was confused, "Who taught you that?" Stephen quickly responded "Joceline the ghost". Mom laughed, "There are no such things as ghosts!"

"Look behind you mom!" instructed Sammy. Mom did just that, then she spotted Joceline, "a ghost?" Joceline replied "Yes!" Mom slammed on the brakes, screamed, and pulled her car off to the side of the road. Once stopped, the mom quickly grabbed the two children and ran swiftly away from the car, leaving Joceline alone in the car. She left everything behind as she continue to scream. The alarm continue to go off signaling the need to go back. All Luis wanted to do was eat.

Luis reminded his lovely wife about the alarm. If they ever wanted to leave here, they needed to finish their business on earth. Joceline was fascinated with all the food signs but did not know anything about their food, "Home of the Whopper", "We have the meats!", "over 1 billion served," "best hot dogs in Chicago", Joceline picked the over one billion served.

They flew through the door as everyone stared. Joceline read the menu as she waited in line, people stared at the two. Luis whispered to Joceline, "I think they can see us". Joceline was not so sure and tapped the older lady standing in front of her, the lady turned around, "Can you see us?" Frozen and unable to move or talk, the lady just shook with fear.

Seeing the whole situation, a little boy strolled up to Joceline and answered the terrified older lady, "Of course we can see you, are you a ghost?" Hesitantly, Joceline and Luis timidly replied, "I think we are!" The little boy quickly returned to his mother at the back of the line.

The little boy whispered into his mother's ear. The woman's face immediately turned pale. Very slowly, very calmly she put the boy back on the ground, very bravely she took a deep breath and yelled, **"IT'S A GHOST! RUN FOR YOUR LIVES!"**

It was a stampede that took all of ten seconds. In an instant, every man, woman and child had evacuated from the fast-food restaurant. Half-eaten cheeseburgers sat on tables; ice cubes melted in freshly dispensed soda cups, hot salty crispy French fries became soggy, this once thriving restaurant now became a ghost town.

The alarm continued to blare uncontrollably, making Joceline very nervous. However, Luis was hungry, he had not eaten in over 170 years. He saw a tray of unopened food on the counter wrapped sandwiches. The alarm kept getting louder, Luis knew he needed to grab the food and head back to the cemetery. He ended up grabbing two spicy chicken sandwiches, chicken nuggets and some French fries. Joceline's stomach was happy.

Being new at this ghost thing, Joceline and Luis got back to the cemetery very quickly. There was nobody, the gates were locked, the normally quiet cemetery was dead. Luis did not like being here, it was eerie, it was dark, it was not a good place to spend eternity in. Luis had always had a good head on his shoulders, so he knew the alarm meant something.

Joceline and Luis had a great relationship, after four, I mean 174 years of being married, they knew making decisions together was the right way to go. They talked and knew the only way to go was to defend whatever was by plot 252 marked Dulany, this was their only way out of purgatory. Luis agreed, Joceline agreed. But where was plot Dulany 252? Joceline and Luis had to find it before anybody else did, Luis knew this had to be the best bastion ever.

Joceline was the over thinker between the two. Luis kept it simple, defend plot Dulany 252 and soon they would be where they belonged. Joceline wanted to know why they were defending plot

Dulany 252. Joceline wanted to know what was in plot Dulany 252. Joceline wanted to know where plot Dulany 252 was. Joceline wanted to know who this Dulany character was in plot Dulany 252. Joceline was not happy, Joceline had questions, Joceline wanted answers.

Princess Emily was not used to this, she always had the strongest, the smartest, the fiercest warriors helping her defeat evil. Princess Emily had a reputation for stopping, for squashing, for controlling the sinister characters of the world. Princess Emily was mystified, flabbergasted, bewildered at this group of warriors that Uncle Bruce bestowed upon her.

Princess Emily was at a loss for words. However, she was impressed how fabulous the girls looked in their pink uniforms. It did not matter if you were at a state dinner, you looked your best! It did not matter if you were cooking dinner, you looked your best! It did not matter if you were planting a garden, you looked your best! Win or lose, Valerie and Nicole looked fabulousa!

Having no plan, Princess Emily was a bit apprehensive about looking for the cemetery plot marked Dulany 252. Princess Emily always had and followed a plan, there was no ignoring it. When Princess Emily saved the little old lady from being run over by the school bus on Main Street, there was a plan. There was the time Princess Emily saved the train full of people going to work from derailing after someone stole a rail, there was a plan. And when the bank robber stole all the money from the vault, there was a plan. What would she do without a plan?

Valerie struggled with Princess Emily's inability to be strong without a plan. Was not having a plan Princess Emily's kryptonite? Almost lethargic, Princess Emily struggled to move without the plan. They looked all around the room hoping to find the plan and focus on saving Valerie, under the cat, behind the cat, and beside the cat, there was no plan, right now there was no plan. Princess Emily had no idea what to do without a plan.

Nicole stood shocked at Princess Emily's demise, barely under her breath she called Princess Emily a weenie. Valerie heard her cousin and encouraged Nicole to be more empathetic. Nicole did not understand why Princess Emily needed a plan to get the next clue. Princess Emily sat on the bench unable to move, unable to think, unable to be the great superhero she truly was.

Valerie and Nicole searched high and low for the plan. Nicole checked the chocolate chip cookie jar that was filled to the brim with fresh baked goodness, not in there. Valerie looked in the stack of old mail that sat on the kitchen counter, a coupon good for a free blizzard, a free submarine sandwich, not in there. Nicole looked in the kitchen garbage hoping she put her toilet paper in there, not in there.

Valerie knew what she did with the plan, very slowly, very purposefully she went into the bathroom hoping by some small twist of fate. a miracle that could only be explained by a higher power, that her used toilet paper was still there. Afraid to know the truth, Valerie squinted her big brown eyes and opened the toilet seat with her feet, nothing, crystal clear, nothing floating in the bowl, thank goodness. However, she did notice a few pieces of crumpled up bathroom tissue crumpled up on the ground.

In a momentary loss of sensibility, Valerie rushed down and got on her knees so she could reach behind the toilet. Knowing there was a chance, small as it was, a chance of her finding the plan, Valerie grabbed the four pieces of trash and rushed backed to Princess Emily. Princess Emily sat there motionless. Valerie prematurely yelled, "I FOUND THE PLAN! I FOUND THE PLAN! I FOUND THE PLAN!"

Back at the cemetery, Joceline and Luis found Dulany plot 252 with ease. It was a simple grave all alone on a small hill. The dingy beat up grave simply stated Dulany, Born December 21,1860 died August 12, 1954, six ball in the corner pocket. Together they hovered over their designated bastion grave. Luis promised Joceline under no circumstances anyone would get near their grave, their very own bastion.

Joceline wondered how they would be able to defend the beaten-up old grave. Luis was no fighter; he did not like to argue, and he hated confrontation. This was going to be tough, Joceline was easy going and extremely happy, the best thing she could do would be to kill them with kindness. This was going to be tough, Luis finally remembered they were ghosts.

They did not have to fight anyone; they would fly around and act like ghosts, they could scare, they could prank, they could have lots of fun. Joceline and Luis could just scare anyone who might want to mess with the gravesite. Everyone was afraid of ghosts, defending Dulany 252 on a hill was going to be easy. They would be out of here sooner than later. They patiently waited behind the old tombstone as darkness took over the cemetery.

Valerie rushed over to Princess Emily with the wadded-up piles of toilet paper to show her they had found the plan. Now with three hours left before time ran out, they had a chance of saving Valerie. Excited, Princess Emily grabbed the first wad and opened it, it turned out to be a shopping list for the grocery store, milk, eggs, bananas, cereal, soda, and a whole lot more. Nervously, Nicole opened the second wad, somebody started saying congratulations and spelling it wrong, garbage.

Thinking she had the golden ticket Valerie smiled from ear to ear and opened up the large wad of paper. There was a small lake of blood wrapped inside the large wad, somebody must have had a bloody nose. "EWWW!" Valerie screamed. Surprisingly there was no plan in any of the wads of paper left on the floor.

As Princess Emily sat unplugged at the thought of having no plan, Nicole knew there was a solution to the problem, but could not figure it out. She sat there and pondered some of the solutions but remembered the book she read in first grade, "Think Think Think!" Valerie knew without Princess Emily this journey would be a bust. Valerie asked herself why everything was so difficult, "Why, why do I have such bad luck?"

CHAPTER 20

TIMOROUS

(Full of Fear)

Joceline and Luis prepared for battle as they hid behind the tombstone. They were not timorous, they were brave, they were determined, they were ghosts. Patiently they waited in the darkness for somebody, something, or someone to appear. Deer crossed their paths, a skunk wandered by, and a pack of racoons scampered past the tombstone marked Dulany 252, but no humans.

Valerie had had enough, what kind of superhero was Princess Emily? A simple plan was all that stopped her from being the great superhero she was destined to be. Valerie did not want to vanish, Valerie did not want to be another statistic in the family folklore, Valerie was timorous, but was determined to break the curse. Valerie enlisted Nicole and together they swiftly produced a new plan based on what they thought would work.

Nicole quickly helped Valerie read the impromptu plan to Princess Emily. Would it work? Nicole and Valerie nervously waited as Princess Emily came back to life. First her eyes blinked, then her arms began to move, then she was able to use her legs. Princess Emily was coming back to life; her mind began to process the plan.

With under three hours before elimination, Valerie was ecstatic Princess Emily was operational. Without warning Princess Emily got up and asked the two girls if they were ready to take care of things now that she had a plan. Both girls smiled knowing they had averted a major catastrophe.

Some say Princess Emily took her "plans" too seriously, she was too rigid, she followed the plans to closely leaving little or no margin for error. However, she was human and did make mistakes. As they drove, Valerie noticed Princess Emily driving east on North Avenue, the cemetery was west, "Aren't you going the wrong way?" she asked.

Princess Emily quickly interpreted the question and replied, "The plan you gave me says get dog food for Luna, cranberry juice, chicken wings, donuts, and tea. The grocery store is just down the street on the left." "What about the cemetery?" asked Valerie.

"Did somebody die?" asked Princess Emily. Valerie was confused but immediately answered, "NO!" Valerie was confused and asked Princess Emily if Nicole had downloaded anything into Princess Emily's plan for the day. Princess Emily responded with, "A trip to the grocery store." You could see the windows began to fog up as steam started to build in Mt. St Valerie.

Nicole was hesitant, but knew that was her shopping list, the shopping list that was on the backside of the plan for Princess Emily. She must of inadvertently, gave Princess Emily the wrong information. Nicole confessed her crime to Valerie. Mt. St. Valerie blew instantly spewing hot insults. Nicole was caught off guard and was burned many times with rude comments.

Princess Emily was stunned by the powerful force of Mt. St. Valerie; she had never seen such a reaction like this before. It was one of the few times that Valerie was not herself, but the pressure was on, in a little under three hours Valerie would be gone, lost forever somewhere in this big universe. Nicole tried to be emphatic, despite years of therapy with Dr. Trongwatarangasig, she was still tired of Valerie always getting her way with her temper tantrums.

Valerie had had enough, she decided to be in control of her own destiny. She has had much help during this awkward and difficult quest, but they were dropping like flies. Uncle Bruce fell down the stairs, Taylor was exhausted, Angelica was fed up, Princess Emily was lethargic, and Nicole was no longer her friend, let alone her long lost cousin. Valerie felt this was the time, this was the place, this was the opportunity for change.

Change is hard for most people, but Valerie decided it was change that this group desperately needed. She remembered what her neighbor, Mr. Dulany told her once, "If you cannot fly then run, if you can't run then walk, if you can't walk then crawl. The important thing is you have to keep moving forward." With three hours left, she had to keep moving forward.

The first and most important thing to change was her relationship with her cousin Nicole. With plenty of timorous, she took a big deep breath and swallowed her pride. she slowly ambled herself over to her cousin. Nicole was done with Valerie, everybody thought Valerie was so sweet, but in reality, she was not, not even close. Valerie knew this was not going to be easy.

Standing very remorseful for what seemed an eternity, Valerie thought about what to say to her cousin. She thought about the Captain of the Titanic, when everything was done, he gave an hour speech apologizing for hitting the iceberg. She thought about the man who embezzled millions of dollars from all his friends in Russia. He spent the next twenty years writing apology letters to each one of his victims. She thought about the group of bully's who stole the Girl Scout cookies from the little girl. They spent the next five summers selling cookies door to door to apologize.

Valerie thought about what she could do, say, or for Nicole to apologize. In her big brain she started thinking of a long-winded speech, too long, it would never work. She thought about writing her an apology letter, no stamp, would not work. She thought about making Nicole dinner, she could not cook, wouldn't work. What could she do?

She stood there puzzled, flabbergasted, mystified as what to do. Despite the dire possibilities that lay ahead, Valerie decided to put her friendship, her kinship, her relationship with her cousin first. No more thinking about the handsome new boy in school first, even though his golden hair was gorgeous, his smile was irresistible, and his baby blue eyes were to die for. Nicole would be the first thing on her mind. But first she had to figure out how to apologize.

Valerie was very brave, not timorous in searching for answers. That poor girl used every cell, every nerve, artery in her brain to try and solve Princess Emily's problem of no plan. Valerie thought for a second and wondered how Princess Emily survived, does a superhero always need a plan? Who is the planner? Valerie wondered if Princess Emily planned to make a plan for herself every day. Valerie thought about what was on the plan. Valerie thought some more of plan, who was on the plan? Valerie wondered why Uncle Bruce was on the plan. Valerie wondered where the plan was.

Then like an eagle swooping down on a poor church mouse, it hit her. BAM! Like an ice cream bar on your tongue on a hot summers day, it hit her, BAM! Like walking outside on a cold 20 degree below zero day and the wind hitting your face, it hit her BAM!

Joceline and Luis' alarm continue to ring, however they saw nothing and heard nothing. Luis started to complain and wanted to go home, this is not the afterlife he imagined for him and his lovely bride of 174 years. Bored out his mind he started to make jokes, Joceline he asked, "Did you know a will is a dead giveaway?" Joceline just stared. Luis tried again changing the subject just a little, smiling he asked his lovely bride, "Why do ghosts ride the elevator?" He waited patiently for an answer, Joceline did not bite, she was timorous of the answer. Luis proudly answered, "to lift their spirits!"

At first Joceline did not budge, then she couldn't hold back, she smiled at the stupid joke, then she started to laugh. Luis laughed with her. In a quick reversal of emotion, Joceline quietly yelled "Shush!" and covered her husband's mouth. "I hear footsteps, two people coming. I am scared!" she admitted to her husband.

Luis was scared too, this was their job to protect the grave, but ever since he met Joceline he would do anything to protect this beautiful maiden. He was her knight in shining armor, there was no time to be timorous, no place to be timorous, no room to be timorous. Ghost or no ghost, he had to be brave, he guided his maiden behind the grave as they heard the footsteps approach closer and closer.

It was dark, Luis could not see a thing, the four footsteps approached quickly. His mind raced wildly at all the options. He had no weapon; he could not decide if he should use his powerful muscles to fight the intruders, should he use his powerful mouth to talk to the intruders, or should he use his spirit and scare the intruder? The footsteps quickly approached.

"Fight? Talk? Scare? Fight? Talk? Scare?" he kept repeating to himself. He was scared, he did not know what to do. The footsteps stopped in front of plot Dulany 252 . It was go time, now or never, he could be Joceline's knight, or he could be her stable boy. "Decide Luis! Decide!" he yelled at himself. The footsteps did not move. Luis decided.

In one quick sudden burst, Luis jumped in front of the beast. Luis did not know what it was, it was hideous, it had six-inch teeth, big bulging eyes and two giant antlers that were the size of Texas. Luis was timorous and screamed; the beast was timorous and screamed. In a strictly reactionary moment, Luis closed his eyes and bravely yelled "BOO!"

Nicole saw the expression on Valerie's face when it hit her. You know the look, drinking an ice-cold cup of ice water after moving the lawn on a 100-degree June day, pure satisfaction. Studying hard for a final exam, getting the test back and getting an A, pure satisfaction. Waiting in line for the latest and greatest pop music band concert tickets all night and getting the last two front row tickets, pure satisfaction.

Valerie knew there was no guarantee but had enough confidence to continue. Without being arrogant or big-headed Valerie went in for the chance of redemption. The clock was ticking, but Valerie wanted to leave this planet with no regrets, no remorse, no sorrow.

With her heart beating fast, sweat pouring off her brow and her black hair tangled, Valerie went in to apologize.

It had been years since the big Barbie debacle, Nicole had gone through intensive therapy, traveled all over the country, endured countless ridicule and harassment from her family and friends, Valerie was timorous. She slowly backed away in fear of Nicole's reaction. Valerie knew if Nicole knew how timorous she was being she would call Valerie a weenie.

Valerie was being a weenie. She looked at Nicole and noticed how pretty she was, she saw how nice and helpful Nicole has been in this ordeal, she noticed how funny Nicole was. Valerie mustered up the courage and started walking toward Nicole once again. It was hard, step by step, in her head she practiced what she was going to say, but would she freeze up and forget everything she wanted to say.

Nicole was confused, Valerie had always been a little bit different, odder, smarter than most children her age, but what was she doing now? Pacing back and forth, she watched as Valerie came closer and closer to her. Nicole knew Valerie would not hurt a fly, so Nicole wasn't timorous, but she was extremely curious. Finally, Valerie stood in front of Nicole, with her head down and a tear in her eye, Valerie said those two magic words, "I'm sorry!"

Smiling from ear to ear, Nicole calmly asked, "What?" Embarrassed she did not speak loud enough, Valerie raised her head and repeated herself, "I'm sorry!" Now almost laughing, Nicole looked at Valerie and humorously replied, "What?" Valerie knew what Nicole was doing but did not have time for her games. Valerie walked away knowing she did the right thing, before leaving Nicole yelled out "Fine!"

"Where does the time go?" Valerie asked herself as she headed towards Princess Emily. "How does a superhero get to be so high maintenance?" she thought. Valerie was now down to a measly 90 minutes before she suddenly vanished into the great beyond with her other family members who miserably failed so many years ago.

After searching for what seemed like a lifetime, okay 30 seconds, for the greatest female superhero, whoever graced the planet earth, Valerie found Princess Emily. Yes, I say, Princess Emily was prettier, smarter, and stronger than, Wonder Woman, Storm, or Black Widow. Like all superheroes, Princess Emily had a weak point, Princess Emily's kryptonite was needing a plan.

Valerie knew this and had been quietly working on a plan for the superhero. She really did not have a clue as to how to write a plan, so Valerie made it very simple. Go to the cemetery, go to plot Dulany 252, and get the clue. Valerie gave the piece of paper to Princess Emily. Her senses came alive. Princess Emily was recharged, now they could head to the cemetery.

After scaring the beast, Luis was exhausted, totally spent of every drop of energy. Luis fell to the ground, unable to move on that cold October night. Joceline came from the tombstone and thought Luis was hurt, she ran hoping Luis was not dead, but she thought he was already dead, he was a ghost. The beast laid motionless on the ground, and although sore, Luis was not dead again, he was still a ghost. Joceline, who is an avid animal lover yelled at Luis wondering why he would ever hurt such a beautiful animal.

Despite being extremely aggravated at Luis for hurting the poor beast, Joceline helped Luis up off the cold dusty trail. With her back toward the beast, Joceline started to lecture her husband on the importance of being kind to animals. She brushed the dirt off his shirt as she concentrated on telling him how to properly feed animals. He just stared at what was going on behind his wife.

Joceline brushed and brushed the dust off the shirt of her husband all while lecturing her husband on scaring animals. Luis just stared at Joceline. She thought he was goofing around so she told him, "This is serious, you killed this poor defenseless animal, what are going to do with the body?" He stood there frozen. "What do you think he is just going to get up himself? Luis continued to stare, but now he began to stutter and point.

Tired of his shenanigans, Joceline turned around thinking Luis was having fun with her. Joceline just stared at the eight-foot beast in horror, she was timorous. Unable to move, unable to breathe, unable to think Joceline was a sitting duck. Luis was also terrified and frozen in fear. In an unprovoked show of supremacy and domination, this creature let out a giant roar, ROAR! And attempted to scare the pair of ghosts.

The four-legged creature rose to his feet groggy, trying to get his senses back. Still dizzy, the large beast swung his hairy arm to the right, nothing, then a swing to his left, nothing. He growled, he drooled, he roared. Luis grabbed his bride of 174 years, and they ran into the darkness hoping the creature had no desire to catch either one of them. Joceline and Luis struggled to find hiding places, but after running in a circle, they seemed to have lost the beast. They continued to hide behind Dulany 252 Tombstone.

Princess Emily's senses were working once again, she had her plan, that is all she ever wanted. Nicole was excited, she finally got her apology, that is all she ever wanted. Valerie was excited things were actually happening, that is all she ever wanted. Princess Emily pulled up to the cemetery gates. Valerie tried getting a copy of the map, but according to the sign, new maps would not be available for another week. Valerie got mad and asked, "Why, why do I have such bad luck?"

CHAPTER 21

OBFUSCATE

(Making something more confusing)

Joceline and Luis cowered behind the tombstone. Despite working out several times a week, the beast was tougher than them. Once again, the alarm began to ring in both of their ears and Luis began to worry, he realized he was no match for the beast and admitted to himself how confusing it was when he ran screaming like a little girl, eventually losing him.

Joceline knew her husband had doubts about his confrontation with the beast and wanted to reassure him, "Honey, the beast is a beast who has been a beast his entire life. His mother was a beast, his father was a beast and a beast he will always be. He did not grow up to be a goldfish, or even a pet turtle. The beast is a beast. There is no denying it, it was the truth, that thing was a beast." Luis was confused, his lovely wife had just obfuscated the whole situation.

Luis wanted to do better, his job was to protect this tombstone, why? What was so important about this Dulany character? He died so many years ago, why isn't he protecting his own tombstone? What does "Six ball in the corner pocket mean?" Why does he have that carved on his tombstone?"

Joceline saw her husband thinking and wondered how she could help him without obfuscating any plan he was working. They were always a team; they always had each other's backs and they always supported each other. Frick and Frack, Laurel and Hardy, Peanut Butter and Jelly, Joceline and Luis, some things just go well together.

She gently reminded her sweet husband they were ghosts, "Ghosts have special abilities, right?" Luis really did not know. They had only become ghosts this morning, so he did not know. He was always working so he never read anything educational about ghosts. He could not tell you the difference between a ghost or a spirit, Casper and Uncle Billy, a helpful ghost, or an evil spirit. If Luis was going to protect Joceline he needed to figure these things out. Unfortunately, all they figured out was they had to figure the last clue out, quickly.

Joceline heard them first. Marching side by side, Princess Emily brought her two sidekicks, Valerie, and Nicole to get the last clue for the diamond necklace. Step by step, the ladies in pink marched toward plot 252, where the clue was. Luis and Joceline hid behind the tombstone and held their breaths as the enemy approached.

86 minutes were left before Valerie vanished. 86 minutes were left before Valerie knew her future, 86 minutes before the world would be without Valerie. "There it is, on top of the hill!" exclaimed Nicole. Valerie started running up the hill to see what was on the tombstone that was so special, without warning Princess Emily yelled "Stop! It could be a trap!" Valerie did not move.

Princess Emily pulled out her UV-3247 anti-ghost contraption. She looked to the right, nothing, she looked to the left, nothing. Princess Emily signaled to Valerie to stay quiet, but to slowly continue going forward. Princess Emily held the UV-3247 weapon very firmly. Dr. K.B. Kutenheimer recently developed this vacuum type gizmo, specifically for occasions like this. However, it was still in its initial testing stage.

Valerie, as instructed, slowly inched closer and closer to the tombstone. Joceline and Luis knew it was now or never. Valerie took another step closer; Luis took a deep breath and out of nowhere Nicole came running up the hill screaming. Everybody freaked out, Luis popped out and screamed "BOO!" Valerie was frightened beyond recognition. Joceline went up ten feet and growled, forcing

Princess Emily to scream, "Retreat! Retreat!" Nicole was forced backwards, losing her footing, and rolling down the hill.

Together Princess Emily, Valerie, and Nicole congregated behind a giant oak tree about one hundred yards from the grave. Joceline and Luis continued to hide behind and protect the tombstone. Luis prayed, they were scared and ran back home, things remained quiet until Nicole sneezed. Luis was not sure what he heard, was it an elephant or a parade with 76 trombones.

Bravely, he stood firm and came out of hiding. He stood tall and walked in front of the tombstone. Joceline was impressed, and asked her sweet husband, "What are you stupid?" Luis ignored his wife's comment. He stood tall, proud, and commanded, "We do not want to hurt you, but we are here to protect the tombstone. Go away before you are hurt!" Joceline was so proud of her husband.

Princess Emily raised the UV-3247 ghost vacuum and carefully aimed it, she pushed the trigger, not close enough. "Push it again!" yelled Valerie. Still not close enough! Valerie cried "Push it again!" Princess Emily fired again hoping the vacuum reached its intended target. Inches away, Valerie asked Princess Emily how to work the vacuum.

Princess Emily started explaining how the transistor relays information to the data processor's circuits and based on the voltage of the heated transponder the panel will transfer enough radioactive power to the motherboard. Valerie stopped Princess Emily in mid-sentence," you are making this obfuscated. How do you work this thing?" Nicole grabbed the vacuum, Princess Emily said "You push this button!" Valerie did not even pay attention. Nicole was worried.

Valerie took her long black hair and put it in a ponytail, then without any warning she stood up yelled, "Cuidado que vengo! (I am coming!), then she played with the buttons on the vacuum and ran towards the ghost. Luis quickly responded by meeting her halfway up the hill. Valerie pressed the buttons hoping she was close enough to suck up the ugly ghost with the special vacuum. Holding the vacuum firmly she pressed all the buttons, the vacuumed roared with power, almost knocking Valerie off her feet.

Regaining her stance, Valerie held on with everything she had, and started pushing buttons, out came bubbles, lots, and lots of tiny bubbles. Valerie stood there mystified. Luis started laughing and swiftly flew right in front of Valerie looked her straight in the eye and yelled BOO! Valerie rolled her eyes and fell to the ground. He looked out, and sternly yelled, "You are no match for my powers, GO HOME!" Luis then went back to the tombstone to be with his lovely bride.

Nicole and Princess Emily simultaneously ran up to Valerie to give her a hand and bring her to safety. Princess Emily immediately started talking about the next plan, Princess Emily's fail safe, best plan ever guaranteed to work plan, called the NH-6121. As Valerie and Nicole regrouped, Princess Emily began explaining NH-6121, "First we distract them with fireworks flown in from China, each color should be separated by size as well as shape and frequency of use. While they are watching the intricate designs of the specialized fireworks, we will have 124, 62 men, sixty-two women, military men, and women approach from the north, east, south, and west.

Valerie and Nicole just chuckled knowing she had obfuscated the whole plan, however as they rested, they decided to let her explain her long confusing plan of action. Now with 49 minutes to go before Valerie disappeared, her and Nicole knew they had one last chance. They did not understand Princess Emily's plan, vacuuming the ghost didn't work, but what would work?

Joceline and Luis were proud they were doing their jobs; it was not easy . Especially considering they were new inexperienced ghosts. They hunkered down hoping no one would try and find out what was written on the tombstone.

With 49 minutes left, Valerie could not figure out the next plan, mostly because she couldn't believe the luck, she had with the ghost vacuum/ bubble blower. Quietly, as others rested and regrouped, she asked herself, "Why, why do I have such bad luck?

CHAPTER 22

PERPICACIOUS

(Good judgement)

The usually perspicacious Valerie sat down on an old rickety wooden bench that had been in the cemetery for a hundred years. Hungry, thirsty, and running low on energy, in her tiny little head, Valerie started to send out invitations to her pity party. The really sad part was she knew no one would come, there would be no presents, no cupcakes, no dancing.

With only 49 minutes left on this beautiful planet Earth, she reminisced once again about the good things in life she had experienced. Her parents were the best parents a young girl could ask for, would not trade them for the world. Vivian was the best sister. Uncle Bruce, although unique in his ways, was an awesome uncle. Kiara was an incredible dog, and shall we not forget Mr. Dulany, he was an incredible neighbor. She smiled just thinking about Grant.

Nicole came up to Valerie and asked to sit down next to her on the old rickety bench. With a tear in her eye, she shook her head yes. They sat awkwardly for a while before Nicole decided to break the silence, "would you like a drink?" Valerie once again shook her head yes. "The only thing I seem to have left is energy drinks, would you like one?"

Valerie never had an energy drink before, but she was thirsty, "Sure!" she replied. With only the light from the full moon Valerie took the can of Wild Watermelon from her cousin. Curiosity got the best of her, and she began reading the ingredients, caffeine, sugar, taurine, guarana, glucuronolactone, cameline, inositol, gingko biloba, sucralose, acesulfame potassium. Valerie asked herself, "What, what and what?"

Her mother had always taught her to read ingredients on food labels, and these made no sense, what was this stuff? Her mother had bought apple juice and the ingredients were apples and water. Unexpectantly, Nicole reached over to Valerie and hugged her. "I am sorry for everything! Can we go back to being friends again? We still have 49 minutes to solve this problem!"

In an unexpected move, Valerie screamed, "That's It!" She hugged Nicole and summoned Princess Emily, who was working on another plan. Joceline and Luis heard the commotion and prepared for battle, once again. Joceline was tired, she wanted this over tonight, she told her husband, "No dejes para manana lo que puedes hacer,"(Do not leave for tomorrow what you can do today). This was their turf, and they were not going to lose to a bunch of little girls wearing pink suits.

Valerie took the can of Wild Watermelon energy drink and put it in her small bag. Nicole had three more cans and Valerie made sure Nicole did not drink them, claiming they were very unhealthy to drink. The usually perspicacious Princess Emily prepared a new plan, it was crazy, it was dangerous and probably illegal in 32 of the 50 states. But with less than 49 minutes on the clock it was now or never. Desperate measures call for desperate times.

As Princess Emily led the march back to the tombstone, per regulation rules, Valerie and Nicole followed closely behind. Unlike regulation, the two girls held hands in a sign of support and love for each other, hoping that they both made it out of this terrible situation, alive and well. As they marched diligently toward the highly defended tombstone, Princess Emily proudly explained her unusual plan.

"It is simple, but it should work. There are two ghosts and three of us. All we need to do is read the front of the tombstone, we do not have to defeat the ghosts, capture them or be friends with those evil monsters, all we do is have to read the clue before 11: 35 pm", Princess Emily explained. Everyone looked at their watches, it was 11:00 pm now. Both Nicole and Valerie were perspicacious, smiled in agreement of this plan.

Princess Emily continued, "So, when we get there, Valerie you run to the right, Nicole you run to the left, do not stop running. I will get the clue.' Valerie was always very respectful to adults, so she was very leery of disagreeing with Princess Emily, but she was so wrong. Fearful of Princess Emily's wrath Valerie spoke up, "I think if you paid attention, when they scream and try and scare you, they stand still, this is where we destroy them. As they are screaming, we spray the energy drink on them?"

Nicole was intrigued, Princess Emily did not like to be upstaged by a seventh grader, "That's absurd!" Princess Emily responded. "Not really, the chemical composition of the caffeine, sucralose and acesulfame potassium is like an explosion just waiting to happen. This combination C6S4P15 mixed with EP3 is highly flammable." Princess Emily was frustrated with Valerie's subordination, "We will do it my way, okay warriors are you ready!" Nicole winked at Valerie.

Luis and Joceline were stunned at the quietness of the cemetery. They wondered if they were better ghosts than they thought. Then a twig snapped, trees rustled, and a scent of humans appeared. Luis went to investigate. The three girls in pink suits were back. The usual perspicacious Joceline thought they were so adorable in their pink suits and wanted to let them see the tombstone. Luis reminded her of the consequences.

The girls approached with extreme caution, finally stopping, and standing in back of the tombstone. Valerie stood poised, Nicole stood poised, and Princess Emily stood poised not sure what to expect. With fifteen minutes left, their hearts raced, they sweated profusely, they bit their lips as they waited patiently for something to happen.

Then in one graceful move Luis flew up, flew across and flew in front of Nicole. Nicole started to shake, scared at this whole situation. After Luis got comfortable, he opened his loudmouth and started to yell BOOOOOOOOOO!! Nicole stood firm. Finally, Princess Emily yelled," Run Nicole Run!" Nicole ran as fast as she could, Luis followed her. Joceline followed suit and Princess Emily yelled, "Run, Valerie, Run!" Valerie ran swiftly through the cemetery.

Princess Emily thought her plan was going perfectly, the ghosts were following the girls allowing her to go to the tombstone. She looked left, no one was coming, she looked right, no one was coming, Princess Emily darted toward the tombstone. BAM! She tripped and fell on a tree root protruding from the ground. She tried to get up, she tried to crawl, she tried to drag herself to the front of the tombstone, but it was no use, her knee had twisted, and the pain was unbearable.

Valerie saw Princess Emily laying on the ground and knew she needed help; she circled back but Joceline was on her tail. In an instant Valerie slammed on her brakes, Joceline did the same. When Valerie turned around, Joceline opened up her mouth and yelled "BOOO!" right into her face. The smell was horrendous, but Valerie stood strong. The spit and slime that came out of Joceline's mouth was disgusting, but Valerie stood strong. The noise was bellowing, louder than a freight train, but Valerie stood strong. Valerie knew this was the time for the energy drink.

Nicole was not sure what was happening. In a frantic run for survival, she worried about herself, but as she swerved, turned, reversed, ducked, jumped, and danced through the cemetery avoiding the ghost, her mind turned to Valerie. Nicole was not sure if it was safe, but she was glad she guzzled the two cans of Wild Watermelon energy drink. She had missed her cousin, her friend, her best friend and decided to go back and see if she could help. At this point she was toying with Luis, it would be lucky if he could keep up much longer.

Joceline continued to scream at Valerie. The noise was unbearable, the smell was unbearable, the spit was unbearable, but Valerie stood her ground. With shaky wet hands she grabbed the Wild Watermelon energy drink and opened it. The sloshing of the can spilled some out, but Valerie was determined to get some in Joceline's mouth. With every ounce of muscle in her tiny hand she held on to the colorful can, she maneuvered her arm, but it was too much, the powerful thrust of air knocked the can right out of her slippery fingers.

She reached down to get the can, hoping there was enough left for the chemical equation to be effective. Valerie slipped and fell down. Seeing Valerie down, gave Joceline an opportunity to quickly compose herself and regroup. Valerie was slimy, exhausted, messy, but was determined to continue to fight until the bitter end. For a few seconds Joceline was resting, but then she saw Valerie moving again. Joceline quickly took a deep breath.

Nicole came running back to the back of the tombstone. She saw Princess Emily wincing in pain, holding her knee, but telling her to help Valerie. Nicole immediately saw her slimed soaked cousin on the floor trying to grab the energy drink and offered her the last can. Nicole got the can out of her backpack and handed it to Valerie. Suddenly Luis appeared, and together they yelled "BOOOOO!" at the two girls.

The powerful blast of air thrust the two girls backwards. Valerie dropped the energy drink on the ground as they were violently relocated. "Get me that can, I need that can!" hollered Valerie. "Are you addicted to them too?" asked Nicole. Breathing heavily, Valerie explained, "Based on unscientific data and unprofessional opinion, my hypothesis is the energy drink should depower the ghosts."

Nicole took a deep breath and wondered what the two cans of energy drink she drank, would do to her. Then in an unusual twist, Nicole felt powerless, lethargic, useless, she was coming down from the caffeine and sugar high given to her by the energy drink. Joceline and Luis continued to blow their hot slimy spit all over Nicole and

Valerie. They blew the girls farther and farther away from the old tombstone. Nicole was exhausted, Valerie was exhausted, at this point they were like ragdolls being blown in the wind.

With five minutes left before the demise of Valerie, the girls felt someone coming. Valerie had an idea, "Play dead! Play Dead!" The two brave warriors stopped moving. Joceline and Luis saw the lifeless creatures and decided enough was enough. They were not mean ghosts, they were not cruel ghosts, they were not evil ghosts, but they did do their job. They flew back to the tombstone content that the girls were incapacitated.

Completely exhausted, completely spent, completely useless, the girls laid on the cold dirty floor of the cemetery unable to move. The approaching visitors had the girls worried. Would they be witches looking for their next victim? Would they be cannibals looking for meat for their stew? Would they be voodoo doctors looking for extra parts for their clients? Hoping not to be seen in the darkness, Valerie and Nicole continued to play dead.

Closer and closer the footsteps came, Valerie hoped they would pass without seeing them so they could get back to finding and reading the last clue. Then it started the constant bickering among the people coming, "You don't know anything!" the one girl said. "You are such a witch!" said another. "Girls, girls, can't we all be friends?" said the man.

Valerie heard those words and knew who it was. Nicole was confused, she had no idea, but out of curiosity and trying to keep things light, she asked. "Is it the Pope? George Washington? Or I know is it the King of Siam?" Nobody laughed. Valerie started screaming. "Over here Uncle Bruce! Over Here!"

Angelica, Taylor, and Uncle Bruce came running towards the two wounded warriors. Nicole immediately wondered, "What are you guys doing here!" Taylor quickly answered, "You guys are our friends, we couldn't just leave you to have all the fun!" Valerie quickly reminded everyone of the time, "three minutes before

Valerie departs the earth FOREVER!" Suddenly everyone got serious.

"Very quickly, somebody get me that energy drink" Valerie said with a sense of urgency. Angelica quickly recovered the beat up can, "You want this empty beat up can?" Uncle Bruce quickly took the can and held it, so it did not keep dripping. The rest of you run around like little children, do not let the ghosts look at you or catch you." Valerie commanded.

"But why?" complained Angelica. Valerie was getting angry and snapped, "Just do it!" she proclaimed. Uncle Bruce wanted to stay back and help, Valerie said she had to do it herself. Everyone started running around like little children, Nicole went east, Taylor went west, Angelica went south, and Uncle Bruce went a tad north. They screamed and yelled, almost waking up the dead. They got the attention of Luis and Joceline, they swiftly flew to catch them and follow them. Valerie stayed back to read the clue on the tombstone and to help the fallen Princess Emily.

Taylor turned east, then crisscrossed north, Angelica started south, but turned and headed west, then east, then west again. Luis tried to follow but was too confused with all the changes. Nicole started east, swerved north, back east, and eventually headed south. Uncle Bruce wanted to stay close, so he went in a little square, north, east, south, west, and back north again. Joceline was getting dizzy following the two. Suddenly, there was a mid-air collision between Joceline and Luis; BAM! They fell to the ground.

Luis apologized to his beautiful wife, "I'm sorry honey, are you okay?" Then it hit Luis, then it hit Joceline, "Who's watching the tombstone?" They stumbled, they tripped over each other, they slid on the wet grass, but they quickly returned to the tombstone where Valerie was uncovering Dulany 252. They commanded Valerie to stop, but Valerie ignored them.

With two minutes left she prayed that the chemical reaction would immobilize Luis and Joceline. Valerie wondered if the chemical reaction of the three parts caffeine, sucralose and acesulfame potassium when mixed with the ecto plasma of the ghost would be enough to immobilize them. It was now or never. She grabbed the can and was ready to throw it at them, that is when the angry Joceline came and pushed Valerie. Valerie fell backwards, hitting her head hard against the ground and knocking her out.

Nicole saw everything and was not very happy, she rushed over to aide Valerie. Valerie still holding the dented can of wild watermelon energy drink, started mumbling, "the energy drink, the energy drink!" Luis and Joceline started to come down and scare away Nicole. She did not see or hear them coming, she was more worried about her cousin. Nicole could not believe Valerie was hurt. Upset and frustrated, she reached in to give Valerie a hug, but the leaky can was in the way.

Completely agitated, the usually precocious Nicole wrestled the can away from Valerie and vehemently threw it as hard as she could behind her back. Bullseye! The energy drink splattered all over Luis and Joceline's ectoplasmic bodies. Valerie, groggy, could not believe she threw the can away, Valerie knew this was the end, the last hurrah, the big finale, she started saying, "Good"… but Joceline and Luis started complaining, "What's happening? We're disintegrating!" they screamed.

Everyone watched in horror as the two ghosts complained of the burning sensation they were experiencing. Valerie was right, the unusual chemical composition of the energy drink began cannibalizing the ecto plasma that the ghosts were made of. Slowly, painfully the energy drink ingredients devoured Luis and Joceline. Soon, there was no trace of either ghost.

"Nicole, you did it, you did it!" Uncle Bruce quickly ran over and read the old tombstone, "Six ball in the corner pocket." With only seconds to spare, Valerie would be okay. Suddenly a cloud of smoke appeared, and a voice appeared, "Congratulations, you have made it this far. Unfortunately, to complete this treasure hunt and transfer the curse, you have only four hours, Valerie's hands must be on the necklace for the curse to be removed from her or everyone in your search party will be eliminated . Good luck, you will need it. Everyone moaned and complained. Valerie sighed and asked herself, "Why, why do I have such bad luck?

CHAPTER 23

LUGUBRIOUS

(Gloomy)

"Six ball in the corner pocket?" asked Princess Emily. Everybody just sat there lugubriously. Uncle Bruce looked around and he saw Taylor sitting on a log lugubriously. Angelica was busy checking out the cemetery plants. He looked over and saw Nicole tending to Valerie looking lugubriously and he saw Valerie sitting there the most lugubrious.

It was close to midnight, 11:48, they were tired, they were dirty, they were overwhelmed with bad news. They had less than 4 hours before they had to find the diamond necklace. Four hours, 240 minutes, 14,400 seconds, it did not matter how you broke it down, that's all the time, before Princess Emily, Uncle Bruce, Taylor, Angelica, Nicole, and Valerie would be eliminated, banished, removed from the earth forever unless Valerie was holding the precious diamond necklace in those tiny hands of hers.

Unexpectantly, Princess Emily's watch started beeping. Annoyed, she turned it off and remained in the group. The watch started beeping again, Princess Emily apologized, struggled to get up and said, "I have to take this, it's the boss!" She maneuvered herself to the side. Uncle Bruce just stared at the lugubrious bunch of young ladies, not sure what to do or how to break them of this evil state.

Princess Emily came back quietly, afraid to tell the small group of treasure hunters the news. She decided she would just say it and let the chips fall where they may, "I am sorry guys, there's a huge typhoon in Japan and all the superheroes have been asked to help with the recovery! Good luck!" Trying to avoid any sad goodbyes, she immediately jumped in the air and flew off to help the Japanese government.

Uncle Bruce was shell shocked, mystified, speechless. Taylor looked at Uncle Bruce and gave him a very rare thumbs down in a sign of disapproval, he couldn't believe it. Angelica threw her hair back and walked past Uncle Bruce in a sign of disapproval, he could not believe it. Nicole looked at Uncle Bruce huffed and puffed, then crossed her arms in a sign of disapproval, he could not believe it. Valerie stomped her foot, crossed her arms, and turned around in a sign of disapproval, he could not believe it.

What did he do wrong? Princess Emily left to save the world; he could not stop her. He looked at Taylor and told her it would be easy to find the necklace, Taylor would not even look at Uncle Bruce. He walked over to Angelica and told her how pretty the flower was, she would not even look at Uncle Bruce. He went by Nicole and thanked her for her bravery, Nicole would not even look at Uncle Bruce. Last but not least he talked to Valerie assuring her they could find the necklace; Valerie would not even look at Uncle Bruce.

Mystified, Uncle Bruce had enough, "If you girls want to have a pity party because Princess Emily left, or because we have less than four hours to solve the puzzle, GO AHEAD! But I will have no part of it. Instead of sitting here feeling sorry for us, I am going to see if I can solve this riddle. I think I can do it, but if I cannot at least I went down fighting."

Not knowing where he was going, he started to walk away. Taylor was the first to react, "Stop!" The five-foot-tall young lady looked up at the six-foot giant. She stared straight into the blue eyes of Uncle Bruce and exclaimed, "You're impatient!" Her brown eyes were extremely powerful, he immediately apologized. Angelica got up next and told Uncle Bruce the first place he could, stop and buy her a Sprite. Not very happy about anything, Nicole exclaimed,

"FINE!" and joined the group. Valerie was silent but smiling as she walked back to the Jeep.

As they walked Nicole and Valerie held back a few feet. At first there was an awkward silence, however both had something to say but did not know how to say it. Nicole reached over and held Valerie's hand; Valerie smiled. Simultaneously they looked at each other and said, "Lo siento! (I am sorry!)" As they fell behind the group even further, the two laughed and gave each other a huge hug.

Valerie started first, "I should have believed you, and I should have trusted you, but I was too afraid, I am so sorry for the pain I have caused you; I was a terrible cousin and even worse friend." "It was a crazy story; I would not have believed myself either if it didn't actually happen to me. I just wish there were some evidence left behind to prove my story", Nicole replied. Valerie could not believe she said that.

"You know we were young when that happened, I was so scared of getting in trouble, (she swallowed), I am so sorry, I found this when you left." She handed Nicole a boys necklace with the initials GP. "Every day I carry it with me, hoping I figure out who it belongs to." Valerie waited for the big bang, but Nicole stayed calm.

I have worked hard with my therapist, Dr. Trongwatarangasig, I forgive you. If I look at it positively and not be a lugubrious person, I have traveled the United States extensively, I have tried many new foods, and I have made many new friends including meeting a very charming man named Mr. Dulany, he lives somewhere near here." Valerie was so shocked she stopped walking.

Valerie's mouth hung open. "You know Mr. Dulany?" Valerie asked. "Quite the charmer, quite the talker, quite the advice giver!" Nicole proudly stated. "I met him when my sister and I went on a Caribbean cruise, he needed help with his cell phone. Very nice guy. Why do you know him?" Valerie timidly replied, "He's my neighbor, used to talk to him all the time, not so much anymore!" Nicole was confused.

It was dark, it was cold, it was late. Where was Uncle Bruce, Taylor, and Angelica? How did they get separated from the group? What happened to their group? Who was going to find them? Why were they lost? The brightness of the moon was covered by the endless supply of cloud coverage, leaving the girls only able to see a few feet in front of them. Taking full responsibility for their poor decision to stay back and talk, they quickly realized blaming, complaining, or whining about their dilemma would be wasteful.

Both Valerie and Nicole were determined to be relentless in their attempt to get back to the group quickly. Valerie decided to take the path they were on and just continue straight. Was it a good decision? Only time would tell. The girls continued to hold hands for support. As they walked, they encountered darkness, darkness, and even more darkness. Nicole could not see more than two feet ahead of herself.

Afraid of attracting the attention of any more ghosts, Valerie called out softly, "Uncle Bruce, Uncle Bruce!" surprisingly, nobody answered. The crickets chirped, the owls who'd, the wind howled, but there was no Uncle Bruce. The two cousins walked slowly, step by step, they followed the trail, step by step they held their breath, step by step they prayed they would find Uncle Bruce quickly.

Nicole thought she heard something up ahead, they stopped, the noise stopped, they continued, and the noise continued. Was somebody following them? Nicole thought it was the headless horseman, Valerie thought it was the abominable snowman. They walked a little faster, Valerie heard a very deep voice traveling through the barren cemetery, they picked up their pace.

Almost running, the two abandoned warriors had their guard up. Nicole jumped at the small branch as it fell from the tree, giving it a quick karate chop before it hit the ground. They walked into a swarm of mosquitos; Valerie squashed six of the nasty bugs before they bit her. Nicole tripped on a small rock; she kicked it into the air then high kicked the rock across the parkway. Valerie was ambushed by a spiders web, she swiped, and she wiped, quickly knocking it to the ground. The girls were ready for anything, anybody, anytime.

The girls felt an untested confidence in their abilities, still wearing their glamourous pink suits, they felt powerful, strong, and invincible. "Remember, when we were young, we both wanted to be the pink Power Ranger?" They laughed loudly as they walked drowning out any other noises. Then under the cover of darkness, they walked into a huge warm wall.

Surprised, the warriors reacted quickly to the huge unwelcomed visitor. The human wall raised its hands, Valerie grabbed the right, Nicole the left and in one swift powerful unbelievable awesome move, they flipped this monster onto its back, dropping him to the ground like a wet noodle. Continuing their unscheduled WWE wrestling event, Nicole slammed her elbow down on his stomach, Valerie copied her move flawlessly, causing the monster to cry out in excruciating pain.

Nicole was getting into this a little too much. She backed up to get a running start and yelled, "Watch This!" Then she ran, jumped, and landed on top of the beast. Then the beast started to move, "Can't we just get along girls?" he said before he fell back down. "OMG!" exclaimed Valerie, "That's Uncle Bruce!"

Feeling like a pinata at a children's birthday party, Uncle Bruce slowly got up. "We are so sorry!" exclaimed Nicole. "What were you doing out in a dark cemetery so late at night? You should be ashamed of yourself!" Valerie exclaimed. Uncle Bruce brushed himself off and said, "I was looking for you! There was a long pause and he said, "Let's GO!" He turned around and started walking towards the Jeep.

It was a short walk, but it seemed to take forever. Uncle Bruce was unusually quiet, he was never quiet, he always had something to say, which made things even worse. Although he claimed he gave up being angry over 20 years ago, his face and demeanor said something else. However, it was late, maybe he was tired, maybe he was upset. The girls knew they were wrong and could handle him being upset, however they hoped he wasn't disappointed in either of them.

With three hours left, Valerie noticed nobody was in a rush. Valerie and Nicole were told to sit in the back, highly unusual, Valerie always sat in the passenger seat, not today, Taylor was there. Valerie and Nicole wanted to stop and get some cheeseburgers, Angelica and Taylor wanted to stop for tacos and enchiladas, they stopped for Mexican.

Uncle Bruce ordered the gourmet nachos, without jalapeños, and a large Pepsi. Angelica ordered cheese quesadillas with a small Sierra Mist. Taylor ordered a chicken burrito and a Baja Blast. Nicole ordered two hard shelled corn spicy tacos and a glass of water. Valerie, who was famished and could eat a horse ordered three nacho cheese Doritos Locos Tacos Supreme and a sparkling water.

Everyone got what they ordered except Valerie, she received three steak and cheese burritos and a large root beer. As they enjoyed their late-night fiesta, they talked, they laughed, they cried. Nobody was lugubrious, nobody except Valerie. Valerie was trying to be a vegetarian, so she refused to eat the burritos, and worried about the time Uncle Bruce refused to go back and exchange the product. All the lugubrious Valerie could do was sit in the back seat and sulk, asking herself over and over "Why, why do I have such bad luck!"

CHAPTER 24

COPACETIC

(In Excellent Order)

The girls ate quickly and dropped crumbs, wrappers, and cups all over Uncle Bruce's Jeep. It was not looking copacetic at all. Valerie, still lugubrious, was not happy. She thought she lost Uncle Bruce's love, because her and Nicole beat him up, and she was STARVING! And to make things even worse, not only was she going to disappear into the great unknown, but she was bringing her uncle, cousin, and several new friends with her now. "Six ball in the corner pocket?" Valerie kept saying to herself.

Nicole wondered where they were going and asked Taylor, "Shouldn't we be looking for the diamond necklace?" Taylor chuckled, "While you two girls were having a heart to heart, the rest of us were trying to figure out the next clue. Uncle Bruce immediately recognized "six ball in the corner pocket" as a billiards table. But where is this antique billiards table? Is in the Glendale Heights Museum? Is it in somebodies basement rotting away? Or being 170 years old was it thrown away? This is what we talked about."

Nicole, who was extremely smart and clever, quickly responded, "This spell obviously updates itself to current events. Remember when it mentioned Valerie by name? Remember when it said our whole group would be eliminated? It is watching us. But the billiards table is out there, out there for us to find!" Everyone was impressed, Valerie started smiling.

Valerie was intrigued, "Nowhere in the history books is there any pool sharks from Glendale Heights." Angelica replied, "So, it's not in any museum!" Taylor responded, "And it's not in the garbage!" Nicole asked, "So, where is it?" Valerie figured it out first, "It's in the Papadopolus house!"

Uncle Bruce slammed on the brakes, heaving everyone forward unexpectantly and causing widespread flooding of soda and water in his precious Jeep. Things were definitely not copacetic. Uncle Bruce, Taylor and Angelica automatically thought it would be in the Glendale Heights Museum, the Papadopolus mansion was on the other side of town.

The side of town where the elite, the few, the very rich live. 1000 Wealthy Court, the name said it all. Mansions big enough for ten families, twenty bedrooms, 15 bathrooms, a theater, a state-of-the-art kitchen. Butlers, maids, mechanics, landscapers, and a personal chef. Six cars, fancy sport cars, an Olympic size swimming pool, basketball courts, tennis courts, a spa, a pool table. The grass was green, and the flowers were always blooming. This was the side of town where Uncle Bruce and his friends only wished they lived.

Angelica Googled the address, 1000 Wealthy Court, and found it was only twenty minutes away. Uncle Bruce had to drive carefully, being stopped by the police would end this quest on a sour note. It was late, 1:45 am, everyone was exhausted, but they had less than two hours to find this diamond necklace. The diamond necklace that would change Valerie's life forever. Two hours, 120 minutes, 7,200 seconds, it seems like a lot, but time moves quickly.

The rag tag bunch of warriors quickly found the huge mansion. Huge was not the right word, maybe humongous, maybe gigantic, maybe large. Uncle Bruce quickly asked, "How do we get in? We cannot break in, that's against the law. And I am too naive to go to jail!" Everyone laughed, but quickly realized they were stuck, how would they get in?

Somebody wanted to get disguises, somebody wanted to pretend to be lost travelers, somebody wanted to act like their car broke down, somebody wanted to sneak through a window, somebody wanted to sneak through the doggie door, somebody wanted to go through the back door. All were lies, all were deceptive, all were wrong.

Valerie stepped up, "I have a way!" Taylor was intrigued, Angelica was curious, Nicole was interested, and Uncle Bruce smiled because she was thinking, trying, not just sitting back, and crying. Ready to bust, Angelica rudely asked, "Well come on girl, spit it out!" Valerie took a deep breath and proudly announced, "Let's be Honest!" Nicole laughed so hard she almost fell off her seat, Angelica quickly said, "What are you stupid?" Taylor sighed and gave her a hearty thumbs down. The three girls all laughed together making fun at the expense of Valerie.

Angelica laughed hysterically even though Valerie was sitting right next to her, it was as if Valerie was invisible. Taylor flashed her thumbs down gesture freely even though Valerie was sitting right behind her, it was as if Valerie was invisible. Even Nicole got in on the fun, poking fun of her naive cousin, she closed her eyes and laughed uncontrollably saying, "What are you going to do? Go up to the front door and tell them you have been cursed?" Nicole could not stop laughing, laughing so hard she almost peed in her pants.

Valerie was unphased as they bullied her, during the last 48 hours she had grown up a little, but the job was not done yet. She looked at her inexpensive simple watch, 2:15 am, it was now or never. She got out of the overpacked Jeep and proudly walked towards the front door, nobody even noticed, she really was the invisible girl.

As she walked away from the Jeep, Uncle Bruce noticed, he just thought she was getting some fresh air. Valerie continue to walk up the long walkway, and Taylor took notice, she thought Valerie was getting some fresh air. Valerie kept walking up the winding walkway and now Angelica noticed, she thought Valerie was getting some fresh air. Finally, Nicole noticed Valerie on the walkway, she thought Valerie was getting some fresh air. They all intently stared at the young lady continuing to walk up the walkway. "How is she going to do it?" asked Uncle Bruce.

Uncle Bruce thought she was joking; he was seeing how far she would go before turning herself around. Valerie kept walking. Taylor watched as Valerie got closer, she had no faith in Valerie continuing. Valerie kept walking. Angelica watched as Valerie proudly continued, thinking she was foolish because the security cameras were watching every move she made. Valerie kept walking. Although very proud of her relentless attempt, Nicole thought Valerie was putting herself in unnecessary danger. Valerie reached the massive French doors. "How is she going to do it?" asked Taylor.

Valerie reached for the doorbell. "What is she going to do?" asked Uncle Bruce. "Don't be foolish!" quietly screamed Taylor. "I double dog dare you!" sarcastically yelled Angelica. "Do not do it! Do not do it!" commanded Nicole. She did it, Valerie rang the doorbell. "How is she going to do it?" asked Angelica.

The huge French door open as the bright luminescent light lit up the front porch. A large well-dressed man stood patiently as he stared at Valerie. 'Valerie stood frozen. "She's crazy!" declared Uncle Bruce. "She's a wild one!" announced Taylor. "She's unbelievable!" said Angelica. "She's my best friend!" declared Nicole. "How is she going to do it?" asked Nicole.

Although Valerie's back was turned, the large man who answered the door faced forward. Uncle Bruce saw him smile. Taylor saw him laugh. Angelica saw him cry. Nicole saw him shake his head. Then they saw it, the miracle, the hole in one, the half-court shot, Valerie waved her hand indicating they should come inside with her. They immediately listened and headed up the walkway to the front door.

Impressed beyond words, Uncle Bruce wondered how she got the man to let her in. As he went by, he asked Valerie "How did you do it?" Taylor was so impressed she proudly held her thumb high in the air as she came in the door and asked Valerie, "How did you do it?" Angelica came in the house wondering who the bad decorator was and asked Valerie, "How did you do it?" Nicole smiled from ear to ear, so proud of her cousin, as she passed by, she asked, "How did you do it?"

Uncle Bruce was the first to guess, "Did you tell him, our car broke down and we needed to use his phone?" "No!" Replied Valerie. Taylor was next, "Did you pretend to be a young hungry child, and he decided to let you in?" "No!" Replied Valerie. Angelica asked her, "Did you pretend to be the horticulturist and say you were there to take care of the indoor plants?" "No!" Replied Valerie. "I know!" exclaimed Nicole, "You pretended to be the backup dog walker and were there to walk the dogs!" "NO!" proclaimed Valerie.

Everyone just stared at Valerie, waiting for her to say something, anything, everything. It was 2:30 am, time was ticking, one hour fifteen minutes before vanishing. Valerie cleared her throat and told her friends, "It was not complicated, it wasn't difficult, it wasn't unlawful. (Valerie paused a second for effect, her friends eagerly awaited) I used something very rare, something not everyone uses,(she paused) I used honesty."

Uncle Bruce's knee buckled, Taylor's glasses steamed up, Angelica was speechless, and all Nicole could do was say "FINE!" "Why?" asked the confused Angelica. Valerie told everyone, "First, it is the right way to go. Second, honesty is the best policy. Remember honest Abe? Enough said. I told Carlos, the overnight butler, all about the two families going on vacation, the necklace, the curse, the lost relatives, my bad luck, the gym, the rock, the cemetery, the ghosts and now the pool table."

"Carlos was intrigued, he thought someone should write a book about the diamond necklace. I told him I didn't know anybody. He suggested Mr. Dulany. I was surprised Carlos knew him, he told me everyone knows Mr. Dulany! But Carlos knew nobody would make up a story like this, so he trusts me."

The group was extremely astonished at Valerie's creativity. Taylor yawned and said, "Thanks Carlos, thanks Valerie!" Uncle Bruce was extremely proud of his niece, even in the time of trouble, she did the right thing. Nicole teased him when she saw a tear fall from his eye.

Angelica was the only one paying attention to the time, "So where is everybody?" she questioned Carlos. He immediately responded, 'they're off on one of their fabulous vacations, maybe New York, maybe Paris, maybe Monaco, I don't know I don't pay attention anymore. They have so much money, they use their jet like a car."

"Interesting!" responded Taylor, "So where is the billiard table? We are looking for a real old one." Carlos thought about it over and over again, finally the light bulb in his head went off. "If I remember right, they found out it was a defective pool table, something about one of the pockets, as well as the set of balls one of them was unusual, heavier. So, they bought a new table and put the old one in the garage."

Valerie gave Carlos a huge hug and asked, "Where's the garage?" Carlos told her, "Go next door, the big Victorian Mansion. It's actually an 18-car garage, they only have 17 cars, the last space is where your pool table is stored. I will turn off the alarm, so there is no problem! Good luck!"

With less than 45 minutes to spend on the earth, the rag tag team of hunters ran out the door and next door to the huge garage, or more like a luxury car lot. As promised, it was unlocked, Uncle Bruce was amazed at the Mercedes, Taylor was impressed with the Porsche Cayenne, Angelica loved the Maserati Quadrate, Nicole loved the BMW X6, and Valerie wanted to drive the Rolls-Royce Cullinan, when of course she got her driver's license.

The garage was copacetic and huge, they passed by a black Hummer, a blue Aston Martin Cygnet, a fire engine red Lincoln MKS and finally someone's obvious favorite, the maroon Cadillac Escalade, but what they saw next was the most beautiful thing in the world. No, it wasn't a Chevrolet Corvette, a Lincoln Corsair, or a Lexus NX, it was an old beat-up pool table.

This scratched up, ripped up, torn up beauty had two problems. First, where were the balls? Second, there were boxes and boxes full of old clothes marked for Goodwill that someone needed to deliver. Angelica and Taylor bravely volunteered to find the balls, or at least the all-important, six ball. Uncle Bruce, Valerie and Nicole decided to take the boxes off the table. Time was not on their side, 40 minutes left.

Angelica looked on every shelf for any indication of billiard balls. Old shoes, Halloween decorations, spring accessories, but no billiard balls. Taylor checked underneath the pool table, Christmas decorations, planters, boxes of school supplies, but no billiard balls. Together they searched high and low.

Then they both had the same idea, the big old toolbox. They both checked each drawer carefully, opening and closing each drawer swiftly. They found hammers, pliers, screwdrivers, saws, nails, screws, drills, and many other tools they had no idea what they were, but no billiard balls. Then they opened the fifth drawer, it was scary, it was ugly, it was horrifying,

Uncle Bruce, Valerie and Nicole, all work expeditiously on removing the boxes marked for Goodwill off the pool table. They worked hard passing the big boxes through their self- made assembly line, knowing full well the clock was ticking. Each box was heavy in itself, but Valerie knew there was no time for whining or complaining. Fifteen minutes until lights out, fifteen minutes until the game was over, fifteen minutes before the final chapter.

Suddenly, they heard police sirens wailing in the background. They all looked at each other with a sense of fear and anxiety, but quickly dismissed the thought of being a target of a police manhunt, so they went in for the last big box on the dirty, dusty, antique pool table. Surprisingly, Angelica screamed, followed closely by Taylor screaming.

Not knowing what was happening, Valerie and Nicole struggled to get the heavy box off the antique pool table without damaging it further. Valerie pulled; Nicole pushed. Valerie maneuvered; Nicole strategized. The heavy box moved slowly across the top of the dust covered pool table. Angelica continued to panic and scream, Taylor followed suit even pointing at times.

With under five minutes, chaos began to downpour. Valerie and Nicole were not going out without a battle, they finally managed to get the bulky oversized box off the table and began carrying it across the room, the police sirens continued screaming in the background often seeming to get closer as the seconds went by. Amid the chaos, Uncle Bruce saw the problem with Angelica and Taylor.

Trying to be funny but instead being mean and insensitive, Uncle Bruce grabbed the eight- legged creature and put it on his palm threatening to let it eat the girls. Nicole and Valerie moved slowly as they carried the box, police sirens continued to wail, Uncle Bruce laughed, Angelica and Taylor ran frantically towards the door trying to evade the "man eating spider". The next few minutes are a blur, almost surreal.

The clock didn't stop, neither did the sound of police sirens in the background, neither did Uncle Bruce laugh, neither did Angelica and Taylor. BAM! KAPOW! THUD! BANG! OW! Were just some of the sounds that were heard as Angelica and Taylor ran into Valerie, Nicole, and the big box. Bodies fell to the ground like dominoes, the box fell upright, but swayed to the right, then to the left. Everybody watched as it settled gracefully still and were equally surprised when the box began to rock back and forth once again.

Angelica held her arm, not so concerned with spiders anymore. Taylor wiped the dust off her face as she wondered if a pack of raccoons were living in the box. Nicole brushed herself off as she stood watching the suspicious box. Valerie stood frozen, knowing her time as well as everyone's time was almost done. 90 seconds, that's all that was left, 90 seconds.

Could it get any worse? Could it get any more dismal? Could it get any more miserable? Unexpectantly, two policeman kicked open the door and told everyone to freeze. The box tipped over and slowly the balls to the billiard table started to roll out, one by one.

Uncle Bruce saw this and whispered to Valerie, "You have to do it! Don't be afraid! You have nothing to lose!" Valerie was terrified but knew she didn't have a choice.

She watched her clock, 60 seconds left, the black eight ball rolled out. The police officer asked, "Who's in charge?" With 50 seconds left, Valerie saw the number five solid orange come out, the police officer asked, "What are you guys doing here?" Valerie stood still with 40 seconds left and a number one solid yellow ball rolled out, the police officer asked, "Where are your parents?"

Nervously, everyone sat quietly on the floor waiting for their ball to appear. Valerie looked at her watch, 30 seconds left, then the number ten striped blue rolled out, nobody was paying attention to the police officer. Then with 20 seconds left, the number six solid green ball came barreling out. The small group cheered; the officer told them to calm down, then called on his radio he needed backup at 1000 Wealthy Court because he had an unruly crowd.

Valerie hesitated for just a brief second before realizing it was now or never, she was in control of her own destiny. Bound and determined, she quickly got up and grabbed the ball. She thought it was heavy but ran over to the pool table and randomly picked the right far corner pocket, she rolled the six ball very intently at the pocket.

Like it had a mind of itself the six-ball stopped and started rolling back, eventually falling into the corner pocket right next to her. 10 seconds left, nothing happened. The police officer asked her what she was doing and commanded her to sit down. Valerie asked herself, "Why, why do I have such bad luck?"

CHAPTER 25

CONUDRUM

(A Difficult Decision)

As Valerie started to turn around, the ancient pool table burped very boisterously, considering the seriousness of the situation, nobody laughed. In an attempt to accept her fate and the fate of her friends she began a countdown. "10, 9, 8, 7." Suddenly from the corner pocket the elusive diamond necklace rose, it was absolutely breath taking. Shining brightly in the distance, it gave Valerie a sense of accomplishment. Rising up like the bright sun, the necklace sparkled brilliantly as it rose above the clutter. "Everybody yelled, "Grab it Valerie, Grab it!" Only Uncle Bruce continued the countdown, "6, 5, 4" There was no conundrum, as if she was in slow motion, everyone watched as Valerie desperately dove onto the table reaching for the diamond necklace. Uncle Bruce closed his eyes as he finished the countdown, "3, 2, 1."

At first, nothing seemed to happen, then everything happened. The lights dimmed, the earth shook, lightning thundered in the sky and then a thick white smoked filled the air and like magic, everyone was gone. The policeman and his partner both agreed they saw nothing. Uncle Bruce looked around wondering where he ended up. Angelica, Taylor, and Nicole stood frozen in time, not sure what to do or say.

Valerie looked at her hand, she was clenching something, smoke started to fill the room. She tried opening her fist but couldn't because she was overcome by the thick smoke. Suddenly, her eyes went blank, darkness filled the room and Valerie passed out.

The Next Morning
Monday Morning
11:32 am

"Valerie, get up, your friends will be here at noon!" called her mother. "I'm going to send Ariana up to help you clean your room and get ready, please get up and help her!" Valerie, still extremely tired from her weekend adventure, just laid in her bed unable to move. Her legs hurt, her arms hurt, her eyelids hurt. Completely and utterly exhausted, she didn't want to move. Valerie put her head under her fancy silk pillow thinking she could hide from the world.

Suddenly, there was a light knock on the door, there was no conundrum, Valerie ignored it. "I'm coming in Ms. Valerie." Valerie heard the door open, and somebody walked in, Valerie peaked from under the pillow, "Who was this strange girl?" she wondered. Valerie kept peeking from under her silk pillow and watched the young lady in a maids uniform pick up assorted clothes that were strewn throughout the large suite. Valerie wondered if she was lucky enough to have won a weekend in a fancy hotel.

This was not Valerie's room; those were not Valerie's clothes. Valerie shopped at Target, nothing fancy, nothing expensive, just nice fashionable clothes at a fair price. She noticed they were clothes from Model Madness, Belle Chic, Clothing Fierce and Morning Glory, places that were far too expensive for the young lady. Valerie noticed purses from Michael Kors and Gucci, bags from Coach. Valerie wondered if she was lucky enough to have won designer clothes.

In one swift unexpected swoosh, the young maid opened the large curtain, letting the beautiful bright sunshine into Valerie's second story suite, catching Valerie off guard. "Valerie screamed, "Close the curtain, it's too bright!" The young lady continued opening the curtain, "Sorry Ms. Valerie, I work for your mother, Ms. Hernandez, and she told me to get you up! Your friends will be here soon, and you need to get ready for the trip to the mall." Valerie wondered if she was lucky and finally had won a shopping spree.

Valerie jumped out of bed; the sun was too bright for the young lady to continue sleeping. She was wearing fancy silk pajamas. Then there was another knock on the door, "That must be your breakfast," announced the maid. Valerie liked the idea of somebody bringing her Eggo Waffles to her room, but was confused, "How many people work here?" Ariana laughed.

"What is wrong with you?" she asked. "You know there are many people that help keep this mansion running. 144 rooms, 35 bedrooms, 21 bathrooms, 2 kitchens, a bowling alley, a home theatre, an Olympic sized swimming pool and tennis courts" Valerie was confused, "I live here? Who works here?"

Ariana took a deep breath and quickly jostled her memory. "Frida is your personalized chef, Alyssa, Caidon, and Alani all work in the kitchen with her. Your personalized waiter staff include Adrian, Brianna, Damaris, and Giselle. Keeping the mansion clean is done by your cleaning staff headed by Crystal and includes Jose', A'Niyla, Daniel, and Jonathan. Samantha and Ethen are your limo drivers. Emma is your mechanic; Anabella is your handywoman. On landscaping duty, you have Kaiden, Fariz, Sophia, and Anyeli. You are quite the lucky person to have such a wonderful staff. Valerie was confused.

Valerie looked at the room, this wasn't her room. Ariana had a nice outfit placed to the side, all picked out for Valerie to spend time with her friends. Valerie quickly changed into the overpriced outfit and then headed out her massive bedroom door to explore the lifestyles of the rich and famous, her new lifestyle.

The walls were adorned by the famous painters of yesterday, paintings by Picasso, Rembrandt and DaVinci were seen by the naked eye. The floors were brilliant, fine woven rugs were from China. The carpets came from the exclusive mills in North Carolina. Every step she took, Valerie saw luxurious expensive items that came from around the globe.

She worked her way to the kitchen, hoping to find some waffles, she quickly realized she should of ate when the waiter brought her breakfast. She passed by a young lady covered in grease and dirt, he apologized for being dirty but told her the limo and her driver will be ready in fifteen minutes to take her to the mall.

Valerie made it to the kitchen and noticed her mother sipping a Starbucks cappuccino, "Would you like one?" asked her mother. "NO, I don't want you to have to go out," sweetly replied Valerie. Her mother laughed, "Always cracking jokes!" Then she clapped her hands, and a Starbuck's barista came out. "What can I get you?" asked the young man. Valerie smiled, there were so many cool drinks at Starbucks, she had a conundrum. After a brief moment of indecision, she jumped up and replied, "A Pink Drink! That's coconut milk with strawberries."

The young man scurried off. Valerie smiled, her luck had changed, she had her own maid, her own limo, her own mechanic, her own driver, and best of all her own Starbuck's barista. She quickly realized she had broken the evil curse. This was just the beginning, what else would this beautiful day bring? It could only get better. She sat down for breakfast and the chef asked her what she would like for breakfast.

This was a conundrum, so many choices, so little time. Valerie wondered if she should go for the usual or go for something different. Valerie had little time for humor, but decided this was a good time, she was going to test this chef of the rich and famous. Trying to get serious, she sat up, cleared her throat, and began ordering, "I would like a Midwestern omelet, with pork sausage from Nebraska, eggs from Michigan, American cheese from Wisconsin and freshly grated hash browns from Idaho. I would like freshly squeezed orange juice from Florida and Irish Soda bread from Ireland, lightly toasted.

The chef began to sweat, wondering how he was going to pull all these ingredients together from Idaho, Florida, Wisconsin, Nebraska, and Ireland. But the one thing he remembered was this Hernandez family had money. Lots and Lots and Lots of money.

Valerie's family had the Midas touch. Not wasting any time, he quickly excused himself to make things happen. Immediately jets flew at supersonic speeds, trucks barreled down the highway, warehouse workers walked faster and soon the delivery truck pulled up to the kitchen door. What the Hernandez family wanted, they got; money was no object.

The chef quickly made the fresh omelet, and the young waitress gracefully served it to Valerie. Valerie was incredibly impressed; she could get use to this lifestyle. Valerie took a bite, she was in heaven, she felt lucky, but was more interested in how they got rich, she pushed her plate away. Choosing her words carefully, she asked her mom, "Can you tell me again how we got so rich?"

Valerie's mom smiled and said "Sure!" Then she became eerily quiet with a confused look on her face. "What's wrong mom?" asked a concerned daughter. Her mom, still mystified, paused for a minute before admitting, "I really don't know, I really don't know, it's like yesterday I remember struggling to pay the bills and today I have money coming out my ears. Maybe I need to go lay down." Her mother went upstairs to lay down.

Ding Dong! Ding Dong! Went the loud doorbell. Her friends were here, thank goodness, she was hoping Angelica, Taylor and Nicole made it back alive, these were the best friends ever. The butler opened the door and in came Julia Tensteel, Samantha Morales, and Veronica Hayward. These were Valerie's friends?

These girls absolutely could not be the friends Valerie was going to the mall with, these girls were in a league of their own. They had money, lots of money and they let people know it. They were pompous, arrogant, and pretentious, and those were they're good points, but their peers loved them, wanted to be like them and followed their every move on Facebook. Valerie was not like this, was she?

Tuesday at School
Chemistry class

Valerie was still in shock about her families fame and fortune. She learned, her great, great, great, grandfather invested wisely in the phone company, her great, great grandfather invested in the success of automobiles. The Midas touch continued with her great grandfather investing heavily in gas and oil. Money followed money.

As the years went by her grandfather invested in computers and her father continued the lucky streak by investing in cell phones. The Hernandez empire continued to grow, they bought land, diversified into many different businesses, yet they maintained a positive community image, often donating thousands to the poor.

Valerie wasn't sure what to expect in chemistry class. After a very adventurous weekend full of ups and downs, she was ready for some routine chemistry problems. She liked Ms. Crystal, but she really needed to see Grant, there was something about him that made the world better. He was kind, clever, he was sweet, and he had a great sense of humor. It would be nice to sit next to him for 55 minutes, but something went wrong, Grant was absent today and would not be returning to school. Valerie was devastated. She asked Ms. Crystal if she knew what happened, but Ms. Crystal didn't have a clue.

Ms. Crystal suggested going to the office and asking, they kept all the information there. Worried sick, after school, Valerie walked swiftly down the two flights of stairs directly to the main office. She waited patiently for one of the secretaries to acknowledge her, nobody did, back to being the invisible girl.

Finally, old Mrs. Brightser came up and tried to help, but told Valerie it was confidential information and couldn't help her. Valerie refused to take no for an answer, so the spunky Ms. Louisa stepped up and politely asked Valerie to leave. Valerie stood there in shock, unable to get any information.

Nobody would give any information to Valerie. She sat down on the bench, buried her head between her knees and started to cry. Ms. Alice' came from behind the counter to comfort her. As she hugged her, she whispered in Valerie's ear, "Everyone leaves at 5, meet me back here at 5:01, the office will be empty." Valerie wiped her face and quietly left.

5:01

Valerie very hesitantly walked back into the main office. It was cold, dark and to be honest, a little creepy. Unexpectantly, Ms. Alice' walked out into the shadows and told Valerie, "Come on Valerie, let's see if we can help you! What's his name?" Valerie stood frozen, like a deer in the headlights, unable to move, talk, or breathe.

Ms. Alice' was not sure what was wrong with Valerie, little did she know she was experiencing crime fright. It's like stage fright but it's with crime, Ms. Alice' liked bending the rules for the children as long as it was for a good cause. "Okay, who are we looking for?" asked Ms. Alice' as she turned back on her computer. Valerie still did not answer. "Come on, talk to me!" Ms. Alice' politely commanded.

She saw the look in Valerie's eyes and immediately knew she had been fighting for a crime. Valerie was always a goody too shoes and breaking any rule would cause her to have this reaction. Ms. Alice' was good with children and immediately knew what to do, "Listen to me Valerie, I give you permission to be in the office, you will not get into trouble!"

It was like magic, Valerie came to life, first she started to breathe, then her eyelids blinked and then she began to dance. "So, what's his name?" All Valerie said was "Grant." Ms. Alice' rolled her eyes and quickly replied, "Grant who?" Poor Valerie didn't know. Ms. Alice' took a deep breath knowing she had her work cut out for her.

Sit down Valerie. So, what class do you have with him? You do have a class with him, right?" sarcastically asked Ms. Alice'. Valerie was slightly offended, but answered without attitude, "Third period chemistry class, Ms. Crystal is our teacher." Ms. Alice' smiled, finally having some information to start the hunt. She started typing fiercely on her computer; however, her computer was old, and the screen kept flashing on and off. "Ahha!" proclaimed Ms. Alice', 'I found it!' Then the computer screen went dark. Ms. Alice' assured Valerie the information would come back.

Valerie saw Ms. Alice' write down the letter P. Valerie decided to be silly and draw a heart, inside the heart she wrote the letters GP & VH. She smiled, was she in love? She didn't know. Then it hit her, "OMG" she proclaimed. Was GP the boy that caused the trouble between her and Nicole so many years ago? Was he the boy who destroyed her Barbies? Was he the boy who ran out blaming Nicole? Coincidence?

Trying to stay positive, Valerie patiently waited for the computer screen to work, "There it is, his name is Grant Papadopolus. Valerie almost peed in her pants, "OMG! Grant Papadopolos? The rich family who lives in that huge mansion, at 1000 Wealthy Court, across town?" Valerie asked. Ms. Alice' shook her head in agreement.

"What happened?" asked a curious Valerie. "This is all confidential, but the dad called this morning, saying they were in financial ruin, he invested heavily in DVD players, lost everything over the weekend. Even though they didn't have a hotel bill they put all their souvenirs on credit cards, understandably they were denied. They had four flat tires after they ran over screws on the ground from a truck carrying screws that swerved to avoid a moose on the road. And today they were forcibly evicted from their house. It's such a shame how their luck changed.

Valerie knew what caused their luck to change, she had taken the diamond necklace, Valerie had a giant conundrum, does she tell everyone who the diamond belongs to now or does she keep quiet? Only time will tell. What do you think she should do?

THE END